Blue

Moon

By: S.L. Kotar and J.E. Gessler

Ahead of the Press
Grand Rapids, Michigan

Library of Congress Cataloguing-in-Publication Data

/S.L. Kotar/ author/
/J.E. Gessler/author/
      Blue Moon

ISBN	KINDLE	978-1-950392-52-0
ISBN	PAPERBACK	978-1-950392-51-3
ISBN	HARDBACK	978-1-950392-95-7

Ahead of The Press Publishing
Grand Rapids, Michigan

TABLE OF CONTENTS

Blue Moon

Dedication

This novel, which might never have seen the light of day if it wasn't for my publisher, is dedicated to that individual who oversees the day-in and day-out operations of Ahead of the Press. Not only that, she's my go-to cover artist and webmaster. She also answers queries, suggests new approaches, sees to it that unknown authors get a legitimate shot at seeing their work in print and bugs me about such things as summaries and dedications – which, once you get past Mom and Dad, siblings and pets – is not all that easy.

Thank you for everything you do, AC (*nee* K) Z. You've made our dreams come true. Something I never thought was possible.

SLK

(and JEG, always)

CHAPTER 1

"Fulton's Folly," it was not.

Not after Robert Fulton and his partner, New York Chancellor Robert R. Livingston successfully negotiated a contract to own exclusive steamboating rights to the Mighty Mississippi.

The first steamboat to successfully navigate upstream had been called the *Clermont*. Named after Livingston's estate on the Hudson River, the "infernal contraption" had steamed 150 miles from New York City to Albany on August 17, 1807. Appearing more like a Long Island skiff than a modern invention of momentous significance, the *Clermont* was 133 feet long, with an 18 foot beam, and a 7 foot hold. She measured 170 tons. The boat was powered by a Boulton & Watt engine. The single wheeler, mounted on the side, was equipped with twelve huge paddles.

In the likely event of engine failure, her inventor, Robert Fulton, had provided the boat with two masts from which sails could be hoisted.

The engines did not fail, the trip was completed in thirty-two hours and the erstwhile "floating tea kettle" turned jeers into cheers.

Fulton himself wrote, "The power of propelling boats by steam is now fully proved."

He had steamed his way into history, which was fine as far as it went. New Yorkers hailed the inventor as a hero.

Hero worship, as they say, is cheap.

What Robert Fulton and his partner really wanted was a patent, guarded by the full and absolute power of the United States government.

They also wanted to take their "backwoods sawmill mounted on a skow" and bring her where she was meant to navigate: the Mississippi.

In 1807, the new country was bursting at her seams. To accommodate westward expansion, two items were essential: the acquisition of the Indian territories and improved transportation to bring the vast riches of the west to the hungry consumers of the east. The birth of the steamboat made both a reality.

Running from New York City to Albany was exciting, but the tame old Hudson was the not wild, swift-currented Mississippi. The real test of steamboating would come after a "home-made" boat was constructed near one of the newly emerging cities on the Ohio and steamed down that river into the Mississippi.

To accomplish that would be a feat worth noting.

It would also be the most lucrative journey ever taken, for once achieved, the owners of the exclusive rights to the river would be wealthy men.

The execution of this dream began with Thomas Jefferson's appointment of William C.C. Claiborne as governor of the Orleans Territory, a huge hunk of land generously carved out of the Louisiana Purchase. Governor Claiborne's earliest effort to promote his new territory was to visit New York City in 1810. There, he met with the inventor and the financial backer of the steamboat. Impressed with what he heard, the governor invited them to introduce their new invention to the vast western waterways, so vital for the transportation of goods and passengers.

Fulton and Livingston were prepared. They demanded exclusive rights before investing the tremendous capital required for such a venture. This, they were granted.

With one territorial governor on their side, if not literally in their pocket, the partnership wrote to other territorial governors, demanding similar considerations.

On April 11, 1811, the legislature of the Orleans Territory passed an act, granting Fulton and Livingston "the sole and exclusive right and privilege to build, construct, make use, employ and navigate boats, vessels and water craft, urged or propelled through the waters by fire or steam, in all the creeks, rivers, bays and waters whatsoever, within the jurisdiction of the territory, during eighteen years from the first of January, 1812."

The United States Congress, however, had other ideas. In the spirit of competition, it passed, in April, 1812, a resolution directly addressing Fulton's monopoly. Legislators demanded, as a condition of statehood, that Louisiana agree "the river Mississippi, and the navigable waters leading into it, and into the Gulf of Mexico, should be common highways, and forever free, as well to the inhabitants of that state as to those of the other states and territories of the United States, without any tax, duty, impost or toll."

Things being what they were, the Congressional mandate was ignored.

That worry behind them, plans were immediately implemented for Fulton and his partner to rule the western waters.

Nicholas J. Roosevelt was sent by the Fulton/Livingston partnership to Pittsburgh, Pennsylvania, a growing city on the Ohio River, where he was to oversee the assemblage of a new steamboat, constructed to the specifications of their exclusive patents.

In a newly created boatyard on the Monongahela, a mile from the "Point," the *New Orleans,* so named after her hoped-for destination, was born.

William Hanna was in his late thirties when he first met Captain Roosevelt. Without substantial means to become an investor in the new venture, he nevertheless believed in the dream.

"Take me as a passenger," he offered. "You will need witnesses; men of faith to travel with you. I am such a man."

Mr. Hanna faced no competition. The *New Orleans* was designed to carry passengers as well as cargo, housing a forward cabin for gentlemen and a smaller, aft cabin for ladies. There was no possibility of his being crowded, however, for men were terrified of the boat and of the idea steam could safely transport anything. Roosevelt accepted the offer. They sealed the deal with a handshake and one stipulation.

"I am taking my wife with me," Roosevelt said. "It would please me greatly if your wife would accompany you. That way, the ladies will have pleasant conversation and I will have an added incentive to invite you."

"Mrs. Hanna shall be honored, sir," he was assured.

Mr. Hanna felt free to speak for his wife, inasmuch as she was expected to do as she was told. Her acquiesce was a foregone conclusion.

"Very well," Mrs. Hanna said, when informed she would be a passenger on the maiden voyage of the *New Orleans.* "When do we depart and what shall I be expected to bring?"

"The boat will be ready to leave in two weeks. Pack what you will."

The fact Mrs. Hanna was only two months away from her expected confinement held scant concern for her husband. Birth was as natural as death; babies were born on horse-drawn caravans, on ocean-faring ships, in cramped rooms atop tea shops. If she were unlucky, a mother might have her child in an alley or a cotton field.

All things considered, Mrs. Hanna was fortunate.

Her husband did, however, pause to consider her natural feelings before departing for a business meeting he had scheduled for later in the day.

"Mrs. Roosevelt, too, is in the family way. I expect that will give you a starting point for conversation with her."

"Is it her first child, Mr. Hanna?" the wife quietly inquired. Despite her calm exterior, she was shaking inside at the unexpected trip. While she had been aware of her husband's growing fascination with the possibility of shipping freight by steamboat up and down the Ohio River, she had not expected him to offer himself and his family as "proof" of the viability of this new mode of transport.

"How would I know? Ask her yourself."

"Yes, sir."

She bowed her head. She ought not to have asked. She knew better. Mr. Hanna was an exacting man with a head for business. As such, he was a good provider. Elizabeth respected him. She could do no less, for she had seen far worse.

The morning of October 20, 1811 dawned bright and clear. Mrs. Hanna had packed all she deemed necessary to provide her herself and her child, should it be born somewhere on the river. Her belongings fit into a small leather trunk, weighing exactly five pounds.

Mr. Hanna's personal belongings, including his writing material, a score of blank contract papers and sundry books came in at thirty pounds, making the Hanna's "personal belongings" equal the grand sum of thirty-five pounds. This was important, for part of how the *New Orleans* was judged would be in her capability to transport cargo. Everything, then, of the most insignificant weight, would be a credit.

A huge crowd gathered on the wharf to see the boat off. Glimpsing her first sight of the craft as she was directed through the throng caused Elizabeth to gasp. Like most others, she gawked at the peculiar "monster," already belching steam at the waterfront. She was immediately reminded of tales heard in childhood; stories her mother had whispered in her frightened ears about Scottish sea serpents, Irish demons and Welsh dragons.

Elizabeth believed those stories, as her mother and her mother before her had believed them. She was of the blood which espoused faith in wee people, giants and flying creatures. The boat she was to set foot aboard was a combination of all those tales she had heard as a girl, and yet somehow more terrifying, for it was the product of man's hands, not God's.

The distinction was a fine one, but palpable. A living thing, no matter how frightening, might be reasoned with. This insensitive thing was soulless.

It seemed an evil omen, filling her with the presentment of doom. Her fears were not allied by what she heard from the crowd.

"'tis the work of the Devil!"

"Man was not meant to travel by steam."

"It's ag'in nature."

"God will not be pleased."

Trying her best to ignore the doomsayers who were shouting no more than she thought, the lady clutching the small leather trunk was grabbed suddenly by the arm and halted by a spectator.

"You ain't goin' aboard, is ya?" he asked in horror.

"I am," she replied. Her heritage was the shepherds and the fishermen of the Old World; the brave men and women who had withstood famine, wars, invasion and harsh elements, eking out a living for thousands of years. She could do no less than uphold that tradition.

"You'll never live to see yer infant an orphan," he predicted.

The man's words were well-meaning but unappreciated.

"I go where my husband goes."

It was all she could think of to say.

"The boat will sink befer she ever gits to Cincinnati."

"God's will be done."

The very words her mother had spoken to her before she set out, a newly married bride, for the New World. That had been three years ago. Since that time, Elizabeth Hanna *nee* McGwinn, had traveled across a vast ocean, settled briefly in New York, then traveled from that teeming metropolis, half way across the United States.

God had protected her over five thousand miles. If He saw fit, He would protect her and her unborn child 1,000 more miles.

If He did not, the man's words would be prophetic: she would never live to see her child an orphan.

A band was playing as Elizabeth broke free of the stranger's hold and continued on her journey. Mr. Hanna had gone ahead, either not seeing or not caring about his wife's dalliance. It was his day, a day of days. He wanted to be the first aboard, the first to stand upon the deck and look back as the boat steamed her way into history.

For what was he born, if not for this?

He, too, had come five thousand miles. Aboard the *New Orleans,* he would be the first merchant to come to terms with those hungry, desperate buyers and traders along the route. He had already established his contracts with Roosevelt's *line;* the rest was up to him.

It was a time when fortunes were made. No longer would he be a shopkeeper in the fledgling city of Pittsburgh. Soon he would be a major merchant, a shipping magnate, a wheeler and dealer.

It would be something for which a man could look up to himself and be proud.

A reporter for the *Navigator* was squatting on the dock making a sketch of the boat as the first passengers arrived. His eyes were wild with excitement. Of the crowd, which was unevenly divided between those who thought the boat would explode, killing all aboard, and those who believed the *New Orleans* would steam triumphantly into the city for which she was named, he was decidedly on the side of the latter.

"My God, it's like living in a novel!" he reverently swore. "We live in exciting times." Seeing Mr. Hanna, he stood and inquired whether he were going aboard.

"I am," acknowledged the shopkeeper.

"May I have your signature, sir? On this sketch? I am going to collect all the names of the passengers for posterity."

Mr. Hanna paused to sign his name, in pencil, by the depiction of the hold. He noted that Nicholas J. Roosevelt, along with engineer Nicholas Baker, had signed before him. There was also the scrawled name of Andrew Jack, pilot.

The captain had signed by the wheel house, the engineer by the exposed smokestack in the center. The pilot had placed his name over the boat, signifying his guiding hand. It seemed only appropriate Hanna place his name in the area where cargo would be stowed.

The other passengers, including "six hands, two female servants, a man waiter, a cook, and an immense Newfoundland dog named 'Tiger'" were not invited to sign.

Neither were the wives.

It was, after all, an adventure for men of importance.

Men of commerce.

Hanna had not been the first aboard, as he hoped, but neither was he the last. That distinction belonged to Mrs. Hanna. When she was brought aboard, the passenger list was complete.

Joining her husband, Elizabeth turned and faced the crowd. Rare were the eyes not blinking back tears as the great paddlewheel began churning the waters of the Ohio.

"God bless!"

"Godspeed!"

"God protect them what don't know no better."

It was a time for piety.

Captain Roosevelt removed his hat and doffed it to the crowd. His wife held onto a small white handkerchief and waved it back and forth. William Hanna stood, hands at his side, savoring the moment. It was only when the boat pulled away from her moorings that he condescended to smile. His wife had no one to wave to and knew no one she cared to smile for.

She was, it might be styled, enduring with dignity.

Elizabeth might have been more excited, for she was a woman of courage and fortitude, had not the baby, inside her womb, taken that moment to begin kicking. His tiny feet, she thought, were emulating the paddlewheel.

He was to be a boy of the river.

A boy destined to look upon the mighty waters traversing the country as his mother and his father.

For so it had been prophesied.

CHAPTER 2

The *New Orleans,* a head of steam up, moved into the current and churned upstream, the first such craft ever to use man-made power to do so on western waters. It was a bit of bravado, moving against the river. Then, to the waves and well-wishes of those on shore, the boat turned and chugged past again, this time in the proper direction.

It was an historic moment.

On shore, the old rivermen, who were seeing their way of life irrevocably altered, shook their heads and held their breaths. It was not until the boat disappeared behind the headlands on the right bank of the Ohio they dared expel their pent-up emotion.

The times, they were a'changin'.

Which did not necessarily mean for the better.

"Might I have a map?" Mrs. Hanna inquired after her husband safely stowed her into private quarters. Had the boat been "full up," Mrs. Hanna would have had to share the accommodations with other women aboard. But as she was the only passenger, Mrs. Roosevelt staying with her husband, she had the suite to herself.

It was a luxury for which she was not unappreciative.

"A map?" gasped her startled husband. "For what do you want a map?"

"To follow our journey. I hear so many strange names mentioned and I do not know what they mean, or where they are. The 'Great Kanawha,' for instance. I have heard those words spoken. What, exactly do they signify?"

"You could not read a map," Mr. Hanna tartly replied. "How could a woman expect to read a map?"

"I am fluent in –"

"It is not a question of language," he interrupted. "It is a matter of mechanics. You might as well ask me for an engine to dissect, so that you will understand how steam propels this boat."

From which Elizabeth inferred her husband did not know the meaning of "Great Kanawha," and feared, if given a map, she would soon learn more than he.

Mrs. Hanna did not begrudge knowledge or even the withholding of knowledge from Mr. Hanna. He ran the household and consequently determined the proper order of things. She therefore silently acquiesced and privately asked Mrs. Roosevelt for a map.

Mrs. Roosevelt did not ask Mrs. Hanna why she required such an educational tool. Had she inquired, Elizabeth would have supplied her with a different answer than she gave her husband.

"I should like to know where, exactly, my baby is born. I cannot tell him, 'Son, you were born on the water.' He will not be satisfied with such a reply. So, I should like to be able to say, 'You were born exactly one mile from the Great Kanawha, which drains into the Ohio River between Pomeroy and Portsmouth," a fact she had learned from overhearing the pilot speaking to one of the crew who was, it appeared, also curious.

"Are you close to your time?" inquired a sympathetic Mrs. Roosevelt, instead.

"I feel... peculiar. I wish to be prepared."

Mrs. Roosevelt squeezed her hand. She, too, was very near her time but had never considered the problem of explaining to her offspring exactly where he was born. It gave her something to think about.

The weather remaining fair, both women spent time "on top," watching the amazing boat propel her way downstream.

"So much can be achieved with steam," the captain's wife explained to her eager listener. "My husband might have been the first to own the patent," she declared, staring into the swirling water. "He was an early inventor, himself. He knew Mr. Livingston before Mr. Fulton, I believe, and commanded his own boat, the *Polacca,* a dozen years before the *Clermont.* With the proper backing – the financial support the Chancellor eventually gave Mr. Fulton – he could have been famous."

"What happened? Did his boat sink?"

"Indeed it did not." The captain's wife paused to readjust her bonnet, turning away from the hot sun before continuing. "Mr. Livingston promised to help finance additional work, but he and my husband quarreled over the proper structure for such a vessel. When Mr. Livingston went to France as minister, Mr. Roosevelt diverted his attention to selling rolled copper to the government. Unfortunately, the Administration changed and his business failed. He could no longer afford to work on experimental boats.

"But he *was* the first. I wish you to know that."

"I will make note," her companion replied. It never occurred to her to question the verity of the statement. She trusted Mrs. Roosevelt and appreciated her support.

"And your husband?" probed the lady.

"Mr. Hanna and I come from Scotland," Elizabeth explained. "He wished to start a business venture in a new land. We might have gone to Ireland, where he was born, but he decided to come to America.

"We lived briefly in the state of New York before traveling by wagon to Pittsburgh. There he has established himself as a merchant. He, too, has great faith in the power of steam. If all goes well, he will operate the steamboat *line* from that city, as well as owning certain contracts for himself."

"You are a brave woman."

"No more so that you."

Mrs. Roosevelt laughed and shivered with excitement.

"I do not think of myself as brave. We are on a great adventure. Nothing would have kept me away. But you – why have you come?"

Mrs. Hanna had a more truthful answer than she gave.

"To be with my husband."

"We shall both bear a child on this trip. Ours will be great explorers, do you not think?"

Mrs. Hanna did not have so easy an answer for that question.

"Yes," she finally agreed.

It was as truthful as her previous response, but not so easily given.

She would have liked to be more confident but was not.

It was enough to imagine him born.

"Look there!" shouted Captain Roosevelt. "They have come out for the show."

He pointed to a group of woodsmen gathered on the edge of the river. The men stared in shocked amazement, more closely allied with fear, at the steam-belching boat sailing down the Ohio.

"The Devil is upon us!" they heard one man shout.

Instantly, the trappers fled, to the merriment of those aboard the *New Orleans.*

"We shall hear a lot of that and more, besides," Mr. Jack observed. He had come down from the pilot house to observe the men observing them. "They fear what they do not know."

"Cowards; backwoodsmen," said a contemptuous Roosevelt.

"Perhaps. But men are most dangerous when they see what they believe to be the spawn of evil. A man may shun a Red Indian because he is a savage, yet attack a monster he is terrified of, in the name of God."

"I see no reason to tremble from the likes of them. Or Red Indians," countered the captain. "If there is trouble, I have arms aboard. Let them come and we shall see who goes flying into this good night."

"I was not questioning your prowess with a musket, sir."

"You forget – I have been this way before. I know these people. I have seen Red Indians and I have spoken with these 'white natives.' We have nothing to fear from any of them."

"You have never seen them from the deck of a steamer."

"Your point is noted." Jack turned, but the captain summoned him back. "You were going to make a suggestion?"

"Merely the thought of setting a guard at night."

"We are not from the Devil, sir," came the tart rejoinder. Jack saluted and returned to his duties.

The boat passed other small groups of men, drawn to the water's edge by the sounds of the laboring engines and the tell-tale smoke from the boiler. The pilot made no more suggestions and the passengers ignored the wild stares and shouted statements from shore.

Mrs. Hanna noted that her unborn child kicked with greater urgency at those times, so she made a point of going below when spotting sightseers.

"Settlement ahead!" came the call. The boat's bell changed with frenzied urgency and everyone aboard, including the dog, rushed topside as the steamboat pulled into the protected shoreline.

"Hallo!" called Captain Roosevelt. "Hallo, on shore."

He need not have shouted, for nearly one hundred people, comprising the entire settlement of Point Pleasant, rapidly gathered to greet the amazing-looking river craft.

"What in tarnation is that?" called a man from shore.

"It is a steamboat," announced the captain.

"Where's yer sails?"

"She is powered by steam."

"By steam?" came the incredulous reply. "How does steam power a boat?"

"Come aboard and see."

The invitation caused exactly one half of the crowd to take a step back. Brave was the man who would set foot on a smoke-spewing monster, threatening to explode at any moment.

"I need wood. Is there any man here I can buy it from?"

"Woods are full of it. Hep yerself," came a helpful voice.

"Cordwood, if you please. Chopped wood. Is there any who can sell me some?"

"What are you gonna pay fer it with? Steam?"

A wave of wary amusement rippled through the crowd.

"Gold," shot back the answer.

Few men were adverse from accepting gold, even if it were from a madman aboard an even madder-appearing craft.

"Come ashore and dicker," called another. Captain Roosevelt donned his best blue suit and hat and accepted the offer.

"How much?" he inquired, stepping foot on shore.

The man he addressed jumped back and held out his hands in a gesture of friendly warning.

"Not too close, sir. Not until I'm sure you're a man."

"And what might I be, if not a man? A woman, perhaps?"

Roosevelt laughed at his own joke. A crowd gathered around him. None of them laughed.

"A river serpent."

Roosevelt was astonished. He pounded on his chest to declare himself sound, then held out his hands, displaying ten fingers.

"Do I look like a river serpent? And see – I have no tail."

He turned around to prove the point.

"That beast yer ridin' on, then."

"It is not a serpent, but a man-made river craft. Have none of you ever heard of Robert Fulton and his 'Infernal Machine'?" No answer. "Fulton's Folly?"

He had better luck with that. One man removed his beaver cap, scratched his bearded face, then nodded slowly.

"I've heerd of it. Back east, weren't it?"

"That's right. Mr. Fulton piloted the first steam-powered boat from New York City to Albany."

"I'd call it a 'folly,' too, iffn that's where I sailed fer."

It was another man who spoke. Roosevelt turned his attention to that speaker. He was short, stout and plain-faced, with long black hair and a leather vest hanging down to his knees.

"You sir, appear to be an educated man. Might you oblige me with cordwood?"

The long haired man turned to his companion and shook his head.

"He thinks I'm an ed-u-ca'ed man because I know where Albany is – and where it ain't. How about that?"

"Where is it?" his friend inquired.

"Nowhere."

It was an old joke. Both local men chuckled heartily before the first turned back to a perplexed Roosevelt.

"I might have wood to sell. Iffn you make it worth my while."

The captain smiled. With the long strides of a man who knew what he wanted and how to obtain it, he joined the pair.

"Let us have a talk. Is there a place we may retire for a drink shared 'round a bottle?"

"There might be."

"Lead away."

The captain returned in an hour with a signed contract to purchase wood and a broad addendum scrawled to the bottom.

"What'd you agree to?" asked his engineer as the captain re-boarded the boat.

"Nothing more than a fair price and the promise to promote the 'Traveller's Rest,' his inn, to the rest of the world. The 'world' being anywhere we stop on the Ohio and Mississippi. A simple matter of business."

"Don't that tie the pup," Mr. Baker muttered to himself, walking away.

Engines, he decided, made sense. People he would leave to others.

"Come, my dear," Mr. Hanna urged his wife. "The captain is inviting the entire population aboard to have a close look at the ship. I wish us to make an appearance."

"Will many come?" she asked with trepidation. Mrs. Hanna was not feeling well and dreaded the thought of "entertaining."

"Some will, I suppose. There appear to be men of intellect there; men of business," he added, though he need not have. She sighed and put on a stoical face.

"Surely, Mr. and Mrs. Roosevelt would care to do the honors by themselves."

"Not a bit of it. Come, hurry and get dressed. This is the reason I am aboard – to make new contacts; establish myself as an important man. Those who see me with the Roosevelts will remember me. When the time comes, it is to me they will bargain."

"Time comes," was perhaps a more apt expression than he intended. Elizabeth's unborn charge was reminding her of his presence. Deep inside the innermost reaches of her body, his little fingers were tapping out a message only she could hear.

Time comes, I shall come a'calling, he said.

It was a gentle, persistent reminder. Her baby was asking not to be forgotten.

His time was nigh.

Despite her presentment of imminent birth, Mrs. Hanna did as her husband commanded. She dressed as conservatively as possible, then wrapped a shawl around her shoulders. The October wind was chill and she feared catching cold.

Coming aboard the *New Orleans* were seventeen men, all with eyes agape. These brave citizens of Point Pleasant roamed the craft from stem to stern, asking questions, pointing with wonder, nodding their heads wisely and jumping when the slightest current caused the boat to shift.

"Never thought I'd see one of these in my life," declared the innkeeper. "But you're going with the current, Mr. Roosevelt. It's another thing entirely to go ag'in it. You'll never be seed in these waters ag'in."

"Then you have bargained your wood away for nothing."

"Nothing an' a most generous price," he agreed.

"There will be great opportunities for men like you," the partner of Fulton and Livingston continued. "Once we have established our *line,* you will see steamboats up and down the Ohio every week."

"Reckon that'll happen," came the dubious reply.

The group was lead on the Grand Tour. No cabin was left unturned and Mrs. Hanna was glad she had not begged off and remained in bed, for the idea of privacy had certainly given way to that of novelty.

"Why is it you have womenfolk aboard?" asked a young man with obvious skepticism in his voice.

"Once the feasibility of rapid, two-way travel is established, families will flock from east to west, looking for a new start, seeking land and opportunity. It is westward expansion," he added. "These paying passengers will constitute a great portion of the cargo our *line* will carry. We cannot house the gentleman without their ladies. It would be unthinkable. But we do insist on separating the genders."

"Wouldn't want no one to call it a floating whore house," someone from the back dryly observed. His comment was ignored out of deference to good breeding.

"The *New Orleans* is a side-wheeler," Roosevelt continuing, leading the tour back on deck. "She is sound for a three-hundred ton burden."

"And what's them things?"

"Those, sir," the proud operator explained, ignoring the levity in the man's voice, "Are sails. In case of trouble. I do not wish it said I exposed my passengers to danger."

"How much it cost to build one of these machines?"

"This boat cost in the whereabouts of $38,000 to construct, my good man."

Which caused the visitors to be more respectful.

Below decks, they peered into the yawning opening where fuel was stoked, shuddering at the heat still radiating from the furnace.

"This thing catches fire, you'll all be meetin' yer Maker sooner'n yer expectin'."

"Yes. Fire is a very real possibility, I have to admit. But the boiler is watched at all times."

"Satan's breath." The speaker stepped back and shook his head. "God never meant for man to rise above his station like this."

"My good man, God gave man a brain to use. If it were not for far-thinkers such as Mr. Fulton and myself, where would the world be today? You live in an age of modern wonder, sir. Inventions are changing the face of the world. Imagine what the steamboats will offer mankind."

"Never, by God!" swore a man whose arms resembled bands of iron. "I ain't ready fer it an' the river don't want it. I'm a keelboatman an' I'd as soon you and yer crew all drowned befer I see these damn boats takin' over my river."

His words were meant as a threat and taken seriously. The keeler and his type made their living drawing keelboats and barges upstream by dint of sheer strength. They were the kings of the river, the men who ruled the waters. They were tough, mean and contrary. Roosevelt had met their type on his previous voyage down the river on an exploratory trip by flatboat and understood perfectly the danger he was in.

With little respect for law and less for human life, these brawlers would not go quietly. What they saw as the end of their dominance would compel them to fight like alligators. Worse than Red Indians, they were the new savages, bound and determined to replace the old.

"Might be, one night a river rat slips aboard and slits yer throats," he pursued. "Wouldn't make me sorry."

"Perhaps not, sir, but you cannot stop progress by slitting throats."

"Wanna bet?"

Mr. Roosevelt decided he did not want to bet, knowing he would never live to collect.

"I thank you, gentleman," he said with a smile. "The tour is now over."

The men piled off the boat and the boiler was restocked with wood. With a ringing of the bell, the *New Orleans* chugged away on her epic voyage.

At the rear of the boat, in a cabin fit for four, Mrs. Hanna wrapped the shawl closer around her shoulders and mumbled a prayer.

They had come to a harsh new world and she was going to bring a new life into it. As if reading her thoughts, the baby kicked.

It was not for attention, but to agree with her sentiment.

Harshness would be a word this child knew well.

Better, in fact, than his own name.

On the river, priorities always took precedence.

CHAPTER 3

When the *New Orleans* arrived in Cincinnati two days later, the boat was welcomed with wild enthusiasm. It was not that the citizens of this burgeoning new city had more faith in steam than those upriver. It was that many remembered Nicholas Roosevelt from his prior trip, and the promise he had made.

"The next time you see me, I will be commanding a boat powered by steam. The same steam, boiled in the same manner as a tea kettle."

Mr. Roosevelt and his steam-powered tea kettle had kept the promise.

The wharf was filled with men, women and children, each wanting to see a piece of floating history. White handkerchiefs fluttered in the breeze, men waved their hats, babies cried at the loud, unfamiliar sounds.

A man's word was his bond and Nicholas Roosevelt's word was worth a great deal. He had kept a promise no one expected he would. That was much in this city situated on the edge of forever.

Not enough to encourage any to book passage for the ride to New Orleans, however. That was left to more intrepid souls – and their wives. It was enough to know the businessman had kept faith. It would be asking too much for others to share in it.

After purchasing wood and replenishing the galley with fresh meat and drink, the boat puffed away, leaving behind her the tell-tale trail of grey smoke, white-churned water and red faces.

Everything was going according to schedule.

On October 24th, near midnight, exactly sixty-four hours after leaving Pittsburgh, the *New Orleans* drew up at Louisville. The half-moon was especially bright, illuminating the water so that any man might have thought it day. This brightness allowed the crew to pilot the steamboat during the night.

Captain Roosevelt and his passenger, William Hanna, were standing on deck as orders were given for the reduction of speed.

"We'll stay a week; maybe longer," the commander decided. Then, turning to Hanna, he continued with a grin. 'Never pass up an opportunity to make friends. This will become an important city if we live up to our promise of establishing a steamboat *line*. There will be lots of cargo to pick up and dispatch here. They also have a newspaper."

Hanna smiled. He understood the power of the press.

"Shall you invite the respectable citizens aboard, as you did at Point Pleasant?"

"Oh, we shall give the rich and powerful of Louisville a reception they shall not soon forget," he promised with a wink. Then, turning to his wheelhouse, Roosevelt gave a silent command. Immediately, an ear-splitting roar escaped into the night. "Nothing like the power of steam – whether it be 'making waves' with forward movement or noise – to impress."

"You will wake everyone up!" exclaimed Hanna.

"Exactly my intention."

In less than fifteen minutes the dock was filled with men, some of whom had rushed out of their houses in nightshirts. Everyone wanted to see the cause of the terrible belching noise. In their wildest nightmares, none of them could have dreamed up what met their eyes.

"At furst I thought it were on fire," confessed one man to another standing beside him. "All that smoke and noise. Sounded like all hell broke loose."

"And so it has," agreed his companion. "The world has never seen nothing like it."

The *New Orleans* continued to shake and dance in the water like a live thing as her boilers were shut down. With her decks illuminated by moonlight and every oil lamp on board brought up on deck to celebrate the midnight arrival of the wooden leviathan, the atmosphere was charged with expectation.

The very foundation of wood and earth upon which Louisville's citizens stood, trembled from escaping power. The passengers aboard had grown used to this phenomenon, but for those who had never witnessed it, the sight was nothing short of miraculous.

"Miraculous" in the sense of wondrous, rather than from any religious connotation.

"I don't believe it. It ain't right."

The speaker was a tall man, dressed in black. He did not join the crowd waiting to greet those disembarking from the strange visitation, but lingered behind, staring with calm, though narrowed eyes.

He did not speak again until the small procession was making its way inland. Then, seeing a woman, very obviously in the family way, struggle to keep up with her husband, he stepped forward and placed a hand on her arm.

"God has a message for you," he hissed through clenched teeth. "He has blessed you once by bestowing a child into your womb. Do not go back aboard that boat, or your life will be in danger."

The woman he stopped was Mrs. Roosevelt. She grabbed her arm back and shoved the man aside.

"Kindly do not block my way," she advised. "I have as much faith in that steamboat as I do in God. My life is not in danger from either."

"I had a dream," the preacher persisted. "A warning."

"Do not drink milk before retiring, sir, and I expect you will have no more premonitions."

"No good can come to any child born aboard that boat. He will be cursed. Believe me. His life will be plagued by demons. He will be the harbinger of ill fortune for any who cross his path."

"He. He. He," Mrs. Roosevelt repeated. "And what if I am carrying a girl child?"

The man's answer was lost to her as she hurried away. The question had been meant as rhetorical. The wife of the west's first steamboat captain did not have time for foolishness. The man clearly did not understand the difference between God's message and dyspepsia.

After a brief ceremony conducted under torch light, there was much hand shaking and head wagging. Not everyone was convinced of the wonderfulness of the new arrival, however, or of the source of the gigantic noise which had come close to breaking the ear drums of those unfortunate enough to live at the water's edge.

The headline in the two-sheet newspaper next morning read, "Comet of 1811 strikes near Louisville."

The text of the article, written by a Mister H. C. Leeky, went on to predict dire consequences for the future of steamboats.

"They are noisy, creating false rivers of current on the water. Belching huge clouds of dirty air, this new-fangled boat arrived in Louisville last night, coinciding exactly with the crash of a great comet to earth.

"The Bible states that the End Of The World is nigh when such beasts as Steamboats make their appearance in God-fearing cities. No Greater Proof of this can be had, then the Nearby Crash of a Great Comet."

"It was not a comet," Captain Roosevelt patiently explained to a group of influential citizens at breakfast. "There was no comet crashing to earth. The noise, I tell you, came from the release of steam. No more than that.

And if God had not wanted men to make steamboats, he would not have created trees to fuel them."

It was a good joke and everyone laughed heartily.

When told of the captain's wit by Mrs. Roosevelt, Mr. Hanna laughed too. He had been unable to attend the breakfast due to his wife's condition. She had taken ill during the evening and required his presence.

"Come, Mrs. Hanna," he encouraged, pausing to check the time on his pocket watch. "Your color has returned. Tell me you are feeling better and I will still have time to go ashore and meet the men Captain Roosevelt entertains. That was the purpose of our coming," he added.

"I am feeling better," she urged him. He did not require a second confirmation.

"Fine. Keep in good spirits. That is very important. I would not wish the disposition of our child soured by your bad thoughts. You know what influences a maternal mind has on an unborn infant."

"Yes, husband."

"Then smile, so he will be a cheerful lad."

She smiled.

"That is better. And do not listen to town gossip. I have been assured by the first mate no comet fell last night. It was only the roar of the steam which scared these superstitious people. No more than that."

"A comet is an ill omen," she dared whisper.

"Then it is as well none fell."

She did not bothering explaining to him that an hour before arriving in Louisville, she had seem a shooting star streak across the night sky.

Such thoughts were better left unsaid.

Three days later, a public dinner was offered by the leading men of Louisville to the captain and his passenger. Inasmuch as the ladies were not invited, they stood together on board, watching the setting of the late autumn sun.

"It was the most peculiar thing," Mrs. Roosevelt remarked. "The preacher said any child born aboard this boat would be the harbinger of ill luck. His life would be cursed. What nonsense. My child will be as brave and stalwart as any ever born on land."

Mrs. Hanna nodded her head and said nothing. Apparently Mrs. Roosevelt did not remember or take into account her own similar condition.

Or perhaps she thought Elizabeth would feel as she did.

In that, Mrs. Roosevelt erred.

Elizabeth Hanna was frightened. Not for herself and not of idle threats.

"There," she said, pointing upward. "The moon is half full."

"Yes. It is beautiful. I think I have never seen it so bright."

"There will be a blue moon at the end of the month."

For once, Mrs. Roosevelt was puzzled.

"What does that mean, my dear?"

"It is also called a harvest moon; the second full moon in one month. They are very rare."

"How interesting. I wish I had been invited to that dinner."

Mrs. Roosevelt was a woman who knew what she wanted and how she would obtain it. Every moment of her life was calm, calculated and served to promote her goals. She was involved with her husband's business ventures, excited about everything connected with steamboats and not adverse to danger. She was hardly, as some were apt describe the weaker gender, a woman given to fancies.

Mrs. Hanna was cut from a different cloth than her fellow passenger, but she was no more fanciful. Of stout, long-suffering Scottish-Irish stock, she understood danger as well as the next woman. The difference being, she did not view it as a challenge. Nor did she face the dire premonitions of the preacher man with an eye toward either her own safety or that of her husband's.

It was her unborn child which caused her concern.

Across a journey of five thousand miles, from her home on the shore of lochs so deep they went to the very core of the earth, Elizabeth McGwinn Hanna had learned a thing or two, remembered others told her by women far older and wiser than she. Dreams were visitations from God. Cloud formations always told stories. Revealed in the scattered tea leaves on the bottom of cups lay the mysteries of the future.

There were good signs and bad signs. There was a right and a wrong way to do everything. Luck was dependent upon which way the wind blew and dried leaves could be spun into gold by wee people.

A man with a premonition was one visited by the Spirits. What he saw and how he interpreted his visions were not always correct, but always demanded consideration.

A falling star was an ill omen.

A comet crashing to earth meant great change.

Together, a premonition, a falling star and a comet meant unrest in the universe. That which was, that which had been, that which would be, had subtly altered. The rules had changed. God was putting His people on guard.

Take nothing for granted. The rivers would flow backwards, roosters would lay eggs, the sun would not rise and the moon would not set.

A new day was dawning, whether it be to darkness or to light, Elizabeth did not know.

The blue moon was the key. In her life, she could remember only one other time there had been a blue moon. Then, she had been a wild lass, carefree and full of spirit. Ignoring her grandmother's warning to stay inside during the three days of the full moon, she had gone alone to the lochs, to swim in the luminous light of the celestial night beacon.

Three eventides she had swum in the ancient waters. On each night she had seen her reflection in the water. The features which stared back at her were strong, handsome, sensitive, yet not her own at all. They belonged to another, a stranger she had never met.

There was a familiarity in the eyes, in the cut of the jaw, in the color of the hair. When the image was very clear, she could see the freckles on the nose, dotting the cheeks, creeping into the hairline, so like her own, but not her own. Closing her eyes, she could trace the ears and knew they were her ears, touch the warmth of skin and recognize its feel.

This stranger was her and it was not her and she did not understand.

It was a youth's face Elizabeth saw reflected in the water, magically transformed into reality by the faerie light of the blue moon. What she saw was a boy's face, impish, loving, trusting, then changing just as suddenly into expressions of bitterness, impatience and anger.

She had thought, at first, the countenance she stared at was to be the face of her lover. She laughed, teased, cajoled the unknown boy-man from loneliness into happiness. She sang to the rippling reflection of his face, whispered stanzas of poetry, foolish rhymes that came to her lips so spontaneously she knew not where they originated.

She called him Blue Moon, because he had come to her with the rays of that far away heavenly body. She stared into his deep brown eyes, kissed his freckled forehead, ran her long, slender fingers through his flowing red locks and called him her own.

He was her secret, her elf, her love, her purpose for living.

For three days she lived only for the night and during those three nights of the blue moon, she lived a lifetime.

On the morning of the fourth day, her grandmother died. Elizabeth was not able to return to the loch for a fortnight. When she did, no boyish, red-haired, freckled face came to welcome her.

He was gone.

Vanished with the blue moon.

Elizabeth McGwinn never forgot that boy. Never stopped loving him.

Never whispered a word to a living soul about her visitation.

She did not know everything, but she understood this much: To tell a dream is to spoil it.

Elizabeth had returned to the water, swam in its deep bosom, searched with frantic urgency for his strange yet well-known face and did not find him. She did not think she would. He was from a time out of context.

Nor did she complain when William Hanna came to court her. He was not her freckle-faced boy of the blue moon: he had not his red hair, his changeable moods, his piercing brown eyes. Mr. Hanna was an old man, a man of thirty, and she a lass of sixteen. He was stiff, unyielding, hard.

Mr. Hanna was a man seeking a young bride. With her parents' permission, he had married her and taken her away from the lochs of her birth. She had gone with him without protest.

That was the way of the world; a world without blue moons.

She had never thought to see another, yet soon it would rise in the night sky like a vision, a promise. A blue moon, so many miles, so many years removed from her home and her lochs and her dreams.

Elizabeth knew now whose face she had seen in the luminous water.

The face of her child, bearing her bright red hair and her freckles and her ears.

He had come to her in spirit because she would never have him in flesh.

A premonition, a falling star and a comet.

And soon a blue moon.

The world was changing again.

The mother-to-be left the side of her companion and retired to her cabin. There, from the depths of her small leather traveling case, she brought forth a cameo. It was not her face depicted thereon, but she had never seen anything like it. When she had cried so at first seeing such a treasure, William Hanna bought it for her. It was not like him to be so generous, yet she had accepted his gift without question and without thanks.

Like reflections in locks, some events in life were unfathomable.

Taking the brooch out, the woman wrapped her fingers around the oval piece of jewelry as though it were the body of her child she was embracing. Kissing it with her lips, blessing it with her flowing tears, she sat down suddenly and wrote two words on the back of the shiny, black stone base of the cameo with a pencil.

Blue Moon.

A message from beyond time for a boy she would never know.

CHAPTER 4

The *New Orleans* delayed her departure due to low water, allowing Captain Roosevelt to be wined and dined by the citizens of Louisville. He was the man of the hour, a man with the future beneath his feet. He was the harbinger of all new and wonderful tidings, and William Hanna shared his glory.

Commerce was the key to opening the west and steamboats were that promise of prosperity. On the night following one large party ashore, the Captain and his lady gave a scrumptious dinner for the same men who had so graciously entertained him. It was not the food, however, for which this party would be remembered.

"It's moving! Good God, the steamboat has slipped anchor!"

Forks were frozen in mid-motion as the guests turned their ears toward an easily discernible rumbling.

"Fire! Fire!"

Cries of alarm spread like flood waters. Guests and crew alike jumped to their feet and raced up the companionway, the fear of being trapped below spurring them on.

As the assemblage reached topside, the men from Louisville cried again, this time by having their original suspicions confirmed.

"She's moving! We're adrift!"

"Someone save us!"

"My God, we are headed for the Falls! No boat of this type can pass the Falls without breaking up!"

Before any of the terrified guests could make the decision to jump overboard, the man of the hour, their host and the harbinger of Things To Come stepped forward, arms outstretched.

"Gentlemen. Gentlemen," he cajoled them. "Do not fear. Your captain has everything under control."

"But we are moving, sir," gasped one, his hands noticeably trembling.

"Indeed we are."

"The boat is out of control!"

Mr. Roosevelt's smile widened.

"If that were so, would I be standing here like this, enjoying your consternation?"

It was, perhaps, a poor choice of words, but in his moment of triumph and their terror, the social *faux pas* was overlooked.

"Then what is the meaning of this?"

"Have I not invited you all to dine aboard the *New Orleans?*" he graciously inquired. "And is the *New Orleans* not a steamboat? What do steamboats do, gentlemen?" Without waiting for an answer, he supplied one himself. "They travel the great western waterways."

There was a momentary lull in the panic as deep breaths were drawn in, then exhaled.

"Please be more clear, Captain," begged the mayor. As the head of the delegation, he felt it behooved him to clarify the mystery.

"Being the accommodating host – and keeping in mind my duty to the *line* – that is, to introduce the uninitiated to this new and exciting mode of travel – I have played a small prank on you."

"Prank?" gasped a man clutching his heart.

"I am giving you a ride. Free of charge," he added, a simple acknowledgement to priorities.

"Do you mean to say, sir, this was all planned?"

"Of course. There is no fire and the *New Orleans* has not slipped her anchor. I gave orders to Mr. Baker to weigh anchor near the end of dinner. I hope I have not frightened any of you too much?"

The question was a direct call to his guest's manhood. It was a summons none dared refuse. A tittering of nervous laughter supplied their support for his "prank."

"And please note: we are not headed for the Falls. That dangerous journey I shall ask none of you to accompany me on."

It took several minutes for erratically beating hearts and rasping breaths to regulate. Time, and the repeated reassurance the boat was paddling in the opposite direction from the Falls calmed the civilians.

None wished to have their courage called to question. And a boat ride, free of charge, was an exciting opportunity, after all.

"How wonderful!" the mayor exclaimed.

"Something to tell our grandchildren," whispered another, glad to know he would have the opportunity of living to see his progeny.

Having been forewarned of the short journey the boat would make this night, Mrs. Hanna remained in her cabin. Her stomach was not well. She had made her excuses early, fearing the consequences of Captain Roosevelt's prank. In their rush to get safely ashore, she might have been trampled in the melee. She did not express this concern to her husband, however, knowing beforehand he would not approve.

This was business, after all, and nothing had a right to stand in the way of progress.

More spirits were consumed after the incicent, allowing the non-paying passengers to relax and praise their host.

"Delightful."

"Extraordinary."

"A once in a lifetime opportunity."

The latter sentiment, it was hoped by the crew, was merely an exaggeration.

The party was declared a great success and written about next morning in the local newspaper. The word "excitement" was substituted for "panic."

Low water continued to prevent the *New Orleans* from attempting a passage through the Falls of Ohio, a difficult area of swift current, hemmed in by steep rock, immediately below Louisville. Dreaded by all rivermen, it was deemed best to wait for higher water before making the attempt. If steamboats were to prove their worth, they would routinely have to traverse such navigational horrors. If the boat were broken up on her maiden voyage, not only would a great deal of investment capital be lost, so, too, would the *line* of Fulton and Livingston stuffer demoralization.

Time was not important on this first trip.

Timing was.

It would not be underestimating the situation to declare it critical.

After a brief trip upstream to Cincinnati and back, rain in the upper Ohio Valley finally rose the water levels to an acceptable point. Good-byes were said, prayers uttered and the traditional "Godspeed" shouted from those remaining on shore.

Mrs. Roosevelt, who had not been seen all morning, came on deck and waved her handkerchief. Dressed in loose-fitting clothing, her condition was not readily apparent until the boat was underway. It was only then, after the celebrating died down, that she announced to her husband he had become a father.

"That is wonderful news!" Captain Roosevelt cried. "I am glad the baby has been safely delivered and you did not have to miss our departure."

"I should not have missed it for the world," she agreed. "This is high adventure."

Elizabeth Hanna remained below with another woman's newborn and the maid. She was out of sorts. No one missed her absence, she not being required to mark the summons, "All hands on deck!"

The crew of the *New Orleans* took aboard an experienced "rapids pilot" in Louisville. He stood in the bow with Mr. Baker as the anchor was weighed and the boat left her moorings.

With a full head of steam for added speed, should the boat lose control in the swift current, the next fateful leg of the journey began.

Following the example of those around him, William Hanna grasped the railing with both hands. Already accustomed to the shriek of the safety valve, he stared straight ahead, looking to the future with grim determination. A man was called upon to have faith. His did not desert him. No tall tales of barges and keelboats breaking up in the wild water of the Falls could shake his courage. Not even the stories of how men drown or were battered to death by timber torn lose from their own boat could deter his enthusiasm.

This is what he had come for; this was the Opening of the West.

If a price were to be paid, he was good for it.

Any price.

The boat made a wide circuit for the Indiana Channel, then turned in a cloud of billowing steam and headed downstream.

As she picked up steam, spray was cast upon all those who stood on deck. Never had the boat made such rapid progress. Steep overhangs of rock flashed by with lightning rapidity. The *New Orleans* lurched, driven by the current, sending the crew flying from location to location as they skidded on the deck, now slippery as glass. The roar of the impending Falls made speech impossible. Orders were flashed by hand signs.

"Great Jesus, we're not going to make it!" came a high-pitched scream. The words echoed eerily off the steep cliffs, coming back each time fainter, yet no less poignant.

Great Jesus, we are not going to make it.

Distorted by hysteria, twisted by the whip of angry water, smothered by the churning of the paddlewheel, the speaker's voice was unidentifiable. It could have been anyone aboard, either a man or a woman. The only living soul who was exempt from this patent loss of faith was the Newfoundland, Tiger. He could not speak English, but as he cowered between his mistresses' legs, he put on no braver front than his human companions.

The passage was over almost before anyone knew what happened. The *New Orleans* shot past the dreaded Falls and settled herself into the safer waters of the Ohio. No one breathed, no one cared to move or make idle shouts of triumph. Not until they were sure.

That sureness took a minute, five minutes. Ten. It was only when they had readjusted their hearing to block out the sound of the Falls, now cascading behind them, and once more grew accustomed to the steady, faithful rotation of the driving paddlewheel that they truly believed in their accomplishment.

In this awesome stillness, the one discernible, distinct sound making its way upward from the bowels of the boat was the wail of a newborn babe.

It carried with it the reminder of both life and death.

"Very well," Captain Roosevelt declared, wiping his damp hands on his even wetter trousers. His steady, controlled voice was belied by the fact his face was ashen white. "We shall have a jolly time describing this adventure to our partners."

His words signaled a return to normalcy. Orders were given to "round to." The rapids pilot departed, his pockets full. He spoke not a word. If it were not for the fact he made idle chatter coming aboard, the passengers might have thought him mute.

"Smooth sailing ahead," Roosevelt declared, speaking to the waters of the western river. "We accepted your challenge and beat you. Never again shall you hold us in terror."

Proving prophesies and predictions were the realm of seers and not riverboat captains.

Their journey continued in much the same fashion as it had above the Falls. Terrified calls of "The British are coming!" rang through the trees, as old soldiers, remembering their not so far-distant enemies, described the smoke-belching floating "sawmill."

When the *New Orleans* tarried for wood or stopped to explain their "contraption" to the backwoodsmen who gathered on shore, there was time for rest and relaxation. Fresh supplies were purchased. Aided by the promise of "smooth sailing" ahead, good time was made.

"Exactly on schedule," for they had no schedule, the steamboat passed from the Ohio into the Mississippi, an Ojibway Indian word meaning "Great River." And great she was, for it would be on these waters the *line* of Fulton and Livingston would steam to a new world.

But as though to prove any new world had links to the old, Mother Nature stepped in, least she be forgotten, along with the era of keelboats and barges.

It began at night, while the *New Orleans* was at anchor. Like the party at Louisville, the tremors began quietly, then increased in force, rattling the boat from stem to stern. The cable attached to the anchor jumped like a writhing snake, rousing the slumbering passengers into wakefulness.

Going with her husband, Elizabeth Hanna ran topside, casting anxious glances toward the smoke stack. It was cold and dead.

"Fire in the boiler," she head a man whisper, but that could not be right. The night air was fresh and clean, the stars shone bright. No smoke bellowed from below, no acrid half-burned particles stung her nose.

Fire, it was well known, posed the greatest threat to a steamboat. But like prophesies and predictions, that which is well known is not always true.

The engineer came up the companionway, shaking his head.

"No fire," he declared.

"Check again. There must be."

He disappeared, then returned with the same message.

"No fire."

The trembling persisted, growing stronger, more insistent, more demanding with each passing moment. If Mrs. Hanna has to describe it, she would have likened the feeling to being on a sailing ship at sea, tossed relentlessly about by wind and wave.

Clutching hands to stomach, she stifled a groan, suppressing an insistent nausea, not entirely the result of the heaving boat.

"What is it?" she heard Roosevelt ask. His question went unanswered, hanging in the air like mist over the lochs she remembered so well.

Elizabeth Hanna did not need to know the scientific explanation for the mighty hand of nature playing with the *New Orleans* as though it were a child's toy.

A shooting star.

A comet falling to earth.

An earthquake.

All premonitions came in threes.

She had been waiting.

Her time had come.

With a low cry of pain, she doubled up, nearly losing her balance as the ship quivered beneath her. She steadied herself against a railing, then groped her way along it, barely making it to the foot of the stairs before another, far more powerful tremor shook the boat.

Her absence was not noticed as she descended the steps, one at a time. At the foot, she paused for breath, then cried again as a spasm of agony shot through her body, wracking her slight frame.

"Merciful spirit," she prayed, not to God, but to the soul of her long dead grandmother. "Have pity."

"Have pity," the unspoken portion of her prayer meant, "Not for me, but for the new live I am to bring forth."

She half stumbled, half crawled to her stateroom and shut the door. There was no time, no opportunity to summon help. She was alone.

As isolated here as she had been while swimming in the loch.

As she knew she would be.

Elizabeth could have shrieked from the torturous pain of giving birth, but did not. Her reticence was not from fear no one would come. She wanted no one. She was silent now, saving her tears.

Tears she would cry for her lost love.

There was no way of telling time and no need. She writhed on the bed, clutched the sheet between her teeth, bore her agony as she had once born her loneliness.

In darkness he had come to her and in darkness he came again. Not in the guise of a boy or a man or an elf, but in the shape of a baby. She felt the head pass, then the shoulders and the body. As the earth twitched and upheaved its terrible force upon the world, a son was born to her.

In the preternatural gloom of a world turned upside down, her infant cried, taking in his first breaths of air to the accompaniment of the shaking earth and the crashing of the waves of the Mighty Mississippi.

She did not have to see him to know what he looked like. He had her red hair, her freckles, her nose.

He had her destiny.

He had come to take her place in the world.

In sorrow thou shall bring forth children.

Her sorrow was not for herself but for her baby.

With shaking hands, Elizabeth took the cameo from the pocket of her dress and affixed it to a blanket which covered her child. Cradling the precious bundle to her bosom, she stood and walked unsteadily to the port window. There, she held him out, baptizing him in the rays of the full moon.

The blue moon.

CHAPTER 5

There was blood splattered over the floor of the cabin. William Hanna nearly slipped on the fluid as he walked in, calling for his wife. His first thought was that spray from the wildly breaking waves had come in through the port hole. He cursed under his breath.

"God damn it, why didn't you cover the window?"

His answer came in the form of a plaintive cry. It originated not from his wife, but from his newborn son.

"Mrs. Hanna?" he called. Then, more demandingly, "Mrs. Hanna! Speak to me. What has happened here? I expected you on deck. We are experiencing an earthquake. The captain says it is from the 'New Mah-drid' Fault. We are sick on deck; nauseous from the effects of the boat shaking."

For his patient, if excited explanation, he received no reply.

It was the continuing wail of the baby which finally alerted him to the ominous nature of events.

"Mrs. Hanna – are you asleep? Have you Mrs. Roosevelt's child?"

The slight form representing the true nature of the tragedy was shrouded in blackness.

Having no lucifer matches on his person with which to light a lamp, Hanna was forced to go topside to obtain a light. Returning with a lantern, the businessman and adventurer sucked in his breath at the carnage before him.

His wife lay on the floor by the open port hole she had negligently forgotten to cover. Her head was twisted at an unnatural angle, her legs bent at the knees, as though she had been overcome and fainted. In her arms she grasped a blanket, which, upon first glance, appeared to be alive.

Subsequent investigation revealed a tiny, red-haired infant tucked into its protective wool.

Mr. Hanna did not touch his wife, nor did he make any attempt to retrieve his child from the arms of its dead mother. This was woman's work. He backed out stiffly, summoning Mrs. Roosevelt with a preemptive call.

The task of cleaning the room, cutting the limp, dead-white umbilical cord to separate mother from son and preparing both bodies, one for life, the other for death, fell to the maid.

"This is a tragedy," Mrs. Roosevelt declared, wringing her hands in an unusual display of emotion.

"It certainly is," her husband agreed.

"The young mother is dead. There is no one to feed the baby."

"First a comet, then the earthquake. These superstitious backwoodsmen and rivermen are apt to blame it on the *New Orleans.* What terrible timing. Add a death to the first two and you have three remarkable occurrences. Three is a Holy Number. There will be trouble. We must see to it the blame is placed elsewhere," Captain Roosevelt stated.

"You will have to ask Mr. Hanna to get off the boat and take the infant with him."

"I cannot do that. I have an agreement. He is to sail with us as far as New Orleans."

"What shall we do with the body? It must be buried."

"If we take it to a settlement, there will be questions. People will talk."

"Bury her along the side of the river."

There was a short pause while the captain thought the matter over. He had weighty obligations to consider.

"Along the river? In unconsecrated ground?"

"We shall pray over the grave."

"And the child? We will have to get a wet nurse for it, I suppose?"

"Yes. We can say we need the nurse to feed our own babe. That will allay suspicion."

"The crew is already upset; do not speak of this to them. If we are careful, they need not know. Mrs. Hanna seldom went topside. They will not miss her until we are at the mouth of the Mississippi."

Burying Elizabeth Hanna, *nee* McGwinn proved more of a problem than the Roosevelts anticipated. Because of the violent trembling, water in the river rose to flood levels. Earth along the banks was either washed away or submerged, making a landing out of the question.

The intense heat from the boiler precluded all possibility of placing the body below decks. Leaving it in the women's stateroom was only a short-term solution, for the heat of the day would cause the flesh to rot and subsequently fill the room with noxious odors.

After a brief consultation with Mr. Hanna, it was decided to wrap the body in a blanket and drop it overboard. This measure was no less than the dead woman would have received at sea.

There was some speculation that the infant, tiny and sickly, would die before the body was disposed of. That would eliminate the need for a search in quest of a lactating mother. The unnamed son, for so his gender was identified by the maid, did not die, and the body of his mother was sent to its final reward without him.

Captain Roosevelt was correct in his suspicion that the queer, ungodly steamboat with its dark clouds of wood smoke and wild, unnatural noises would be blamed as the cause of the earth tremors. Men standing well back into the woods waved their fists at the apparition, cursing it as the spawn of the devil.

"Ignorant fools!"

Dangerous, ignorant fools.

The men of the river who did not stand on shore and curse posed a far different problem. One the commander had not foreseen.

"Take us away!" they begged. "Take us out of here before the river rises and we are all drowned."

"The end of the world is nigh. Let us come aboard before the Great Mississippi swallows us whole."

"The wrath of God had shown His mighty power. Take us with you."

The steamboat was equipped to carry eighty passengers. The captain might have consented to grant that number of requests, but as they traveled down the river, they encountered three times eighty men, women and children pleading for escape.

"I am not God. I cannot choose who lives and who dies," he informed the supplicants from the bow of the boat. "If I take some, those left behind will feel cheated."

Better to cheat the many then the few.

It was a command decision he did not make lightly.

There would be much to account for.

Three days later, as the full moon slipped into old gibbons, the crew of the *New Orleans* was roused to action by cries of warning. Rushing topside, Mr. Roosevelt saw a large canoe of Chickasaw Indians paddling toward them in mad abandon.

As an arrow shot past his ear, lodging in the wood behind him, he waved an angry fist.

"Full speed!" he cried to his engineer. "We must outrace them."

As the steam was crowded on, the boat surged ahead, yet could not seem to put the fierce Indians behind them. Those on board were outnumbered five to one. If the savages came close enough to board, it would be a one-sided fight to the death.

"Faster! Faster!" came the command. The crew worked diligently, throwing their hearts into the task, for they were well aware of how Red Men treated captives.

Nip and tuck, the steamboat and the canoe flew through the swollen waters of the Mississippi, dodging floating debris, half submerged tree trunks uprooted by the rushing current, fighting hidden eddies strong enough to drive a boat toward shore and certain destruction.

It was an hour, perhaps longer before the screaming savages tired of the chase and disappeared. Not content to savor his victory before he was certain they were safely away, the captain of the *New Orleans* churned at her mad pace till darkness fell and further travel became unsafe.

Mooring the boat in a protected cove newly carved from the river bank, captain and crew turned in, bodies exhausted, raw nerves exposed.

There was to be no sleep this night, for no sooner had the men retired than the cry of alarm roused them. Fearing another attack by Indians, Captain Roosevelt grabbed his sword and raced out, determined to fight to the death for what was his.

Instead of facing a human enemy, however, he saw, to his abject horror, that the boat was on fire. It was not from below where the boiler was housed, but the forward cabin. Exhausted men fought this most deadly and feared enemy till morning before the fire was finally extinguished.

Leaning against the bulkhead, Roosevelt put a trembling hand to his face and wiped away the soot. For a man who had predicted "smooth sailing" past the Falls, he had proved to be a poor seer.

"But how did it start?" demanded his mate. "How did a fire start in the forward cabin?"

The captain shook his head, too tired to care. The boat was safe. Reasons would have to be worked out at a later time.

"Mr. Roosevelt," came a voice from behind him. Turning, he saw the flushed face of his wife. In her arms she held her infant.

"The baby? Is it safe?"

"Yes. Thank God," she informed him. The look on her fine features prompted him to inquire further.

"What, then?"

"The other," she said. "The Hanna boy. He is gone."

"Gone?" came the astonished question. "Explain yourself."

"I cannot. He has simply vanished."

"Fallen overboard?" whispered the captain.

"He was in the forward cabin."

"He has burned up, then."

She shook her head.

"I have looked. There is no body there. He has been taken. By the Chickasaw. It was they who started the fire to hide the deed."

"They have taken the baby?" Incredulous.

She nodded solemnly.

"So be it. God is just," he said slowly. "We have been spared."

"How so, sir?" she inquired.

It was as plain as the nose on his face.

"The Indians meant to do us harm. To hold a most precious hostage. They have failed."

She understood.

"They took the wrong baby."

CHAPTER 6

The sun was beating down with unrelenting heat. The man at the helm removed his navy-blue captain's cap, revealing a unruly headful of red hair. The hair matched his face, for he carried enough freckles on his sunburned countenance to make it appear as though a musket had exploded, leaving its mark in a thousand tiny red spots.

Either that, or he suffered a continual case of measles.

The pilot had heard all the jokes before and it was an unwise man which tried them again on Captain Blue Moon.

Squinting into the swirling water of the mighty Mississippi, he tried to decide which obstructions were real and which mirages. Make a mistake and the riverboat he commanded and incidentally owned, would sink like a rock.

A heavily underinsured rock at that.

He did not trust anyone but himself at the helm and only reluctantly gave over control of the huge steering wheel to his helmsman, a man with twenty years more experience than he, and by far the better navigator.

Captain Moon, as he was called, was a stubborn man.

He was also known to be a fool. But no one said it to his face.

If was his Scottish temper and not his "Irish mug" which cautioned men to stay on the good side of Blue Moon's temper. He was as quick with his fists as he was with his words, and had been known to take on four rivermen at one time.

He had not walked away from that fight, but lived to tell the tale.

And in the retelling of tall stories, the man who retained both his front teeth was often made out to be the hero.

"Steady as she goes."

There was not a living soul within ten feet of the captain but that had never mattered to him. He had lived alone so long, it was alleged, he developed the habit of talking to himself.

And answering, too, if his crew were to be believed.

Captain Blue Moon would not have disagreed.

"I'm my own best company," he had said once. And meant it.

In a world of loners, rivermen and solitary frontiersmen, Blue Moon was an island.

He was also a character.

A river legend.

Not like Captain Henry Miller Shreve, commander of the *Enterprise.* Shreve single-handedly broke the Fulton-Livingston monopoly on the Mississippi, then ran the British blockade of New Orleans for Andy Jackson in the War of 1812. The following year, in 1815, Shreve and his famous riverboat helped repulse the British at the Battle of New Orleans. No matter the war was already over: no one in the Southern seaport knew that at the time. It made Shreve famous and inscribed General Jackson's name in the history books as being the first soldier to utilize a riverboat in combat.

Moon was not like Shreve and less like Jackson, although it was whispered in barrooms up and down the river, there *was* a similarity between Blue and ol' Andy's alligator.

They both had teeth and a lot of growing up to do.

No one had ever actually seen President Jackson's alligator but they had seen Blue Moon's teeth.

He could bite like the devil and was not above taking a chomp out of an opponent's hide. All in the name of fair fighting, and to the winner belonged the spoils, no matter how obtained.

Blue also cheated at cards and once bragged he had taken the coins off a dead man's eyes.

And used them to buy drinks for the house, which made him a very popular man along the waterfront.

Blue Moon was twenty-three years old, going on thirteen. He had never grown to the stature of a great oak tree and never would. There was still that boyish air about him which reminded men of his early days as a "wooder" on "No Name Island Number Three." Older captains still possessed maps of the river which bore the penciled notation, "NNI#3, Blue Moon, $3/cord."

No one on the Lower Mississippi knew where he came from or how he got to "No Name Island Number Three." If he were a day over ten years when he first appeared on shore in a grow'd man's coveralls rolled up to his knees, and shirtless, demanding "ta git paid fer any wood I chopp'd on dis island," no one would believe it.

That Blue Moon, no Christian and no surname given, was a man who had grown up on the river, was common knowledge. That he knew more about riverboats than any man alive was questionable. That he spoke "Injun" like a Redman was accountable to his "red hair." His army cussing, it was surmised, came from exposure to troops being ferried up and down the Upper Mississippi.

That his parents were white folk could not be doubted, for his complexion was as fair as a girl's. Had he been a "breed," his skin would have been of a darker hue. Not even near-constant exposure to the Louisiana sun could color him beyond a cranberry red.

Blue said he did not know what a "cranberry" was and that his father was a warrior of the fierce, uncivilized Fox tribe. He also said he had been with Lieutenant Zebulon Pike when that explorer first reached the head waters of the Mississippi. But that had occurred in 1806, before Blue Moon had been born.

When asked to explain this seeming contradiction, then further elucidated by having it explained Henry Schoolcraft was the man given credit for discovering Lake Itasca, the true mouth of the Great River, Blue had shrugged his shoulders and called his skeptics "fools."

Which was better than they had a right to except.

The skipper of the *Dogtow,* an old man who began his career as a poller on a keelboat, then bought his way into steam by working for Robert Fulton himself, had known Blue from his earliest days on NNI#3. He once had a contract with the lad to purchase "all the wood he could chop" from the opening of the season until the final days, when ice made further river travel impossible.

The deal had been signed with a handshake, an advance of three mouths food stuffs and a fatherly pat on the head for "Baby Blue."

One afternoon in mid-April when Capt'n Daugherty maneuvered his crude, old-fashioned steamer into No Name, he was disappointed to find no wood waiting for him. Thinking, perhaps, the "corder" had gotten lonely and gone home, the captain ordered his crew out to do their own cutting. It was only then he saw Blue, ancient fowling piece in hand, guarding six cords of neatly stacked wood the lazy crew of the *Dogtow* had fastened their eyes on.

"What's the trouble here, son?" Daugherty asked, relieved to discover Blue had not somehow gotten himself drowned or eaten by river pirates.

"I ain't yer son," the mighty giant, made so by his gun and his coppery red hair, replied.

"I thought we had an agreement. You'd chop wood for me all season and I'd pay you three dollars a cord. Left you with victuals, if I remember a'right."

"Deal's off," replied the lad.

"Why is that?"

"I don't chop wood fer them what's calls me names."

"What name did I call you?" the skipper asked in some surprise. While it was true he had called the youth a number of unflattering things, it had all been in the spirit of good fun, and in the strictest confidence.

Good wooders, after all, were hard to find, and this one worked like a serpent.

"I ain't gonna repeat it," came the prompt reply. Daugherty could not fail to see the boy's lower lip protruding, however, and knew someone had squealed on him.

"Then how about my advance back?" he had demanded, hands on hips.

If he thought to intimidate Blue, he was sadly mistaken.

"Them's all ete up. You want ta collect the residue, ya kin go down to the sink hole an' clean it out."

No amount of pleading, threatening, bribery or the offer of $3.25 a cord dissuaded Blue from his position. Captain Daugherty was forced to leave without his wood, cursing the boy to "blue blazes."

Once aboard his boat, the captain gathered his officers together and demanded to know which of them had gone behind his back and told Blue the unflattering expletives he had been called. All pleaded innocent and proved their loyalty by reminding the captain none had been away from the *Dogtow* long enough to have gotten to NNI#3 and done the deed.

"Then you repeated what I said on shore and one of them rascals carried the tale."

Again, there were loud protestations of innocence.

It was only after some careful soul-searching that the skipper was reminded he had casually referred to the boy as "Baby Blue" after sealing the bargain.

"What's a matter with that?" Daugherty demanded. "He ain't but half grow'd. If he makes it to my shoulders by the time he's thirty, I'd be surprised."

In all fairness, Captain Daugherty stood six feet tall.

Everyone agreed with their skipper's assessment, diverging only in the idea of "Baby Blue" ever reaching thirty years of age.

"If he makes it to double digits, I'd be surprised," the mate commented. It was as well for him he was not overheard, or his name, too, would have been inscribed in the "black ledger" young Blue kept.

Kept in his head, for he could not read.

No one ever referred to Blue Moon as "Baby Blue," again. At least no one who ever intended to buy wood on No Name Island Number Three.

Blue ran his fingers lovingly over the wooden steering wheel of his ship, caressing her as he might the arm of a woman. Besides his dignity, the riverboat was the only thing he had ever owned all to himself. She was his pride and joy and while she would never win any beauty contests, there was a bond between man and craft that transcended anything he had felt for a living thing.

Blue Moon did not believe in love. He learned early in life that when an object was so treasured, it died. He had therefore vowed, at a tender age, never to love anyone or any thing. That included himself, for he intended to live a long, prosperous life.

When asked, he denied that he loved *Blue Moon,* the name he had bestowed upon the boat after he had won her in a hard-contested log-chopping contest. "Love," he declared in contempt and with an Irish brogue no one heard in his voice before or since, "Was for story books and dreamers."

Since he was illiterate and presumed to be ignorant of the finer things in life, including ladies, the older and wiser men hid smiles behind their hands and shook their heads.

"Wait till he's grown," they predicted. "Some gal'll come along and steal his heart. Then we'll see the *real* Blue Moon. He'll give up the river and his old riverboat and settle down to be a right peaceful citizen."

That is, if he lived long enough and stayed on shore for any length of time. Marryin' gals were notoriously hard to find on riverboats.

Blue turned the wheel two degrees to port, then cursed and replaced the cap over his head. The heavy rains had washed away a good three feet of shoreline and many young or poorly anchored trees had been washed into the river. Striking one of those waterlogged obstacles could make a serious rent in the hull. Repairs were both costly and time consuming. Add to that the price of a tow, and that would be enough to scuttle most captain's dreams of profit and adventure.

Profit being the more important of the two.

"Deke."

The first mate of the *Blue Moon* moved from the companionway where he had been lingering and reported, touching hand to brim of cap. Deke

Miller was a man who came with the boat. When Moon won it, the riverman's contract had been transferred from one owner to the next, like cargo. He did not resent Blue, but neither was he a friend. He was, as the skipper pointed out, "Twenty dollars a month, for the season."

After which, Deke was free to find other gainful employment.

"Take the wheel."

The mate did as ordered. He was accustomed to acting as navigator and did not understand why the captain choose to perform that task himself. Especially when his mate was better at the job than he.

Blue made his way to the bow and leaned down, over the railing. Something was not right and he was ill at ease. The water was not moving correctly, sluggish at one point, rapid at another. He knew in his bones there was some sort of obstruction ahead. He just could not put his finger on it.

"Check the charts," he ordered. There was no one standing by to carry out the order. Deke adjusted the wheel a notch, then pointed that fact out to the captain, who was known to be half crazy.

"Half" being rather more relative than actual.

"If it's a sandbar you're looking fer, there ain't none at this point in the river."

"Heavy rain's changed all that."

Which was true at other points along the Mississippi, but not here, in deep water.

Blue interlaced his fingers behind his back and began pacing, never, however, taking his eyes from the water line To some men, she was life, itself. To others, the Great River was a friend, an ally. For most who commanded boats, whether they were steamboats, keelboats, barges orthe occasional flatboat, she was a partner.

To Blue Moon, she was the enemy.

He could not explain his feelings, nor could he understand the kinder thoughts of his fellow rivermen. They had their way and he his. If they wanted to view their world with the eyes of a romantic, that was their business. Let them go east, giving travel lectures to wide-eyed youths and ladies in fancy dresses. Let them decorate their riverboat parlours with patriotic streamers and serve imported wines.

Let them invite gentlemen of quality and women of registered blood to visit the wilderness. It was of no consequence to him. Encourage journalists to write about the beauties of nature, describe the majestic oak, enumerate the varieties of cottonwood, hackberry, black walnut, cherry, mulberry, hickory and blue and white ash found along the banks. It was nothing to him.

For Captain Moon, the river was for transport of goods and supplies. Passengers were a necessary evil and more trouble than they were worth. Let one complain to him and he would as soon drop them on the nearest outcropping of land.

The wind, the rain, the changing of the currents, the deadly, shifting sandbars were difficulties enough. Let him get his cargo from point A to point B and get paid for his services and to hell with nature's bounty.

Ask the Injuns about bounty. The invading white man had stripped away the bounty of the land and reduced the native savage to begging for handouts.

"Bounty" was also the price put on a man's head.

If it were high enough, Blue would go after the scoundrel himself.

The captain took a piece of weighted wood from his pocket and tossed it into the water, watching its descent with the eyes of an eagle. When he did not lose sight of his depth marker, he knew his instincts were correct.

"Hard astern!" he called. Then, not trusting the mate, repeated the order. "Hard astern."

The man at the helm did as ordered, not because he believed there was an obstruction in the water but because he was paid to follow orders. If Captain Moon wanted to play navigator, that was no affair of his.

If the damned fool jackknifed his boat on shore, he could damn sure push it off himself.

A loud, grating sound awoke Deke's sleeping nerves and his head shot up faster than if a cannon had been discharged an inch from his ear.

"Tree trunk," he grunted under his breath. He had not meant to be heard, but the man with the ears of a coyote nodded his head in agreement.

"Big one. Waterlogged and sunk but enough to take the bottom off this boat."

"Aye, sir. Are we clear?"

"No."

"Must be a redwood."

Deke had never seen a redwood but a man traveling back from the shores of California had once described the tree to him. The depiction of its vast size had made a lasting impression and found its way into his personal vocabulary. To Deke, everything larger than a dugout canoe and smaller than Blue Moon's pride was referred to as a "redwood."

Blue pulled the cap off the "Captain's Hole" and spoke into the mouthpiece of the long, narrow tubing which served as his inanimate, unpaid orderly, allowing him to communicate with the engineer.

"Let off steam."

There was a momentary delay, than a loud burst of billowing smoke filled the air, while a screech of protest announced the impending decrease in speed. This noise obscured the second clunk of wood against wood, as the *Blue Moon* scraped along a fully submerged limb of the invisible tree. Blue felt them hit and cursed.

Without bothering to give the order, he ran to the wheel and turned it himself, unceremoniously shoving aside his mate. Ordinarily, Deke would have resented the action and had words with the captain later. There was a protocol aboard ship and an unwritten rule of respect between officers. As Blue acknowledged no such law, however, and as Deke was bound to the boat "for the season," he swallowed his anger and said nothing.

There was no sense creating an atmosphere of open warfare. And as Moon had been correct about something not seeming right in the water, he would lose the complaint, in any case.

More for his own sense of worth than any concern for the craft, Deke went to the bow and peered into the water. From this new angle, he clearly saw the felled tree, which had obviously lost its footing in the floods and found its way into the Mississippi, no more than a day gone by.

"There's still dirt in the roots," he observed to his commander. "With the way the current is running, I'd say it come from upstream about five miles. Couldn't have been in the water more'n a day Mebbe less."

"Five minutes is all it takes."

"Yes, sir." Deke waited, cocked his head, then scratched his ear. None of his machinations rewarded him with what he wanted to hear. "Captain –?"

"What is it?"

"The whistle, sir. Ain't you goin' to blow it?"

"Why would I do that? We are not near port."

He was being purposely obtuse. In a contest between floods, flash fire, engines exploding, non-paying passengers, wet cargo and Blue Moon, it would be a neck and neck contest to see which was more dreaded by rivermen.

"To warn other boats."

"Do you see any other boats?"

"No, sir, but —"

"Then why should I bother?"

"There may be others followin' in our wake. It would seem only right to raise a warning."

"If there is another boat in our wake, the chances of it hauling cargo of a similar nature to ours is good. Why should we help the competition?"

Everything was a contest to Blue Moon.

"Because that's the law."

"What law?"

"The law of the river. The way it's a'ways been done."

"Not always."

"When weren't it?"

"When barges and keelboats navigated the river. They had no whistles."

"That was before the time of the riverboat."

"You said 'always.'"

"Then, I mean, since the time of steam."

"Don't say what you don't mean and we'll get along better. Take the helm."

Blue stepped aside and stood in front of his mate, compelling the man to pass before him, in a breach of shipboard etiquette, or backtrack and pass behind. Deke swore an oath and crossed to the rear of his superior officer.

"Just so we understand one another," Captain Moon observed.

"I understand one thing, Capt'n."

"What is that?"

"When it comes time to bury you, the only one what'll be there is you."

"Don't believe in funerals. When it 'comes time to bury' me, throw my body over the side. Or tie it to a tree and let it rot that way."

Deke shuddered and averted his head.

"No one would do that," he said. Then added, in a lower voice, "Not even to you."

"It's an Injun custom."

"Why?" the mate asked, despite himself. Or just to see if Blue had an answer.

"It is believed by the Injuns that seeing dead remains so displayed reminded others of the deceased's worldly prowess."

"What does 'prowess' mean?"

Blue did not answer. He began whistling a tune and disappeared down the stairs. He could be heard all the way to his cabin. It was only when the music faded that Deke, first mate of the *Blue Moon,* lashed out with his foot and struck the deck a mighty blow.

"You don't know what it means, either," he growled, thus assuaging his hurt. He waited another minute, then reached out and drew down the wooden handle of the ship's whistle. He let it sing a full ten seconds before releasing the handle and repeating the process.

It would cost him five cents off his month's pay, but it was worth it.

In his private stateroom, Blue took out a pencil, licked the dull point with his tongue and made a mark on a greasy bit of paper he had found in the refuse bin behind the End of the Line Saloon.

"Five cents," he said. "By the time this month is over, you'll end up owing me money."

As if Deke heard his warning, the whistle blew again. Moon made another mark.

A man must always be made to pay for his transgressions.

CHAPTER 7

It was raining cats and dogs when the *Blue Moon* pulled into Natchez. Save for the near miss of the "redwood," the two hundred and seventy mile trip from New Orleans had been uneventful. Captain Moon hoped to unload his cargo and take on another before half his crew deserted.

Not that he would have missed any of them personally. There were riverboat men aplenty in Natchez. He simply did not want to take the time to hire any.

Time was money and money was the object of the trade.

Wrapping an oilskin cape around his shoulders, Blue drew his cap down to the level of his brown eyes and attempted to wipe away a rivulet of water destined to carve its way down his back and soak his shirt. Being wet reminded him of being hungry, and being hungry was the worst thing which could happen to a man.

Short of having his nose plastered to the back of his head.

Or running afoul of The Bank.

While he had never actually been inside a Bank, he had heard enough horror stories to equate a Bank Official with an Indian Agent.

Both being worth the powder to blow them to hell.

"I'm going ashore," he announced to no one in particular. "No one else is to leave the vessel until the cargo is unloaded, or he doesn't get paid." Blue took a step down the rickety wooden platform leading to the dock, then called back over his shoulder. "Did you hear me, Mr. Miller?"

"No, sir," Deke responded.

Blue ignored him. He expected his wishes to be carried out, whether or not they had been heard. If they were not, it was too damned bad. He would unload the cargo himself and save the price of "hired help."

There were seventeen buildings directly along the waterfront, ten of them being either saloons with girls or cat houses serving whisky. The remaining seven establishments were owned by men who bought and sold goods catering to the river trade.

Blue knew most of the wheelers and dealers in Natchez. It was a small, tight-knit community, entirely dependent upon the commerce coming and going to New Orleans. While once craving the distinction of being a great seafaring city, it had slowly resigned itself to an existence as a stop-over for the New Orleans-Louisville trade.

Making his way through the sleeting rain, Moon sidestepped a stray cur seeking a handout, then wallowed through a calf-deep puddle before coming out on what was called, for no reason he could fathom, a boardwalk, inasmuch as there were no boards and nowhere to walk.

Horse manure, disintegrated by the rushing tide of rain water, floated in half-congealed piles, adding to the stench of the city. Dead fish, overflowing outhouses, discarded animal parts and the accumulation of trash made up the rest. Most men were offended by the stench, but Blue breathed in the odors with a small smile of contentment.

This was civilization as he understood it. Complaining about the smell compelled a man to do something about it. Accepting it made a man at home.

Pushing his way through the half-closed double doors of the End of the Line Saloon, he shook himself like a dog and stamped his feet. The floor was already too wet for him to leave tracks as he sloshed his way over to the bar.

"Afternoon, Capt'n," the bartender greeted him. "Heard you was in. What'd you bring this time?"

"A cargo of molasses. Five hundred barrels."

"Goin' all the way to Saint Louie?"

"No. Unloading here."

"Why is that?"

Blue snorted and removed his cap, sending a spray of water flying over the dulled and pitted bar.

"That's all the money the owner had. Enough to get the hogshead here. He's hoping to find a buyer to take them off his hands."

"Own a piece of it yerself?"

"No. Why?"

"Might know a fella what's interested "

"No matter to me."

The bartender shrugged and poured him a shot of whisky. Blue downed it in one swallow, then belched and wiped his mouth with the back of his hand.

"Nasty weather."

"Have much trouble comin' upriver?"

"Some," he admitted. "The damn water's full of trees."

"Just heard the *Bell Bottom* struck a tree and sunk. She was right behind you. A traveler come in on horseback with the bad news. Said he seen it all."

Blue laughed. Hearing about other men's troubles always put him in a good mood. It was no more or no less than they would accord him, and he was not known for his charity.

"What was she carrying?"

"Dunno."

"What about salvage?"

"Can't say. Might be worth your while to take a look."

"I'll do it."

He was righteously satisfied that his mate's effort, which had cost the man ten cents, had gone for naught.

There were some that said there was no justice in the world.

"Justice," Blue Moon was heard to pronounce, "Was where you found it."

If he unloaded his cargo and set off by first light in the morning, he could be back at another man's disaster within a day.

"Any hands go down?"

"Didn't say."

"Engine blow?"

"Not that he heard."

"Where is this fellow?"

"Over there."

The barkeep pointed to a lone man sitting at a back table. Blue nodded his thanks, ordered another drink and took it with him as he crossed the room.

"Mind if I sit down?" he asked.

The stranger looked him over then shrugged. Blue joined him.

"Name's Captain Moon," he introduced himself. "Of the *Blue Moon.* Just got in. Heard you saw the *Bell Bottom* sink."

"Went down like a felled tree," he agreed.

"Engine blow?"

"Heard an explosion. Could have been the main engine."

"Too bad."

Blue meant to convey his total lack of sympathy and succeeded. The man looked at him with renewed interest.

"You said you were Captain Moon?"

"That's right. Blue Moon."

Blue sipped his drink, then made a show of wiping his mouth on the soggy sleeve of his navy jacket.

"Been up the Mississippi? To its head waters?" the stranger asked.

"What's it to you?"

"I'm an explorer. I heard you were familiar with the Upper Mississippi. I am looking for a guide."

Blue finished his drink and pushed back in his chair.

"Buy a book."

The newcomer reached out a hand and placed in on the captain's arm. He immediately regretted his action when the youthful riverman draw an ugly Bowie knife from his belt and pressed it against the attacker's Adams apple.

"I don't like to be touched," Blue growled. The man nodded. The knife was slowly – regretfully – withdrawn.

But not sheathed. It served as a silent conversation piece sitting on the table between them.

"Just so we understand each other."

"My apologies. I meant no disrespect."

The stranger raised a hand. Immediately a bottle was brought to the table. A glass was set in front of the man paying for it.

"Drink?" he invited?

"Two's my limit."

"Really?" Then, less casually, "That's not what I heard."

"Man hears a lot of things on the river. None of them are true."

"None?"

Blue snorted, then helped himself to a drink, remembering the lecture he had so recently given his mate.

"Not many."

"My name's Kress. Andre Kress. Pleased to meet you." He offered his hand, then thought better of it, remembering the last time he had touched the rough riverman.

"What's your interest in me?" Blue pursued, altering his bland expression into one of acute scrutiny.

"I heard it said you know Indians. I am a researcher."

"What the hell is a researcher?"

"A man who investigates things. Someone who delves into the history of the country. An historian. As a matter of fact," he continued, hoping to impress, "I have written a book. On Hernando DeSoto."

His listener was impressed. Despite himself.

"Who is he?"

"Was he. A Spaniard. He was the first white man to set eyes on the Mississippi."

"What's a Span-yerd?"

"A native of Spain."

"Where's that?"

"Where is Spain? Why, Spain is a foreign country. It's across the Atlantic."

"I don't know any river called the At-lantic."

"The Atlantic is not a river. It is an ocean."

"What language are you speakin', anyway?" Blue complained. He had the suspicion the stranger was setting him up for yet another question, and he had already asked his fill.

"Forgive me," Kress retreated, pouring himself a drink, then leaving it untouched. "An ocean is a vast body of water, thousands of miles wide. Here, let me show you."

He took a leather-bound case from his pocket and opened it, revealing a sheaf of white paper, all cut to fit snugly inside. A pencil was attached by a silver cord. He removed it and made a hurried sketch.

"See here," he explained. "This is the Mississippi. It transverses – cuts through – the country. To the east are a number of states. The country ends on the shores of the Atlantic Ocean. The ocean is three thousand miles wide. A man sailing these waters in an easterly direction reaches what is called Europe. This is England – you have heard of England?" Blue remained immobile. "England is the country our forefathers fought in the American Revolution. The English are governed by kings and queens, while we have a president.

"Here," he continued, receiving no encouragement, "is the rest of Europe. This is the country known as France. This is Spain. All three countries were instrumental in exploring the wilderness, as it was then known to be, of America."

"So?"

"Hernando DeSoto represented Spain. He was an explorer. Returning from Peru, where he served with Pizarro, he was appointed governor of the island of Cuba. Not content to live a sedentary life, he assembled an expedition and landed in Florida. Seeing the riches of this New Land, he and his army of 620 men pushed inland. By 1541, he came to the shores of the Mississippi."

"What riches did he find?"

"He did not find any."

Blue shorted, nodding in satisfaction. He had the suspicion there was no money to be made in "exploration."

At least not along the banks of the Mississippi. Not with an army of 620 to divide it with.

"What happened then?"

"He died."

Blue laughed. He always appreciated a story with a happy ending.

"His body was wrapped in blankets, weighed down with sand, placed in a canoe and set sail down the river."

"That was a waste of a canoe. The sand I'll grant him. The Injuns probably stopped it a quarter mile off, stripped it naked and thought themselves well served. Is that why you wrote the book? To show what a fool this DeeSo-to was?"

"I made him out to be a hero."

"Why? You related to him?"

"No. Because he was a great explorer."

"How much money did you make on the book?"

"I did not write it for money."

"None," the captain interpreted for him. He leaned back in his chair and rubbed his fingers against the red sandpaper accumulation of stubble on his face. It was less a nervous habit than a gesture of contempt.

"You want to be an explorer so you can write about yerself?"

"I wish to collect Indian artifacts." Moon's down-sloping eyebrows prompted him to quickly add, "Indian relics; Indian tools, beads, bows and arrows."

"I know where you're likely to find an arrow and it won't help you write a book none."

"That is why I wish a guide; a man known to the Indians. Someone who can deal for me."

"What are you doing in Natchez?"

"I came up from New Orleans. I had hoped to hire a boat and a guide there but found the city too – difficult to navigate?"

Blue smiled and nodded. That language he understood.

"Too expensive. The riverboat captains you spoke to all smelled money and were offered fish. How much do you have?"

"Five hundred dollars."

"How much of that are you offering me?"

"Half."

"What are you going to do with the other two-fifty?"

He purposely divided the sum in half, least Andre Kress think him ignorant.

"Buy gifts for the Indians."

"Gifts?"

He spat the word out so fast, spittle landed over his business partner's face, compelling the author to wipe his cheek with a linen handkerchief.

"With which to trade for artifacts."

Moon considered a moment, regretting the fact he had not worked up a mouthful of phlegm before spitting. To assuage his feelings of inadequacy, he coughed, then hawked a sufficient amount of mucus to spit on the floor. His effort landed a foot from Mister Kress' boot.

The man thought it best not to move away.

"Five hundred dollars ain't enough."

The would-be explorer let out a sigh of discouragement, then carefully tucked the pencil back into its leather loop. Before he could close the case, however, Blue reached out and took the paper upon which he had drawn the crude map.

"I'll just keep this."

"Help yourself." Then, more hopefully, "You'll accept the commission?"

"I'll think about it," Blue agreed. "Under a different set of terms and for a considerably higher percent of the take."

"The take?"

"You think I was born yesterday? I know all about you 'explorers.' Mebbe you want to write a book and mebbe you want to collect 'artifacts.' But sure as blue blazes you want to make a profit, too."

"I assure you –"

Making a profit was the soul of the enterprise. Writing a book was gravy on the beef steak. A man who already had five hundred dollars in his pocket did not want to return home carrying nothing but Injun feathers and bone necklaces.

"I'll play along with you, if you'll play along with me."

"How do you mean?"

He shook him off and changed the subject.

"Why is it the barkeep said you was interested in molasses?"

"I thought to buy them from you. That would give you a cargo to take upriver to Saint Louis. I could sell the sugar there – at a profit – and have some additional working capital with which   to –"

Blue slapped his hand down on the table and grunted his approval.

"Now that I understand!"

Author Kress smiled broadly. He had made at least one correct assumption.

"I got some salvage work to do. Take me two days, if I'm the first one to the wreck. Then another two days to sell what I took off the bottom. Make it a week. You got that time to spare?"

"I do if you do, Captain Moon."

"We'll talk again when I get back." He rose and straightened, then remembered a thought and grabbed the bottle. "From one explorer to another."

He grinned and sloshed away, content with the knowledge he had found himself a fool.

Diverting his footsteps briefly toward the *Blue Moon,* where he gave orders the hogshead of molasses were not to be unloaded after all, Blue walked back into town. The thought of roaming the decks of his own ship like a ghost, waiting for the morning, or worse still, isolated in his stateroom like a prisoner, did not please him. He craved action. Failing that, he sought a sense of purpose.

Without any destination in mind, Blue found himself standing outside the Page for Page bookstore. He had been in there once before and knew the owner would not pester him with questions about whether he had read So-and-So or what he thought of This-and-That's latest.

Pushing open the door, he cringed slightly as a bell tinkled, then reached out quickly, silencing it with his hand. He was not fast enough, however, for a withered old man wearing a tunic-like jacket with a Chinese collar emerged from the back room. Seeing a customer, he smiled and bowed.

"Good afternoon, Captain Moon. Welcome to my humble establishment. Please make yourself at home."

The last time the bookseller had made that invitation, Blue had asked whether that meant he could help himself and leave without paying. The old man of dubious ethnic origin had merely smiled, held out his right hand and made a sweeping gesture.

Blue took that to mean should he attempt such a theft, the law would be summoned before he got across the street.

Now, he was not so certain.

"I've just come to look," he announced, not wishing to create in this peculiar fellow any wrong impressions. With such a statement, he was challenging the man to throw him out, declaring with an indignant whine in his voice, he was "not running a shop for wet river captains to come in out of the rain."

Moon was disappointed when the ancient shop owner smiled a toothy grin, bowed and walked backward into his study, which was separated from the store by a curtain of beads.

The bookseller's name, if Blue remembered correctly, was Williams. Mister Sing Williams.

He may have been born with the middle of those three names, but he sure as blue blazes was not born with the first or third.

Having the shop to himself, Blue wandered the aisles, staring with rapt attention at the books neatly displayed on shelves. There was not a mote of dust anywhere, and he absently muttered to himself that if "Sing" ever needed a job, he would hire him to sweep out and maintain the *Blue Moon*.

In the unlikely event he ever decided to take on first-cabin passengers.

Taking down a book with bold, gilt-letters on the spine, he riffled through the pages, staring with incredulity at the ten-score of words comprising the book. Some of the letters he recognized, while others were strangers to him. He had no way of knowing whether it was his unfamiliarity with the characters which made them odd, or if they were nonsense.

With a superior shrug, calculated to impress any worldly man who happened to be peering in through the window, Blue made a disparaging remark about the author's "liberal borrowing of Mr. Thomas Jones' work" and replaced it on the shelf.

He had heard a man make that comment once about a politician lecturing from the stump of a tree and never forgot it.

Moon was not certain exactly what "liberal" meant, but he sure as hell knew that "borrow" meant steal.

The comment had done nothing to dissuade Blue from listening to the orator and after the two hour dissertation was over, he had promptly cast his ballot for the man.

Blue had been known to "borrow" any number of items in his own life and thought that similarity made the office-seeker worthy of his vote, if not his patronage.

Whatever office the orator was seeking, Blue reasoned, it was wiser to place a man there whom one could trust to be dishonest, rather than electing some unknown factor.

Better keep to the devils you know, than elect others you do not.

He had not tarried long enough to discover which man won the election.

On a shelf against the rear wall Blue discovered a large quantity of small tomes, no bigger than his fist and no longer than twenty pages. He took one and opened it, lingering at the first page. Unlike other books, this one was filled with large ink drawings which jumped out at him.

Without realizing he was doing so, Captain Moon smiled. Here was a book he could understand. The picture represented a woman holding a child's hand. She was smiling and pointing to a page in a book the boy was holding. Over her head was a large symbol.

Blue turned the page and saw another one full of drawings. There were nine small pictures, each carefully sketched to accurately represent an idea. Bringing his nose closer to the book in order to understand it better, a technique he had learned by watching men read the newspaper, his eyes skipped from one illustration to the next, identifying them.

"Apple." The second he was not sure about, so guessed. "Bridge." Then, Acorn. Arrow." He paused to shake his head. "I never saw an arrow look like that. Kress is right. They need Injun artifacts back east." He continued identifying the pictures, skipping the large character in the middle he did not recognize, as well as the next two illustrations, concluding with, "Anchor. Axe."

He paused in sudden amazement, shocked at himself. He had just read a page in a book. With a sudden shaking of his entire frame, he turned to the next page and "read" that, too.

"Boy." He skipped the large character placed between "boy" and "book." "Book. Baby. Barrel. Flower."

He had read a second page. Suddenly the entire world opened before his eyes. With an eager hand, Blue turned to the middle of the book and recommenced his reading.

"Mill. Animal. Mug. Man." He bypassed the letter. "Man with Injun mask. Mallet. Mouse. Watermelon."

The next page was almost as easy.

"Hazel nut." Then a character he did not know. "Nest. Fishing net. Deer." The last picture he could not make out. He closed the book in annoyance.

"They ought not to make pictures no one can understand," he declared.

"The word is nose-gay," Mister Sing Williams identified. Blue had been so intent upon his new-found ability to read, he had not heard the man come up behind him.

Seeing Blue's surprised look, he bowed and smiled.

"Nose-gay. That is a small bouquet of flowers young ladies carry in their hands. They bring it to their noses and sniff it; thus the word nose."

"Where does the word 'gay' fit it?"

Mr. Williams offered an inscrutable smile.

"I suppose because it makes them gay to have such a beautiful bouquet of flowers."

"Nose-gay," Blue repeated.

"Let me show you, sir. May I?"

Mr. Williams held out his hand and Blue offered him the book. The shopkeeper opened to the first page and pointed to the character Blue had skipped.

"This is the letter 'A.' It is the first letter in the alphabet. These pictures all begin with the letter 'A' to help you remember. See?"

He pointed to the words printed beneath the pictures.

"Apple. Apple begins with the letter 'A.' Arch. Acorn."

"I thought it was a bridge," Blue pointed out.

"It could be taken for a bridge. But the word bridge begins with the letter 'B.' See how the artist has made the structure curled upward? That is an arch. A curved bridge, if you will."

Blue stroked his chin and nodded.

"And the rest?"

"Arrow. Then we have the letter 'A.' This is an 'avoset.' That is a type of bird. Adze. You might call it a hoe. Then we have anchor and axe. They all begin with the letter 'A.'"

"And these?" Blue asked, pointing to the next page. Mr. Williams read them gladly.

"These pictures all start with the letter 'B.' That is the second letter in the alphabet. 'Boy,' the letter 'B,' book, baby, barrel, bud."

"Bud? It looks like a flower, to me."

"It is a flower bud. Flower begins with the letter 'F.' Fffff." He stretched out the sound so Blue could identify the "F" sound with the word. "Fffff. Fffffflower. 'B.' Bbbud."

"I see. That doesn't seem so hard."

"This is a very wondrous book. It is a book of illustrated pictures. All the pictures on the page start with the same letter."

Blue nodded, then remembered something and pouted. Taking back the tome, he turned to the other pages he had read. When he found what he was looking for, he jabbed a forefinger at the illustrations.

"Mill. Animal. Mug."

He sounded the consonants, correcting divining that "animal" did not belong in the group. Mr. Williams beamed proudly.

"Exactly right."

"Then there is a mistake."

He was one up on the author. There was power to this reading business.

"A mistake, if you call the picture an animal. You may also call it a monkey. A monkey is an animal, like a squirrel or a cat. The writer meant for you to say 'mmmonkey.'"

He had been half right.

It was better than being all wrong.

Blue Moon's world had expanded immeasurably.

"Could a man teach himself to read with this book?"

"He might."

"That is, if he couldn't read a'ready."

Mr. Williams nodded wisely.

"I have read this book myself, many times."

"How much is it?"

Blue had never bought a book in his life, and had no idea the worth of such a wondrous thing.

"Fifteen cents."

"Fifteen cents?"

His opinion of books and book writers in particular fell considerably.

It did, however, confirm his opinion of Andre Kress. Kress was a fool. No man could hope to earn a living writing books which sold for fifteen cents.

If knowledge were power, power was not worth as much as he thought.

"I will buy it," he declared suddenly. "For a friend."

"An excellent choice."

Taking the prize possession back from its new owner, Mr. Williams went to the front of his shop, where he placed a sheet of brown paper on the counter and laid the book on top. Before he wrapped it, however, he looked with kindly old black eyes at the student who had discovered 'A' was for 'arch.'

"May I inscribe your name in this book? So your friend will remember who bought it for him?"

"Do so," he was ordered.

"I shall write, 'Blue Moon.' Is that correct?"

"Yes, sir."

Mr. Williams spelled out the words as he wrote them, printing in large, easily identifiable letters. When he finished with the name, he considered, then added one more word beneath.

"Captain. That is your title?"

"Yes, sir."

"There. I have written 'Captain' as well. Captain begins with a 'C.' Blue begins with 'B' and Moon begins with 'M.' You can match what I have written with the letters in the book."

"Captain Blue Moon," the purchaser repeated. It was a wondrous name.

He reached into his packet and removed two bits. He hesitated, calculating the worth of his new book against what it cost to purchase. On impulse, he dropped the coin down on the counter and accepted the package, now secured with string.

"Your change, Captain," the book seller called after him.

"Keep it," he was ordered.

It was the first time Blue Moon had overpaid for anything in his life.

The power of the printed word had risen exactly ten cents in his estimation.

CHAPTER 8

After eating out, a luxury in which Blue seldom indulged, he arrived back at the *Blue Moon* by nine o'clock. They boat was still; aside from a sleepy guard standing by the ramp, there was no sign of life aboard.

Just the way the captain liked it.

Were it in his power, he would sail her with a ghost crew.

Unlike most men, Blue Moon was not afraid of spirits – either the kind which came in a bottle, or those reputed to haunt boneyards and acquaintances of former lives. He did not believe in ghosts, life after death, heaven, hell or religion. Such things were for the superstitious and the confidence men.

With a laugh that startled his crewman into sudden wakefulness, Blue settled in by perching himself atop a molasses barrel. His feet did not touch the deck. To cover the seeming defect in his stature, Blue turned so that one leg was propped against another barrel and thus not left dangling in midair.

"Do you believe in ghosts?" he asked.

The crewman's eyes widened and he nodded vigorously.

"Yes, sir."

"What about God?"

"Yes, sir."

"Even been baptized?"

"That I have, sir."

"How old were you?"

These startling questions openec an entirely new insight into the captain's personality. The guard leaned his back against the railing, eager to talk.

"It was aboot ten years ago, by the best of my recollection," he admitted. "There was a preacher going down the river by the name of Reverend Holly. He had the power." The man, whose name was Tim O'Leary, sighed reverently. "Ya never saw anything like it."

"Oh, I believe I did," Blue wistfully admitted.

"You knew him?" Tim asked.

When Blue nodded, the man crossed himself and whistled.

"Worked for him."

"You worked for him? Worked for Reverend Holly?"

"That I did."

"I never took ya fer a God-fearin' man, Capt'n. I'd right pleased to know you've seen the light."

Blue chuckled while scratching a lucifer against the side of his working-man's shoe. A flame jumped out of the darkness, illuminating the officer's face with a soft, sulphuric glow. What that light failed to catch was the humor in his bright brown eyes.

The captain removed a pouch of tobacco from his pocket, rolled a smoke, then passed the pouch to O'Leary. Pausing for the guard to roll one for himself, he struck another match, lit both, then inhaled deeply. When the effects had worked their way into his brain, Blue tapped a tune on the barrel with his free hand and began to sing.

> Rock of Ages, cleft for me,
> Let me hide myself in thee;
> Let the water and the blood,
> From thy wounded side which flowed,
> Be of sin the double cure,
> Save from wrath and make me pure.

He had a deep, melodic baritone voice, untrained yet not unpleasant. As he sang the religious words, an aura of deep conviction settled over the crewman. With tears in his eyes, Tim mouthed the words he knew so well, craving to be a part of the blessed experience, yet feeling unworthy to lift his voice to the Lord in competition with that of his captain's.

When the song was completed, Tim blew his nose into his red rag handkerchief and stuffed his hands into his trouser pockets.

"Ya got the gift, Capt'n. You surely do. God bless you."

"God blesses those what blesses themselves," Blue acknowledged. Jumping down from his barrel, he readjusted his cap to a more jaunty angle and slipped away, whistling the tune to himself and remembering how he had come to appreciate, if not subscribe to, religion....

The blast of the riverboat whistle woke the sleeping boy and he jumped to his feet, eyes wide with expectation. It was early in the month. Chunks of ice still floated down the Mississippi, some large enough to damage a hull if struck at speeds over five miles per hour.

He had not expected company for a week, perhaps two. The welcoming blast, announcing an imminent arrival filled him with anticipation. His merge food supply had run out a week ago and the youth had lived on little more than boiled latigo and fish bone soup since.

Checking his neatly stacked cords of wood and calculating their worth for the tenth time that day, Blue scrambled down to shore, waving his arms in welcome and ownership. He did not recognize the boat. It was well to announce the island was occupied before trouble brewed.

A captain expecting to harvest his own fuel would not find a wooder a welcome sight. By the rules of the river, he was obliged to pay the fee for wood already chopped or lift anchor and sail away without. If this captain proved difficult, Blue would have to defend what was his with words and rocks.

He had a wealth of both, but neither were particularly effectual against guns and greedy captains, as he had discovered from experience.

"Ahoy on shore!" a voice called from the boat. "Have you wood for sale?"

Relieved but not yet pacified, Blue waved both hands over his head and shouted back.

"Ten cords, at three dollars a cord and a month's grub or yer on yer way empty!"

He saw his offer shouted below decks, then waited while the captain made his decision.

"We'll take what you got and more besides," came the reply.

"You'll take what I got and sail elsewhere fer more," he hollered back.

If the captain sent his own crew to chop wood, Blue would be fortunate to get fifty cents a cord.

He would rather burn the island than be underpaid.

Two short blasts on the whistle told him his terms were agreed to. He fastened his thumbs in satisfaction around the empty belt loops of his trousers. Thirty dollars and grub was a good way to start the season.

The riverboat steamed into the strait of the shoreline, let off a blast of steam to empty the engines, then a series of long planks were shoved ashore. The captain disembarked first, eying the erstwhile owner of "No Name Island Number Three" with a critical eye as he approached.

"Let's see the wood before I pay you," he ordered. Blue marched to his cache, the man following. When satisfied the wood was cut to the proper length and stacked according to regulation, the captain removed a purse from his pocket and held out a handful of coins.

"What's yer name?" he asked before handing over the treasure.

"Blue Moon," came the prompt reply.

"Well, Mister Moon, I got thirty dollars for ya, and a month's grub. I got another five dollars and another two weeks victuals if you do me a favor."

"What's that, then?"

There was suspicion and interest in the question.

"I got a man aboard ship who wants to come ashore. I tolt him he was to stay aboard till I talked to you."

"Ashore to stay?" came the quick, irritated question.

"Hell – Heavens, no," the captain quickly corrected himself. "Not to stay. Least ways no more'n an hour. Mebbe two."

Blue frowned. It would take the crew that long and longer, yet, to load the wood. If the captain's passenger wished to stretch his legs, he did not need Blue's permission to do so.

Although it was an intriguing idea.

"The man's name is Holly. Reverent Holly. He wants to come ashore with ten of my passengers and a handful of my crew to baptize them. Down by the shore. They kick up the devil's own noise," he added.

"So why is it yer payin' me to allow 'em the privilege?"

"They was refused at the last place we put in."

"How's come?"

"There's some what don't take to this holy rolling."

"Fer five dollars an' two weeks grub, I'd let the devil hisself come ashore."

"Deal, then?"

"Deal."

The captain puffed out his cheeks in relief and paid the master his due.

"I'm goin' back aboard. Onest the reverend gets to work, yer welcome to come on deck and pick up yer food."

"I'll do 'er."

They shook hands on the deal and the officer retreated, feeling the eyes of the boy on his back, but disinclined to talk. Blue watched him go, then went about supervising the loading of his wood. It was not until he was certain no additional trees would be chopped in his absence that he untethered his curiosity and went down to shore.

The Right Reverent Holly was a giant, standing well over six feet tall. Dressed entirely in black, from stovepipe hat to polished boots, he was an imposing figure. A growth of black bread bristled from his chin, while long facial hair grew from ears to midway down his neck. He carried a black book in his right hand, directing the gathering by using it as a pointer.

It was apparent he was about to give a sermon. Not entirely unfamiliar with preachers, Blue spat in disgust and prepared to take his leave when the great man spotted him. Aiming the Bible, like a mighty shaft of olde in his direction, the reverend spoke.

"You there."

Blue looked around himself in some surprise, having no suspicion he would be addressed.

"What you want?" he demanded, ruffling his feathers to appear larger and more formidable that he was.

"Are you the gentleman that owns this island?"

Blue's head shot up and his ears pricked with new appreciation.

"That's me."

"A word with you, sir, if I may. In private."

The corners of Blue's face twitched. He squared his shoulders.

"I a'ready been baptized," he announced boldly, drawing a rapid and not altogether erroneous conclusion.

Reverend Holly smiled and flashed a set of teeth which would have a done a grand dame proud.

"I'm glad to hear that. Glad to hear that you have allowed the Lord into yer heart, master."

Reaching Blue's position in a matter of four long strides, the Reverend clasped his hand on the boy's muscled shoulder and squeezed. Finding he would not flinch under the pressure, he nodded religiously and gave him a shove away from the water.

"A word with you in private, sir."

"Ain't got no money. Captain ain't paid me, yet."

Holly laughed and his belly rolled with good humor.

"Don't ever lie to a man of the world, son," he warned, slipping his hand with the speed of a diving gull into Blue's pocket. Before the owner could stop him, Holly retrieved a fistful of coins, running them through his fingers, then dropping each onto the rocky ground as though they held no worth to him.

Blue struggled to free himself, failed, then began cursing. Holly waited for the storm to subside, then shook the boy until his teeth rattled.

"Just so's we understand one another," the preacher declared. "Pick up yer money and come with me."

Blue scooped the precious treasure back into his pocket, then followed the man obediently. When they had walked a quarter mile from the nearest human being, the holy man turned and spread his legs, assuming a smug, superior stance, meant to quail the heart of any sinner.

"My name is Holly. Reverend Holly. I'm working this line for the Lord."

"Good fer you," Blue pouted. He was not a sinner and his body could take a beating.

"I'm also working it, you might say, for myself."

Blue's ears pricked with a different type of anticipation and he unconsciously released his balled-up fists.

"I could use a partner. A silent partner. Know what that means?" Holly continued.

"I seen enough Injun agents to understand what yer sayin'. What ya *mean* is another thing. Say it straight out what ya want of me."

"I'm baptizing men in the Lord's name. An' the Lord helps them who help themselves. Know what I mean?"

"I'm listenin'."

"When a preacher baptizes a grow'd man, he takes him down into the water and dunks him under. What does that mean to you?"

Blue considered the possibilities.

"It means he don't see what's goin' on, on shore."

Holly grinned angelically.

"I can see you're a man of commerce. A man of high intelligence. What else does it mean to you?"

"The man gives money to the Lord?"

Holly laughed at the undisguised hopefulness in the boy's voice.

"Sometimes he knows he does – that's when he pays me fer my trouble – and sometimes he doesn't know. That's where the Lord helpin' those who help themselves comes in. Now, think hard. I need to know if you're the kind of partner I can use in this holy enterprise."

Blue's appreciation of the word "holy" took on a new significance.

"Tell me."

"It's simple, young apostle. What man taking the Lord into his heart wants to walk down into the water with his best clothes on?"

Blue's eyes opened until they were as round and dark as an India rubber ball.

"Blue blazes!" he swore.

The Lord did, indeed, work in mysterious ways.

"Are you with me?"

"Yes, sir," he spoke with reverence.

"What I want my partner to do – what I want *you* to do – is to sneak down to the water line and keep yer eye on those men I'm baptizing. I'll go down the line, blessing them and preparing them for immersion."

"How many do you dunk at a time?"

"On good days there might be as many as thirty converts. Other times, mebbe five or six. You gotta look sharp. They'll be staring at me, waiting for the Lord to hit them like a brick wall falling on their head. As soon as they go under, you scurry out and go through their clothes. Take all that's worth anything – billfolds, watches, chains, money – then run your ass off back where you came from.

"When I see you're through, I'll get them converts outta the water, get 'em dressed fast as they can and herd 'em back aboard before the good feelings and brotherhood of the Lord's wore off enough for 'em to miss their belongings. With any luck and a heap of prayer, the boat'll be off and gone before any of 'em misses their possessions. That keeps me in the clear."

"Damn!"

"Damned if you're caught and rich if you isn't," the reverend agreed.

Blue considered the possibilities, then sighed audibly. He could feel the blessing of the Lord filling his pockets with gold.

"But won't they suspect? Won't them come back after me?"

"There's that possibility, I won't deny. But what river captain's gonna turn back once he's on the river, to look fer a couple of missing billfolds? Not many. Time's money, you know, young gentleman. And besides, there's always a gambler or a lady of questionable virtue aboard. It's been my experience the robbed will accuse them before they'll ever think of you. Or me."

"But they'll search their belongings – and won't find nuthing."

The preacher scratched his head thoughtfully.

"No, they won't. But it just may be they'll find a watch or a chain that don't belong to the accused. The proof, as they say, is in the finding. Then I wonder aloud iffn the gambler or the lady didn't have a hiding place... or mebbe tossed the other valuables overboard when they saw the truth about to fall on their heads. It's been known to happen."

"And then what?"

"They get deposited along the side of the river. Or turned over to the authorities in the next stopover."

"More'n likely they'll taste the paddlewheels."

"Does too much damage. Besides, I'll step in an' save 'em. Beg for their a'mighty souls."

"How do you collect from me?"

"Next time a boat pulls in, you tell the captain you got a package to send home to your folks. He'll post it fer you. Only you won't be sending it back home; you'll be sending it to me. That way, I never have to come near the possessions while aboard a boat. I sell them to a friend I know and slip you your cut next time I'm through."

"Pretty slick," Blue acknowledged.

"Are you in?"

"Count me among the converted."

"Praise the Lord."

"Praise the Lord," Blue acknowledged, feeling the sin of poverty washed from his unholy shoulders.

It was the best season of young Blue Moon's life. He learned the songs of salvation and was even known, on occasion, to sing them while helping load wood aboard the riverboats. He even incorporated several of Reverend Holly's five-dollar words into his speech pattern and memorized entire passages from the Good Book.

When ladies came ashore on NNI#3, wishing the stretch their legs – after incidentally paying a fee of twenty-five cents for the privilege – they were impressed by the lonely inhabitant and his pious ways. Seldom did one refuse to allow the young gentleman to hold her handbag while he aided her in crossing a stream. On one occasion, a matronly woman proposed to adopt the "wild Christian" and send him back east for "a proper upbringing with a God-fearing family."

The offer was refused without due appreciation, it was noted.

If it were discovered, miles away, that a trinket or a coin purse was missing from her bag, the lady would inevitably think she misplaced the prize, never considering the Bible-spouting boy had helped himself to her worldly possessions.

The partnership of Holly and Moon worked well. They ran it for an entire season before too many suspicions were aroused and the Right Reverend Holly moved east to try his hand on the Ohio.

Nor did Blue hold it against him when he did not receive his cut for the last take of the year. That was business, after all. A man took what he could, stole when the opportunity presented itself and cheated whenever possible. There was no such thing as honor among thieves. Blue would have done the same, had their situations been reversed.

All in all, he made over two hundred and sixty dollars that year.

And praised the Lord for His bounty....

Still singing psalms, Captain Moon entered his stateroom and lit his lamp. It had been a good day. He had safely brought his boat to shore, found a new partner and learned how to read.

It never once occurred to him he had sorely impressed his crewman and made a convert to his side.

He was not looking to initiate men to his Cause.

Money was the only soul he wished to "impress."

With a smirk and a deep breath, Blue filled his lungs and sang his good-night praises to the Lord.

> While I draw this fleeting breath,
> When my eyes shall close in death,
> When I rise to worlds unknown,
> And behold thee on thy throne,
> Rock of Ages, cleft for me,
> Let me hide myself in thee.
>
> And let others be blamed for my misdeeds.

CHAPTER 9

Captain Moon stood at the bow of the *Blue Moon* and peered ahead, into the rain-obscured morning. Visibility was down to a matter of feet. With the river running high and fast, there was a great danger of striking unseen obstacles.

It would not suit his sense of the ironic to be sunk while on a mission of salvage.

"Steady as she goes, Mr. Miller," he sang out in his captain's voice. Command did not come easily to Blue. He had grown up alone and his solitary habits tended to make his orders sound terse and argumentative. When he put aside his past and concentrated on the present, however, his voice was authoritative, his words calm and reassuring.

If could not be said Blue Moon was born to be a captain, yet he had attained the rank and earned the right. A few more years under his belt might see him the most respected commander on the river.

Or dead from mutiny or an overdose of pride.

That would not make him the "deadest" captain on the river, for dead was dead and one man could not rightfully be said to be more deceased than the next. But if there ever were a contest in it, Blue would head the list.

The captain sounded the river, testing its depth. His crew did not understand what he was looking for, as the water ran high. They had learned not to question him, however, and saw no harm, if indeed, no help in what he did.

Besides, a subtle alteration had come over them since he had returned from shore two nights ago. Tim O'Leary had spread word of the captain's religious convictions, making Blue grow taller in their estimation.

A man with the Lord on his side could be allowed his idiosyncrasies.

When Moon struck an object with his line of rope and weighted wood, he let out a yell of satisfaction and incidentally raised his eyes heavenward. It was an entirely innocent, unrehearsed gesture of gratitude, directed no higher than the clouds.

If his crew took it for more than it was, that was their affair.

Giving an order to reduce speed and draw up, Blue pointed to shore.

"Mark where we are," he ordered. "In case we drift during the night, I want to be sure and regain this position."

"Aye, sir."

The first mate saluted and squinted toward shore. He could barely make out the trees in the dense fog. If questioned later, however, he would be able to recite any number of intimate details, creativity being one of his stronger suits.

"Light the flares. I don't want to be run down by another boat."

"In this weather? There isn't another riverboat on the water for twenty miles in either direction."

It was Lieutenant Hansen who spoke. Blue did not bother looking at him.

"I want the engineer. Have Scotty meet me on deck in five minutes. You take charge of scavenging the river bottom for the *Bell Bottom's* cargo. Whatever we can glean is pure profit."

He did not have to add, "And one less boat to run in competition with us."

"What was she carrying? Did you learn on shore?"

"No."

"I hope she was insured. Unless we can get her afloat, she'll be a total loss."

"I hope she wasn't insured for a penny."

"Captain Dressher was a good man."

"What's that to you? Or to me, for that matter? And I doubt," he added over his shoulder, "He went down with his ship. So you need not speak of him as though he were dead."

"I don't suppose you would have stopped to pick his body up, had we passed it," Bic Hansen muttered. Blue caught his words and frowned. For a man raised on the river, he could never understand his lieutenant's lack of common sense.

"If we passed his body floating on the river, I would most certainly have stopped to pick it up."

Bic turned back, a hopeful expression in his deep blue eyes.

"I am relieved to hear you say so, sir."

"You're damn right. If we passed it, that would have meant the body was floating upstream, against the current. Quite a feat for a corpse. I could have put in on display and let Captain Dressher pay for his own wake."

Blue laughed at his own joke. Hansen was not amused, which increased Blue's mirth. There was something about the idea which appealed to him. As he hailed his chief engineer, he stored the thought away.

A man ought to pay for his own wake. His money was no damn good to him dead. No sense letting it go to relatives or creditors who would never give him a second thought.

"Scotty."

The engineer, a man of dubious character who spoke with an assumed Scottish accent, sauntered over to his friend, the only one he had on board. He liked Blue because he thought the captain had no scruples. Blue liked the engineer because no one else did.

"Come overboard with me. I want to see if we can salvage the engine. I need you to tell me if it's worth the trouble."

"Aye, aye."

Scotty did not have to ask what was in it for him. He had worked this type of operation with Moon before and knew him for an honest, if not generous man.

Blue kicked off his shoes then stripped, dropping his clothes on deck where they fell. Among the men of the river, there was no such thing as modesty. When a man went into the water, he did so as naked as the day he was born. Which was, incidentally, the same way they buried him.

No sense wasting what a living man could use.

Which reminded Blue of Hernando DeSoto. Imagine wrapping the corpse in a blanket.

Spaniards must be a queer lot, indeed.

Or more wealthy than a riverman.

Without the two inches of heel from his shoes, Blue Moon stood no higher than five foot five, yet his powerful shoulder and rippling arm muscles, aided by the massive amount of red hair on his chest, made him appear like a formidable grizzly bear. If he had not bothered to occasionally have the hair on the back of his neck shaved, and grown a beard, Blue would have been nicknamed "Red," and no matter how he protested, would have been called Captain Red Moon of the *Red Moon*.

Fully clothed, with his hair trimmed to his collar and his neck made barren by the barber's skill, he barely passed for "Blue," and would not have succeeded in that but for his propensity for a fight. The man who called him "Red" was in for it. No one but strangers made the mistake to his face.

In fact, there was nothing "blue" about Blue Moon. With red hair on his head and red fur covering his body, deep brown eyes and an underlying pale skin, he was as far away from "blue" as a man could get.

The joke had made the rounds that Blue's mother was a patriotic woman, naming her son in celebration of the new flag. Inasmuch as he was red and white already, she had merely added blue to the mix to come up with red, white and blue. It was a great disappointment, therefore when Independence Day came and went and "Captain Patriotic" did not so much as set out a flare or give a speech, much less buy a round of drinks for the assemblage.

He had been seen to take a drink or two, but that was explained on other, less patriotic grounds.

Scotty dove off the side, while Blue descended the ladder, jumping into the swirling current only after he had submerged to his waist. He did not follow his engineer under water, but swam out into the river and surveyed the wreck of the *Bell Bottom* from water level.

That was his privilege and no one gave his actions a second thought. The crew would have been surprised to observe their captain never put his head under water and shocked to learn he had an abhorrence of doing so. It was enough to know he could swim.

Not that any of them believed he would dive in after them if they fell overboard. On the Mississippi, it was every man for himself, in or out of the *Blue Moon.*

"She's blown a'right, Capt'n," Scotty yelled to his commander as his head broke the surface. "But I think she's worth the salvage. The main engine won't take too much to repair. If I'm wrong, she's worth pullin' up fer the parts. We kin get two hundred fer her easy."

He did not have to see Blue to know he was smiling.

"What about the boilers?"

"Ya want them, too? They're a'ready second-hand."

No one knew more about engines than Scotty and Blue respected him for that knowledge. The engineer could name every part of every steamboat on the Mississippi and was a walking insurance agent's book when it came to knowing what had been dismantled from one boat and transferred to another.

"How much is it worth?"

"Nary the trouble."

"What about the pitman? How long is she?"

"Too long fer us. Make it thirty-five feet."

Blue swore then splashed water with his hands.

"We'll sell it, then."

He would get three hundred, maybe three-fifty for the engine and another fifty for the pitman. If there was also cargo he could save, the trip would be worth the equivalent of two trips up and down the river from Natchez to New Orleans.

"Did you see any bodies?"

It was Hansen's voice. Or possibly Deke's. Bleeding hearts, both of them. Blue would discharge them the day he saw ice on the river.

"Wasn't lookin'," Scott called.

Scotty was a man wise beyond his years. He also knew how to placate his captain. If Blue Moon ever made his fortune, he intended to be right there beside him.

If he did not, at least he was an employer who asked no questions.

"Mister Hansen!" Blue responded.

"Sir?"

"Send down two men to look for bodies."

"Yes, sir!"

There was no help for it. If Hansen or Miller took it into their heads there were bodies tangled in the debris of the sunken steamboat, they would not let the matter drop until it had been resolved. That would cause delays and unrest amongst the crew. Let them satisfy their own warped sense of morality. Then the work of raising the engine, if not the entire *Bell Bottom* could commence.

A shot from ashore diverted attention from the wreck and Moon swam in that direction, finally striking the bottom with his toes after several long pulls by his powerful arms. He was a strong swimmer and could have stayed in the water for hours without tiring. The distress signal demanded his attention, and it was with no slight degree of irritation that he drew himself up and looked around.

"Hello, on shore!" he called. "Identify yerself. I am Captain Moon of the *Blue Moon.*"

"Moon." The call was spoken like a curse word and Blue smiled to himself. It was always good knowing his reputation preceded him.

"So you didn't go down with your ship, Dressher."

There was the sound of shoes stomping wet brush, then the captain of the sunken boat appeared before him, a musket dangling from the crook of his arm. Dressher's face was dark and swollen from some private malady.

"Thank God you've come." It was amazing how fast word of Blue's religious convictions had spread. "I've got a wounded passenger who needs to be taken to a doctor."

"Don't have one aboard."

"In Natchez, then."

"Don't plan on returning to Natchez until I raise your ship."

"This man may die."

"What's the matter? He owe you money?"

Dressher did not laugh. Instead, he raised the gun and pointed it several degrees to the left of Moon's arm.

"Please, sir," came a woman's voice. Without waiting for permission, a lady pushed past Captain Dressher to plead her case with the stranger. She had not expected to discover him standing naked, however, and quickly withdrew, hand over her face.

For his part, Blue hastily stepped back into the water, blushing furiously. He did not mind showing off his natural endowments to a man, but a woman was altogether another matter.

"Why the hell didn't you tell me there was a female with you?" he spat.

"She's Mrs. Lang, the wounded man's wife."

"I don't give a damn who she is. You had no right –"

"Please," the woman interrupted. She did not repeat her mistake of stepping forward, but hid, back to the water, as she spoke. "You must take my husband to a doctor."

"Lady, I'd like to help you, but I can't." The first part of which was a lie, dictated only by the most basic of custom. "If I leave now, another boat'll be along and claim my prize. The *Bell Bottom's* worth five hundred to me. Mebbe more. You can't ask me to leave salvage for the sake of one man."

"You must," she begged, tears in her voice.

"I'll have one of my men take a look at him," he offered, totally unmoved.

"A doctor?"

"A doctor, sure."

"Thank God," she cried. "You will send him immediately?"

"It might be better if he were brought aboard the *Blue Moon*," Dressher offered. "At least you can put him up in a stateroom, Moon, while the 'doctor' looks at him?"

"What's a matter with the man?"

"His leg was crushed when the ship hit that tree. I am afraid he will lose it, if he is not properly attended to."

There was a long silence before Blue spoke again.

"I'll send a boat ashore. You can load him in?"

"Captain Dressher will see to it, I am sure," the lady tearfully replied.

"He's got nothing else to do," Blue dryly snapped.

It was not until the woman's footsteps could be heard through the brush that Dressher spoke again. When he did, his voice dripped with loathing.

"You're a river rat if ever there was one, Moon. If you try to pass your cook off as a doctor, I'll tell her straight out what he is."

"Suit yerself. It's all the same to me. I don't owe her anything."

"Don't you have any decent feelings at all? Don't you have a heart? This woman's husband is badly hurt. If he loses his leg or if he dies, it'll be on your conscience."

"Decent feelings don't keep a man warm at night. They don't fill his purse."

"Just run him to Natchez. It'll only take you a day and a half to get back here. In this god-forsaken weather, no other boat'll be along."

"That's just the point and you failed to see it," Blue commented. "God-forsaken. I reckon God forsook that poor bastard, or he wouldn't have been hurt. Who am I to stand in the way of God's will?"

"Son of a bitch."

"For that, you bastard, you can stay on shore and rot."

Blue dropped into the water and swam to his own boat, heart hardened by the curse Dressher had left him with. He would keep his word, too, and be damned what his crew thought. If they felt sorry for the captain of the sunken boat, they could spend their night on shore, as well.

And walk to Natchez.

He was aware that Mrs. Lang and her husband were brought aboard, but had no time to spare for them. He had already given orders for "Doc" to fix the wound as best he could. What more did anyone have a right to expect?

It was past midnight when the *Bell Bottom* was raised from its not-so-final resting place and bailed out. With luck and a bit of handling, the *Blue Moon* could tow her to Natchez, where the insurance adjustor for the former owners would pay him a fancy fee for his trouble – or he would sell her at auction. It made no difference to the new owner.

When the knock on the door came, Captain Moon was surprised. Having no other thought than it was one of his crew, he did not bother standing when he gave the command to "Enter." He heard the door open and shut.

After what he deemed an interminable silence, Blue swung around in his chair and started to speak, when his mouth dropped open in abject shock.

"Captain Moon..."

It was Mrs. Lang and not one of his crew, at all. Blue reached for his jacket and shoved his arms through the sleeves, annoyed at having been caught by this woman a second time in a state of undress.

"I thought it was Mr. Miller at the door," he mumbled. Which was as close to an apology as he had ever offered in his life. When she did not respond, he pursed his lips and looked away. "Has your husband been attended to?"

"Yes. Your *cook* did what he could for him."

Blue shrugged and rolled his eyes. He would never forgive Dressher. Never.

He would even go so far as to testify against him, if a case of pilot error were brought to trial by the insurance company. It was something no river captain ever did, but Blue would do so willingly. After all, he had navigated the same waters and brought his boat through safely. If Dressher was close behind and ran afoul of a submerged obstacle, that was clearly his fault.

"Doc has about as much experience as any doctor you're likely to find in Natchez."

"But not in New Orleans."

"I suppose not," he agreed, forcing himself to turn his head and meet her gaze. He had nothing to be ashamed about. He was not a captain for his health. He had taken the injured man aboard his own ship, had him tended to by his own cook and promised to transport both passengers to Natchez free of charge.

She ought to be grateful.

He did not have to look her in the eyes to know she was not.

"I want my husband brought to New Orleans. Tonight."

He did not take her meaning.

"I did not hear another boat come up." He stood, sorely puzzled. "What boat is she?"

"There is no other boat, Captain Moon. I wish *you* to take my husband to New Orleans."

"I am not going there."

She took a step back, effectively blocking the path of his retreat, should it have been his intention to leave the stateroom.

"What price?" she asked.

He was twenty-three years old and unfamiliar with the ways of women. Even less so with the manners and customs of what they had to tempt a man with.

What he did read in her eyes was determination.

Being illiterate, he could have been forgiven for missing the larger picture.

Desperation.

That emotion he was not unfamiliar with. Never having an opportunity to look into his own face when experiencing such fear, however, he did not recognize it in another's.

"A price you cannot afford to pay."

He was talking about money.

"Captain Dressher has explained how it is with you. He said money rules your world. I wonder if he is correct."

She moved closer, placing a hand on the top of her dress. When Blue made no move to stop her, she drew it down over her shoulder, having unbuttoned the back before entering his cabin. It was only then that he understood.

"No!" he gasped, holding a hand out to stop her. "What are you doing? Go away!"

"I love my husband. His well-being is worth more to me than anything I own. I do not have five hundred dollars, Captain Moon. But I do have something which may be of value to you. My body. Take it in payment with no one the wiser."

"Jesus Christ! Get out of here!"

"Not until you have agreed to take my husband to New Orleans. Tonight."

"The river is too dangerous to sail at night."

"At first light, then."

Blue Moon had never been so aroused in his life. While he had been tempted by women in saloons, and once almost drawn into a liaison with a passenger he was transporting from Saint Louis, he had never consummated such a relationship. Money was too dear, or the time had not been right. He had been frightened of his own body and scared to discover himself nearly out of control.

Mrs. Lang was having that effect on him now. Hearing the pounding of his own heart in his ears, he saw his trembling hand reach out with desire.

There was lust in his soul and a driving curiosity so intense he might have harnessed himself to the engines ard powered the *Blue Moon* to New Orleans without need of additional steam.

"No," he gasped, meaning "yes." He did not understand his dilemma, while she was fully aware of his plight.

Mrs. Lang slipped the dress material off her other shoulder, leaving both bare and glistening in the lamp light. This man held life and death in his hands. She would hold him in hers and claim the right to demand a favor.

"Come, Blue," she said. He had never heard his name pronounced with such magic, such all-compelling urgency. His stomach began to work backwards and he felt light-headed. The muscles in his calves cramped and he dropped his hands to his groin, touching himself with passion.

"Lady," he stammered, struggling for air to clear his feverish brain. "Lady, go away. Leave me alone."

In the dimness of the coal oil lantern, Blue's sweaty face appeared no older than a boy's. She had not expected to find him unexperienced. He might have been her innocent son, rather than the man holding her husband's fate in his hands.

But he was not her son and his lack of worldliness could neither be pitied nor used as a weapon against her. Rather, she must turn the fact around and employ it to her advantage.

"Blue. Blue. Undress me, Blue. We have until first light to be together. I will love you as no one ever has or ever will."

She could not acknowledge that she knew his secret, for that would shame him. She would promise, therefore, what he had never had, in other words.

And mean them.

A bargain was a bargain and Mrs. Lang was a woman true to her word. She would tear her own heart out of her breast if it meant saving her own true love.

He turned with a sob and fled from her outstretched hand. While there was no possibility of placing himself in her position, he understood she offered too much. He knew what it was like to bargain at horrible disadvantage and the thought nearly tore him asunder.

"Out!" he screamed. "I'll take you in the morning. It's all the same to me. I don't give a damn if I go to Natchez or New Orleans. Get out and leave me alone."

Get out and go to your husband, he meant to say and did not have the words. He could not express the sentiment beyond his own world.

She had won without firing a shot.

Without even baring a breast.

She had come seeking a man and found a boy. Or rather, she had come looking for an animal and discovered a man.

Mrs. Lang slipped away and returned to the stateroom where her unconscious husband lay. She did not sleep, but wept into unresponsive arms.

Which finally gave her something in common with the hard-hearted Blue Moon.

Bic Hansen saw Mrs. Lang come out of the captain's stateroom and drew back, hiding himself in the shadows. It did not tax his imagination to envision what had taken place. His fists tightened. Nor was he surprised when, at first light, orders were given for the *Blue Moon* to raise a head of steam and sail for New Orleans.

By mid-morning, the entire crew knew of the captain's treachery. Forgotten were his religious convictions and his verve when singing "Rock of Ages." He was what Captain Dressher had called him.

A river rat.

CHAPTER 10

Mad Max Albright was an insurance adjustor. He worked out of a small office on Cat-o-Nine-Tails Lane, so called because he found nine ways to get out of paying a claim. He was a pimple-faced man of forty and had been in the insurance scam business since the advent of sail.

"Too bad about the *Bell Bottom,*" he decided, scratching his head. "A total loss."

Blue shrugged and turned away. He had known beforehand what Mad Max would say and had already made up his mind to sell the boat for scrap. If Scotty were correct, he could get at least three hundred dollars for the engine. Add to that a few pennies for the boiler he had salvaged. With luck, and he would clear four hundred dollars.

"Why is it you didn't haul out the cargo? The shipment of leather was probably ruined but the furniture and cane should have been all right. And all those paying passengers. Left 'em behind with Dressher, I hear."

Blue shrugged and dug his hands deep into his pockets.

"Weather turned bad. The cargo had spilt out, all over the bottom. Wanted to be sure I got the big prize to New Orleans."

"That's not what I heard."

Mad Max winked. Blue spat into the water and shook his head.

"I don't give a damn what you heard. It's a lie."

"Oh. I wondered why Bic Hansen was speakin' so well of you. At first, I thought you was dead."

Moon did a half turn before realizing Max was baiting him. He wrinkled his nose in disgust and stomped away.

It was too late to sail this evening and the sale of the wreck *Bell Bottom* would not be complete before noon tomorrow. That left Blue with nearly twenty-four hours on his hands. He did not want to return to the *Blue Moon,* yet the thought of spending money on a bed in a wharf-side tavern held no allure for him.

He had been as jumpy as a cat on the trip to New Orleans. He had done no more than catnap, and that had come while he stood, propped up at the wheel. He feared sleep now, shunned the thought of it as he would an enemy. In sleep came dreams and in those restless, uncontrollable times, his body was subject to fits of urgency.

He had awoke covered with perspiration, breath ragged, palms itchy. He lost his appetite, took little interest in the workings of the boat as she steamed her way to New Orleans. The only thing to which he could direct his attention was the vivid, palpable image of Mrs. Lang standing in his stateroom, hand to her bosom.

Imagination working overtime, Blue saw her pull down the material, envisioned her naked breasts with their sharply pointed nipples. Worse, he dreamed of her coming to him, arms extended, wrapping them around his waist and pressing her hot, pliable, demanding lips to his.

He heard her whisper his name everywhere he turned. Whether he stood at the bow, handled the wheel or cowered in the head, door propped shut for privacy, he heard her calling.

"Blue. Blue. Blue Moon, where are you? I have something to give you. Come to me, darling Blue. I promised you, and I always keep my promises."

Promised him what? That was the question. While he was not naive enough to misunderstand her offer, he did not fully comprehend the total picture. He had *heard* men mating with women, listened to their grunts and stifled groans, but had never actually *seen* the act performed.

Growing up along the river, Blue was subjected to tales of high spirits and wilder bragging. He had heard of delights he could not fathom, actions he could not envision, emotions which scared and tantalized him.

As he grew older, Blue's curiosity expanded, while his mind worked overtime to make sense of all he had heard, either first- or second-hand. In the end, none of it made any sense and he had literally thrown his hands up in despair, deciding he would have none of it. Women were too much trouble. They took a man's mind off business. They cost money. They reproduced children.

There was not one of them he ever met who could arm-wrassle worth a damn, pilot a boat, predict the weather or stoke the boilers.

Apparently, he held values other men did not.

Now, he was a changed man. Abandoning a shot at the big prize, he had left countless dollars on the river bottom to take a wounded man to New Orleans.

It was all her fault: that Mrs. Lang. She had done something to him, put a spell on him. God alone knew what she might have done, had he refused her request. She had done plenty, as it was. Bewitched him; painted her image behind his eyeballs, so that when he closed his eyes, she appeared, as if by magic.

That was it. Magic. A bewitching. Somehow, in some manner he could not fathom, she made his mind betray him. Turn one way, he saw her reflection in the water; turn the other and in his imagination, she was hiding behind a door, waiting to pounce and drag him away.

If the damage had been limited to his brain, Blue would have tried to live with it. But Mrs. Lang's powers went well beyond mind games. She had reached into his body, curled her long, enticing fingers around his middle and squeezed his insides for all she was worth.

The simple act of relieving himself had become a misery. All he had to do was unbutton his fly and he broke out into a sweat. His hands trembled, his leg shook, his vision blurred. And no matter how hard he tried, he could not pass water.

Which consigned him to a misery of living with a full-to-bursting bladder.

He simply could not spend the rest of his days leaning against the wheel house with his legs crossed.

And there was worse than that.... Much worse. Unspeakable things were happening to him in private areas.

"Hells' bells!" he cursed. His heart was racing, his mind wandering. He had to leave New Orleans, get away before he went stark raving mad.

He tried to tell himself this agitation was due to the fact he had left behind valuable cargo. That had been a foolish thing to do. He should have stayed and rescued what he could from the bottom of the river. Max Albright was right. The weather had turned fair. Everyone knew that. Everyone blamed him for passing on a chance to salvage everything he could from the *Bell Bottom.*

Even his crew had been resentful. When the order to put on a head of steam and head down river was given, they had grumbled to his face and come close to outright insubordination. You would think they were entitled to a percentage.

He would get rid of the lot of them. None were contracted past winter.

He would start fresh in the spring.

Across the wharf a heavy piece of cast iron was inadvertently dropped. Blue twitched like a cat. He was, by nature, a jumpy man, but not like this.

He was ill.

He was under a spell.

There was only one thing to do when a man was bewitched by a woman. He had to have the curse removed. Blue had heard of such things before. If he did not act in a timely manner, his mind would disintegrate faster than a blown boiler and his life would be ruined.

New Orleans was just the place for the cure of mystic occurrences. For five dollars, a man could buy a turn of bad luck for his enemy. For ten dollars, he could have a rival fall into the river and drown. For twenty dollars, he could order a potion sent to a woman which would make her fall madly in love with him.

Perish the thought.

He was not certain what the cost of removing a spell was, but if it was under twenty dollars, he would give it a try.

Any more than that and he would live his life in an ice bucket.

Blue could have hopped a coach but decided to walk. The exercise would do him good. It kept his body too occupied to betray him.

Crossing eleven streets, working his way down a back alley and three blind turns, Blue came out on Hagis Street. Even by New Orleans standards, it was disreputable. The businesses on either side of the two-block dead-end catered to those desperate enough to need a snort, or to men sodden enough not to realize who or what they were sleeping with.

Refuse, ankle deep, lined the sides of the barren street. The road was pitted with holes. A dead dog floated in the water trough. No horses were hitched to any of the railings, a fact which did not surprise him. If a man came to Hagis Street, he took nothing of worth with him.

Unless he was foolish enough to consider his life of value.

The shop Moon sought was the third from the end, on the left-hand side. A half moon, painted yellow, hung from a lopsided chain, so that it appeared to be sinking instead of rising. A large, plaster cast of a head with demarcations of bumps and areas of interest was prominently displayed.

The shop bell tinkled as he entered. The stench inside was so overwhelming he nearly fled. Had it not been for Mrs. Lang's spell, nothing in the world would have induced him to tarry.

An inch high, cone-shaped stick of something smoldering in the back appeared to be the source of the odor. He moved away from that area, holding his breath. He had once come upon a body, a week dead in the hot sun and it had not smelled as bad as this.

A row of jars lined one wall. A curious horror drew him there and he gawked with tingling wonder at the items displayed thereon. One jar held fifteen, or as close as he could count, eyeballs. By the size, he judged them to have been removed from the carcasses of horses. He did not ponder why some of the irises were bluish-white.

Another jar, this one without a lid, held the fetus of a pig. Immediately to the left of it, in a crock, were one dozen black feathers.

In a small wooden crate by the window several live toads were enclosed. Blue removed the wire from atop the box and picked one up. It piddled in his hand and he dropped it in disgust.

He was cursed, for sure.

Crisscrossing the small, cluttered shop, Blue examined a series of life-sized heads, all plaster casts and all with lines and words printed on them. He did not understand the writing, but knew the science, because he had heard it discussed once: Phrenology.

It was French, he decided.

"You are looking for a love potion?"

Blue jumped and spun simultaneously, landing on his feet by sheer luck. He had not heard anyone come up behind him. The voice scared him out of two years' growth.

The speaker was a woman. From her appearance, he deduced she was young, although her hair was hidden behind a scarf and her face decorated with colorful swirls of paint. The speaker wore a long, flowing dress, disguising her figure. On her fingers were numerous rings, all depicting occult symbols.

"I want to see the chief medicine man," Moon boldly declared. While gypsies were as foreign to him as French was alien, he understood medicine men. It would take a great one to rid him of his plague.

"I run this shop," she informed him. He was immediately disappointed. His face fell. He had never heard of a medicine woman.

"Can you tell me where I can find a chief? I have money," he added for emphasis. Everyone, even women, understood that language.

If Blue had gone up the Mississippi with Kress as planned, he could have found exactly who he was looking for without trouble.

If he had gone with Kress in the first place, he would not be in trouble now.

Damn that woman and her evil spell.

"I can help you."

The medicine woman held out her hands. He warily moved away.

"I need someone to take off a spell."

She did not seem shocked.

"Someone has put a spell on you?"

He would have thought any legitimate medicine man could tell that by looking at him.

"Yes."

"A... terrible curse?"

"Terrible," he repeated, nodding his head.

"A curse so terrible you cannot sleep at night?" He nodded dumbly, feeling somewhat relieved at her powers of divination. "A curse all men dread?"

"Yes!" he gasped. She was making a believer of him.

"A curse which leaves you cold?"

He frowned.

He was not cold. He was hot. Very hot.

"A curse which has left you – unmanned?"

Blue was not sure exactly what that meant but he did not like the sound of it. There was the implication he could be beaten in a fight. His fists clenched at his sides.

"A woman has done it to me."

"I see. That is often the case."

"She... wanted me to do something. When I said I would not, she came at me. I felt faint."

"Go on."

"It was then that she did it."

"What did she say?"

"I cannot tell you."

It was too horrible to repeat.

"What did she do?"

He shook his head. His jaw dropped open and his tongue protruded. If his mouth had not been so dry, he would have drooled. "Did she repeat an incantation?" the occult healer inquired.

"What's that?"

He was feeling worse by the second.

"Mutter words you did not understand? Wave her hands? Did she dance, use a potion, make you drink from her cup?"

"She started to take her dress off."

He hung his head in shame. He had not meant to say that but the memory burned deep within him. It also caused him unaccountable agitation. If he did not get a cure soon, he would dissolve into a puddle and never be heard from again.

"And you could do nothing. I see."

Apparently she did not see as well as she thought.

"I promised I would do as she asked if only she would go away." The gypsy started to speak, then held her tongue and stared more closely at the man before her.

"Did you do this thing?"

"Yes."

"She has asked you to do other things?" He shook his head. "She has come to you again?"

"No! I avoided her. When I reached New Orleans, I had my crewman escort her and her husband off the boat. I thought that would be the end of it, but I was wrong."

"Tell me more."

It was all so acutely embarrassing.

"I see her everywhere. In my cabin. On board my boat. In the boiler room. I see her in shadows; in the water. Even when I close my eyes, I see her standing before me."

"What is she doing?"

The question was for form, rather than elucidation.

"Taking off her dress."

"Now I see," the gypsy wisely pronounced. He let out a pent-up breath.

"I cannot sleep. I *dare* not."

He emphasized the word, hoping she would understand. He was out of words.

The medicine woman held up a hand and placed it on Blue's sweaty forehead. She closed her eyes and made low animal sounds. He felt some relief. That was what he would expect from a chief.

"You wish me to purge you."

That was a word he knew. He nodded mutely.

"Come with me. We will go into the back room."

"Can you help me?"

"Yours is... an uncommon problem. I do not have many who come to me with such a curse. I will help you."

He felt a sudden rush of emotion, remembering at the same time, his bladder was full to bursting. He should have made an attempt to relieve himself outside. It was too late now.

If removing the curse did not require much time, he could take care of his pressing problem and be back to his boat by five o'clock. That would give him twelve hours to sleep before he set off for Natchez in the morning.

The medicine woman parted a curtain of beads, indicating he walk through. Stooping low though he was in no danger of striking the ceiling, Blue slipped past her into the inner sanctum. Looking around, he experienced an immediate sense of relief. The room was filled with stuffed birds and animals and smelled vaguely of dung and perspiration.

It was a place where a man could believe a spell would be cast off.

"Sit down."

He obeyed, dropping into an armless chair in the center of the room. She draped a poorly-dressed deer hide around his shoulders.

"What you ask is powerful medicine. It will cost you twenty-five dollars for a cure."

Had he not been comforted by the sight of the animals and the rough feel of the hide, he would have wet his trousers.

Tears came to his eyes and salty gall filled his mouth. Blue shook his leg and came close to vomiting.

It was too late to go back now. The urge was upon him once more. It had miraculously deprived him of all sensation of a full bladder.

Withdrawing his purse from his jacket pocket, the riverman removed the requisite number of coins and counted them into her hand. All thought of sleep vanished from his mind and he felt a peculiar, prickling sensation as his flesh touched that of the gypsy's. He did not have to turn around to see Mrs. Lang's nearly naked shape hovering in the corner behind him.

She was somehow affecting the gypsy, making her move in suggestive ways. The room closed in on him.

He did not understand what "suggestive" meant or why he had thought it.

His mind was definitely affected.

He was as close to death as he had ever been in his life.

Closer. He had been beaten to a pulp and never felt like this.

The walls moved. He pressed his legs together and bowed his head. He did not feel better.

Twenty-five dollars was cheap.

Despite past reservations, he would have paid thirty and called it a bargain.

The medicine woman began to chant. He moaned with her. He did not know the tune, yet was able to keep prefect time with her. She had the power.

If only she would hurry.

Blue had the sinking sensation he would get no sleep tonight.

Or ever again.

Mrs. Lang had made him one of the walking dead.

Better she had tired his body to a tree and let it rot.

The gyrations of the gypsy grew wilder, more intense. He left off chanting with her and dug his fingernails into his thighs. His brain felt as though it were going to explode.

She stopped so suddenly he lost his balance and plunged to the floor, striking his nose on the cold boards. He felt no pain.

When he opened his eyes, she was putting a cup to his lips. He drank eagerly.

"You must take it all," she ordered. The magic potion tasted oddly familiar. He drank it, then eagerly licked the medicine woman's fingers. She hastily withdrew them.

"Go now," she ordered. "Hurry. My potion will purge you. You will think no more of this woman."

Moon got to his feet, staggered, belched then ran from the room. In his haste, he did not see the spirit of Mrs. Lang laughing at him.

Once outside, Blue wildly looked around, tripped in a hole and fell to his knees. Terrible cramps wracked his body. He screamed in agony. His world blurred. Sounds became acutely intensified, compelling him to hold his hands over his ears.

Crawling on all fours, he made it to an alley before his bowels erupted. Without having either the time or the sense to remove his trousers, he soiled his clothes. His groin began to throb. Without the ability or the desire to stop, he began urinating. It was ropey, odd-colored piss. He did not need to stand to relieve himself.

In fact, his legs would not have held him.

Crashing to earth, Blue rolled in the alley, holding himself as he had seen babies do. This, then, was his fate. To be reduced to infancy. He was too drunk from the potion to care.

When his body was emptied, he wept like a baby.

Two doors away, the medicine woman replaced the bottle of magic potion and shut her window.

A good dose of calomel never did anyone any harm.

And occasionally chased away an evil spell.

When Blue Moon awoke, he staggered to the water trough, unceremoniously dumping the dead dog into the street. He washed his trousers and undergarments, though he was as weak as a kitten. Every muscle in his legs ached. He felt like he had walked ten thousand miles.

Uphill.

It was past noon when he returned to the *Blue Moon.*

The cure had been worth the price.

He had not thought of Mrs. Lang in almost twenty hours.

To explain his absence and bedraggled appearance, Blue told his crew he had been fallen on by thieves and beaten.

They, too, thought the cure worth the price.

CHAPTER 11

Little did Blue Moon and the crew of his steamboat know the ultimate price they would pay for their good-deed trip to New Orleans.

Six hours out of the city, the *Blue Moon* came upon a 200 ton riverboat named *One Third Sally*. Chugging along against the rough current, the ancient paddle-wheeler labored in loud distress. If the statement, "In sorrow thou shall bring forth children" were true, *One Third Sally* would soon bear triplets.

Choking from the dense, low-lying smoke belching forth from the floating relic of the Fulton-Livingston days, Blue wrapped a kerchief around his mouth and nose. Waving angrily at his counterpart across the water, he made sharp, chopping motions with his arm, indicating the boat should move to either side to let him pass.

"Can't be done, Moon!" Captain Reynolds shouted back, apparently less intimidated by the noise than his competitor.

"You're floating down the damn middle of the river."

"Safer that way."

Stamping his foot in annoyance, Blue stomped to the opposite side of his vessel. Drawing his cap back on his head, he scratched his brow, shaking away a host of imaginary gnats.

"Hansen," he summoned.

The mate reluctantly moved to his side.

"Sir?"

"If I have to follow that skow all the way to Natchez, I'll lose what little I have left of my mind."

"River widens up ahead."

"Fifty miles up-river. Do you think I don't know where the river widens?"

Hansen made a move between a twitch and a shrug.

"The river's too narrow to pass her here," he continued, anticipating the captain's objection. "There are sandbars and eddies where the water shallows."

"Are you saying we can't pass her?"

"Not unless you put wings on her sides and fly her over."

Anything less and Blue could have ignored the challenge. As it stood, Hansen deliberately set him up for failure. The only way he could win was by successfully passing *One Third Sally*.

He had fifty miles in which to do it.

At eight miles per hour, Blue calculated that within six hours, he would either have established himself as a captain worth his salt, or a jackass.

Retiring to the wheelhouse, Blue pulled his charts and studied the meandering lines of red, blue and black pencil. The task he set for himself was nearly impossible. After the recent heavy rains, banks had worn away, rendering shorelines unpredictable. What a man saw with his eyes was not necessarily true. The first point of shore hid beneath it yards of submerged, sloping land. If he tried to slip past *One Third Sally* and ran aground, it would cost him hours in lost time, a considerable amount of money if he damaged the hull, and a red face.

All three were potential disasters.

There was only one viable place on this narrow, unpredictable section of the Mississippi he might try a passing maneuver. Three miles upstream at a point immediately before a blind, treacherous curve in the river, the banks pulled back far enough for him to slip by Reynold's boat.

Tapping the charts with a rare display of confidence, Blue pursed his lips and whistled a merry tune.

It was a challenge, after all. He who lived by the rules, died by the rules. He who challenged the odds lived to grow rich.

Steaming into Natchez several hours early would not increase Blue Moon's wealth, but it would do much for his sorely-tried self-esteem.

It might also put Mrs. Lang and all her she-devils to rest.

It was worth a try.

"Hansen. *Mister* Hansen," he bellowed in his best command voice. The lieutenant reported, a surly expression in his dusky blue eyes.

"Here. Look at this." Blue pointed to the map, tracing his intended route with a finger. "We can pass her along this stretch."

Despite his seeming lack of concern, Hansen's pupils dilated, until the color in the iris was usurped by round blackness.

"No," he denied emphatically. "That's suicide."

"The river widens enough."

"You'd have to move like the wind to pass *One Third Sally* and get comfortably ahead of her before the banks close in again. Besides," he added through gritted teeth. "There's a steep curve in the river at that point. You'll be steaming around her blind. If there were any submerged sandbars or obstructions in the water, we'd never see them."

"I'll take the risk."

"She's your boat."

"That she is, Mister Hansen."

The first officer moved away, revealing, by his attitude, his lack of care.

It was never a wise move turning one's back on a man known to have little compunction against putting a Bowie knife between one's shoulder blades. It was, therefore, an act of courage, as well as contempt, on Hansen's part.

For which he earned only enmity from his commander.

Bravery had its place. So did respect.

Bravery lost this round.

Blue descended into the bowels of his ship, thumbs hooked over his wide belt, whistling a psalm tune he had learned from Reverent Holly. This particular one he never sang, for there were other lyrics to it he had picked up at the End of the Line Saloon. Had he belted those out, there might have been a mutiny aboard.

He was, therefore, saving them.

They were his Ace in the Hole.

Mr. Scott heard the footsteps before he saw the captain. Wiping his hands on a pair of equally soiled trousers, he scurried away from the heat of the boiler to greet his guest.

"Aye," Scott admitted, clucking his tongue. "The engine is running a bit rough. I thought you'd notice."

Blue scanned the cords of wood neatly stacked by his stoker. Having moved up from the ranks, beginning his career aboard a steamboat as a stoker, he had a penchant for a well-run, unencumbered engine room.

"Is it the wood?"

Scotty shook his head.

"Pressure isn't what it should be. She's got a leak somewhere. We get to Natchez, I'll have to take the engine apart."

"How long will that take?"

"Day or two."

Translated, he meant a week.

"What'll it cost?"

"Depends."

"On what?"

"On what ya made salvaging the *Bell Bottom*."

Which meant every cent he had in the world.

"Bring her up to speed when I give the order."

"Race?" Scotty asked eagerly.

"No."

"Bet?"

"No."

"Lady waiting fer you in Natchez?"

Blue's eyes widened and he winked. They had had this out before.

"Yeah. Mrs. Scott."

Scotty took a vicious swing at him. Blue ducked under it easily, rebounding with his fists up, arms extended. He bounced, sidestepped as his engineer threw another punch, then danced back and held out his hands before the pugilist charged a third time.

"You know I never kiss and tell," Blue taunted him.

"I dinna know any such thing."

"Well, you do now."

"They say you was raised by the Injuns, Blue Moon. They say the Injuns is afraid of you, on accounta when you was born, you brought earthquakes and flood with ya."

"Back off, Scotty," Blue warned, suddenly serious. "You listen to too much barroom gossip. Loose tongues make for grand liars."

"I heard they bought a squaw for ya, but she wasn't no squaw, and you was just a lad."

"Back off, I say."

"Take back what ya said aboot my woman."

Prudence being the better part of valor, Blue backed off.

"I take it back."

It was no skin off his teeth. He would not have touched Mrs. Scott with a ten foot pole.

She was an Injun.

With a loose tongue.

With a sudden determination to dismiss the engineer at the end of the season, along with the rest of the crew, Blue disappeared into the shadows of the hold. He was not ashamed for backing down about Scott's woman. He should not have said what he did. That was pure vanity and more than a little foolishness.

Especially considering his so recent brush with the fair sex.

What struck to the heart of his soul, however, were Scott's words; accusations he had heard for years. In his innocence, he had thought those memories banished from the tongues of men. To hear them now, fresh as a new-born babe, came close to drawing tears from his eyes.

He had not cried in a dog's age.

Not truly wept.

Tears of laughter, tears from getting something lodged in his eye, tears from unendurable pain, rapidly, shamefully wiped away. He had even wept from the effects of the purging the New Orleans gypsy had prescribed for him.

Those instances were forgivable for they had not touched his heart. Crying then meant no more than water leaking from his eyes.

This time was different. Now, as he felt the hot sting of tears stream down his cheeks, he knew he was actually, sincerely crying.

Blue would never forgive Scotty. The next the opportunity arose, he would tell the engineer how a keelboat poller had seduced his Injun.

That would even the score.

If he were truly lucky, Scotty and the Injun woman would kill one another. That would not only stop the vicious lies from being spread, it would save him the cost of paying Scott a season's wages.

Teach that bastard to fool with him.

Blue Moon was a man to be reckoned with. Prattle lies about his background and pay the cost.

Which would be far greater than beads, rattles and Injun artifacts.

Blue Moon emerged from the hold rubbing his eyes. The smoke and heat from the engines had obviously bothered him.

No sympathy was lost between captain and crew.

Once a river rat, always a river rat.

Deke Miller squared his shoulders, stuffed his hands in his pockets and approached the skipper with a sullen look.

"Soon as we get to Natchez, you want I should put up the shingle, captain?" he asked.

Blue gave him a sideways glance. He understood perfectly well what Miller meant.

It was all part of Hansen's dare.

Rather than come out and say he did not believe the captain could pass *One Third Sally* within the next fifty miles, he was pretending the extraordinary feat was already accomplished, and the *Blue Moon* was steaming her way into harbor.

He would show them. He would pass *One Third Sally* if it were the last thing he ever did.

Beyond that, however, he had other problems to worry about.

A rough-running engine and an engineer he no longer trusted.

On the list of things Blue despised, Mister Scott, engines, riverboat captains who refused to pull over and mates, surpassed even Injuns.

His list was as turbulent as the Mighty Mississippi.

"No," he snarled, causing Miller to draw back with a cringe.

It was not so much the word as the way it was spoken. The sound of the man's voice grated on Miller's ears, for he could easily hear Blue and Mrs. Lang behind the closed doors of the officer's stateroom.

The fact no one heard a word of the dialogue which passed between them did not stop the crew's loose tongues. Mr. Hansen had seen her emerge in what he variously described as a "state of undress," "near nakedness," and "buck ass white." The men, with their worldly experience, had no trouble filling in the rest of the details.

It was a far cry from imagining how baby Blue Moon looked sitting on his solitary island singing "Rock of Ages" to those being brought into the fold by the Lord's agent.

"No shingle, sir?"

Miller did not want to ask, for that meant receiving a reply. Had he been able to communicate with the captain by hand signals, he would have done so gladly. But he did not want to be accused of dereliction of duty. That would be galling.

It would also cost him money.

Everything aboard the *Blue Moon* was equated to money.

The fact every crewman aboard knew the finances of running a tramp steamer made no difference. On good years, an owner might clear enough to lay out the winter months in reasonable comfort. On bad years, which most were, the same owner lived in a one room hovel on the waterfront, passing his time playing cards, hoping to make enough of a stake to try his luck again come spring.

The "shingle" was a hand-written announcement of arrival and departure times, scribbled in chalk on a cheap wooden easel. It was easily changed to reflect weather conditions, the amount of cargo contracted and the number of men booking passage.

If business were slow, the rogue boats laid in port, hoping to add a shipment or two before departing. Sailing with half a hold made no economic sense. Despite promised delivery times, a captain was ruled by the Almighty Dollar. A merchant could beg, plead and threaten, to no avail. He could point to the promised departure time on a boat's shingle and demand his already-loaded merchandise be transported immediately.

Demand with nothing to back up his threats, for once cargo was loaded, nothing but an Act of Congress would induce anyone to unload it undelivered.

Acts of Congress were notoriously hard to come by.

And, as everyone knew by experience, frequently ignored.

The only other intimidation a shipper could use was the promise never to contract that particular boat again.

Which, as the owner or the captain knew well, was as hollow as a drunk's leg.

Without being tied to fixed schedules as were the packets and steamboat lines, transient steamers did what they pleased. Since they comprised the bulk of river transport, their devil-may-care attitude was tolerated, if not appreciated.

The ports of New Orleans, Natchez and Saint Louis were not like those eastern bastions of Boston or New York or Pittsburgh. Time held a different meaning for westerners. Timetables meant no more than table manners.

"We'll be laying up for repairs."

"How long?"

"For as long as it takes."

If Moon meant what he said, which was by no means a given thing, a long layover meant he had the right to dismiss the crew.

Worse, it meant the possibility of not getting paid.

"What shall I tell the crew?"

"Tell them to go to hell."

"They have a right to know."

"We're not there, yet. We have a trip to complete. They don't need to know any more than that."

Blue assumed the tension stemmed from his avowed promise to pass an ancient, floating derelict in dangerous waters. That, and the fact his manhood was looked down upon with contempt for his weakness in falling susceptible to Mrs. Lang's spell.

Had he known what they were really thinking about his former passenger, Blue's mouth would have fallen open.

His astonishment would have greatly improved his temper.

Dismissing Miller, Blue paced the deck, hands behind his back. He had worked all his life to earn his captaincy. Now, Fate was conspiring against him to take it away. If he did not succeed in passing that damned boat, his reputation as a captain would be ruined. Even if he did succeed in performing the dangerous maneuver, the engine had a leak. It would cost him every penny he had in the world to repair.

Without money, he could not afford to pay the crew, much less keep himself. He would have to sell the boat and hire himself out to an absentee owner, working for wages and, if he were lucky, a small percent of the profit.

If there were any.

If not, he could not even count on being paid.

Which did not earn him any more sympathy from his own men. A man who worked the river got what was coming to him, good or evil. That was the way it was. He either accepted it or sought work in a dockyard or with a shipping agent.

No one ever said life was fair.

The man who preached that sentiment would find himself tossed overboard, drowned or beaten and robbed.

It was one thing to run a bogus scheme baptizing men in the name of the Lord. Quite another to promise bright times ahead.

Blue should have been an Injun agent instead of a riverman. There was always money to be made cheating the Red Men. He had witnessed it firsthand.

Something to consider on those rare occasions when he acknowledged to himself the veracity of Scott's words.

A shift in the wind diverted his attention from dark thoughts and his spirits lifted. He had been born on the river, damn it. His mother was a comet and his father an earthquake. It would take more than a risky maneuver and a five-hundred dollar repair bill to defeat him.

He was born under a blue moon, after all. He was an anomaly. A man like him was as scarce as hen's teeth. He was better than all the rest. He would show them.

To hell with men's superstitions and fears. He was the bravest of the brave. He had been nurtured on floods and earth tremors. He had been baptized by a falling star.

Not even Reverend Holly could boast that.

A man could touch a piece of straw to his red hair and ignite it.

Who else had that power?

He was a magic man, a legend. A god.

He would prove to the crew he was worthy of his unacknowledged birthright.

Maybe then he could believe it himself.

"Blow the whistle!" Blue Moon ordered. They were coming up on the blind curve in the river. Contrary to his avowed threat to break the rules, he would follow protocol. Warn others he was coming; warn them to stay out of his way. He would do it right; by the book. He knew the rules as well as any man alive.

This time, he would prove it. A right and proper riverman would do no less.

The shrill blast of the whistle stiffened his courage, raised his blood.

"Full speed ahead!"

Running to starboard, Blue waved a fist at the captain of *One Third Sally*.

"Back off, Captain Reynolds!" he warned. "Cut steam. I'm going to pass!"

The skipper shook his head as he flailed his arms.

"Can't be done, Moon. If I lose steam now, I'll never make it 'round the bend."

Which was a bald-face lie if he ever heard one.

A rarity on the river, where most men wore beards or mustaches.

Taking the helm, Blue set his teeth, then gripped the wood spokes in his hand. When he saw the straining paddlewheel dip deep into the water, then felt the surge of added power beneath his feet, he turned the wheel for all he was worth. The *Blue Moon* heaved, shuddered and responded. Throwing spray in all directions, the boat surged forward and to the left, gaining on *One Third Sally* with dangerously little room to spare.

"She'll never make it!" Hansen roared. Blue ignored him. There was no room in his world for disbelievers.

According to his charts, the river widened immediately at the point of the curve. If the recent high water had not filled the bottom with silt, and if the banks had not washed into the river, clogging the sides with young trees and brush, he would just have room to pass.

"Just" was all he required.

Just was the father of *Justice*, and if any man deserved justice, it was Captain Blue Moon.

He had paid enough for the right to claim what was his.

The *Blue Moon* gained on *One Third Sally,* drawing so close beside her, the crews of both boats tossed jeers and refuse at one another. A rotten potato fell at Moon's feet. He disposed of it with a savage kick, sending it flying overboard.

That was another aspect of his heritage.

Claiming the right of savage behavior.

Those who knew, or thought they knew, ought not to forget. Those who did not know, along with those who scoffed, ought to learn.

If their education cost them their lives or their livelihood, it was better than being ignorant.

Another lesson the illiterate, orphan-turned-captain, had learned the hard way.

As though she were an evil shadow, determined to remain attached to his wake, the *One Third Sally* would not lose ground. Going into the bend, she was no more than a foot from his bow, neither gaining nor losing ground. Both could not maneuver the turn in such a fashion. One of the two riverboats would have to pull ahead or they would run into each other. A collision at high speed meant almost certain doom.

"Cut loose! Cut loose! Miller screamed at their kissing cousin. "You're too close."

"It's you who's passin' me," the captain shouted back.

"Give way!"

"You give way, you uninsured bastards!" Reynolds screamed.

Truth will out and Captain Reynolds spoke truth. *One Third Sally* was insured to the hilt. If his vessel went down, he would lose nothing and probably gain by his loss. If the *Blue Moon* were sunk, current insurance policy posted in the wheelhouse notwithstanding, not one penny would be forthcoming.

Not one *red* cent.

Blue swore under his breath. It was a vile oath, spoken in an ancient tongue, summoning the old animal gods' wrath down upon his enemy.

The *Blue Moon* gained an inch, then another. Over his shoulder Blue could see the *One Third Sally* falling back. He shook his fist at Reynolds and laughed.

He who laughs first laughs best.

He was rewriting the rules.

Choking in the smoke of poorly combusted wood, Blue maintained his position, starting ahead, then to the left, then back, gritting his teeth without daring to remove his hands from the wheel to wipe his streaming nose.

"Faster! Faster!" he prayed, leaning forward in subconscious effort to draw ahead.

He was jolted from his position by the force of sudden impact, as the boats made brief contact. Blue lost his balance. Righting himself, he promptly slipped on the wet deck and was compelled to hoist his body upright by the sheer strength of his arms. With a will greater than those around or behind him, Blue regained control of the wildly careening boat and righted her course.

He was solidly ahead of his rival, now, pulling further away. With breath coming in jagged gasps, he dared turn his head to assess the damage.

"Where did we hit?" he called to Hansen.

The first officer made a cry of despair, holding an arm he had broken when thrown to the deck by the collision, then pointed to starboard.

"We've a hole as big as your head."

Which told Moon exactly nothing.

"Above or below the water line?"

"Above."

So much for a swollen head.

"We'll make it."

With its paddlewheel spinning in angry hostility, the *Blue Moon* rounded the curve in the river, coming out two lengths in front of Reynold's boat. Crippled by the collision, then caught in the backlash of river current and steamboat waves, *One Third Sally* was dropping back, her own paddlewheel now rotating at half power. In a minute, she dropped from sight behind the curve in the Mighty Mississippi.

"I've done it!" Blue yelled, raising a fist in the air.

Cheers from his own crew rent the air. It was the first time he had ever been so rewarded. Blue's heart gladdened with triumph.

He had proven his worth.

A noble effort.

Directing a glance over his shoulder, he spat at his defeated enemy.

Had it been in his power, Moon would have tied the dying steamboat to a tree. Not in a display of the defeated boat's prowess, but as testimony to his own success.

Life, after all, was better than death. He who lived wrote his own history while he who died lived only in memory.

The only thing more worthless than memory was an empty whisky cask.

It took only a second, no more, for him to return his sharp eyes to the hull.

One second.

It is said it takes a man one hour to be born and one second to die.

Blue Moon would not have disagreed as he saw death ahead of him.

Coming into the bend in front of him was a riverboat, steaming downriver on a head- to-head collision course with the *Blue Moon.* There was no room for one to pass the other.

In a flash, Blue realized what had happened.

While he had taken the trouble to blow his whistle and warn oncoming boats of his determination to enter the narrow curve, the oncoming boat had ignored it. While Blue was playing by the rules, the other captain was not.

The irony was not lost on him.

He had won the battle, only to lose the war.

With a war cry never before heard from the lips of a white man, Blue Moon performed the only option left him. He cut power and drove his triumphant little riverboat toward shore. She crashed into the bank with a sickening thud, hurtling him over the wheel. He landed on his back and remained prone, the wind knocked out of his body, his senses broken, his mind stunned.

The other crew members were flung from their stations, two of them going overboard as the boat came to ground. No one aboard the *Blue Moon* saw the *Merry Duke* go flying past, her own way now clear to navigate the turn in the river.

It was the last time the son of earthquake and comet would ever play by the rules.

CHAPTER 12

"The hull is damaged. No doubt aboot it," Scott commented, for which Blue was less than eternally grateful.

"I can see that for myself. Can it be fixed?"

"Aye."

"I mean, can you fix it? Right here?"

The engineer shrugged his shoulders and redirected his attention to the gaping hole in the hull.

"The damage is just above the water line," he observed. "If the river was calm and the weather sunny, I'd stuff some blankets and mebbe a mattress or two in the hole and chance taking her up to Natchez. That not being the case, I wouldn't risk it. Another heavy rain, the water levels rise and the hole's suddenly under water. You'd sink like a rock."

"We'd sink like a rock," Blue amended.

"I expect you'd go down with the ship."

Whether he meant that as a warning or was simply stating the oft-parroted phrase of a captain's duty was unclear.

Stamping away, Blue stared morosely at his own footprints in the muddy shore, then turned back, cap drawn back on his head so his bright red hair caught the sunlight, making him look ten years old.

"We'll hoist her up on stanchions so we can work on repairs. Shouldn't take more'n a few days to get her afloat."

"Shouldn't take more'n a few days to get her up on stanchions," muttered Scott. Blue ignored him.

"All right, men. We all pitch in, the sooner we're off. Mister Hansen, take some of the boys out and cut wood. We might as well do some cording while we're here."

"Yes, sir."

The *Blue Moon* was slowly, torturously hoisted out of the sand, revealing the extent of the ugly hole which had been ripped into the hull by the force of impact. It required five days for repairs to be completed, effectively splitting the estimates of captain and engineer.

Between the two of them, neither was placated.

"It's a judgment," Deke Miller complained to his immediate superior. "We passed *One Third Sally* as neat as you please. No captain could have done better. But when God saw to it Captain Blue was gonna make good his boast to get by that boat, He didn't like it. *He* remembered Mrs. Lang and sought revenge fer her."

That was stretching God's vengeance, even for Mr. Hansen.

"I dunno. Let's see what happens when we git to Natchez. Scotty says there's a leak in the pipes. He's gonna have to take 'em apart and buy new. That'll take three weeks if it takes a day. An' there's a god-awful lot of chalking to do on the bottom of this boat.

"If Moon thinks he's gonna dismiss us because he's laid up in port, we'll never see a dime from him."

"Then late one night, one of us ought to shove him overboard and take ownership ourselves."

"Shut up. Here he comes."

Blue saw his officers huddled together and approached, eager to break off the conversation. He had served on enough riverboats and seen enough powwows to know trouble when he saw it.

"We're taking off at sunrise. I want to make a fast run before we get caught in bad weather."

"Yes, sir."

When it became apparent Blue was not going to leave them, Miller sauntered away to supervise the loading of cord wood. Hansen went back aboard ship.

Left to his own devices, Blue walked the shoreline. He was restless and nervous. The thought of getting to Natchez and having his boat dry docked for weeks was oppressing him. He did not think the leak was in the pipes or the tubing. That would be too easy. There was something wrong with the engine. That meant big dollars to repair.

Money he did not have.

Money he did not know how to go about getting his hands on.

There was only one possibility: Professor-turned-Explorer Kress. He had five hundred dollars. If he loaned it to Blue on the promise the captain would take him into Indian Territory, there might be the slightest chance of getting it. While Blue had an utter repulsion about the Upper Mississippi, he knew those waters well. With luck, he could be up and down before anyone was the wiser.

He would let Kress do the negotiating with the Indians. While not exactly hiding aboard his boat, he would not make himself readily visible. He did not want to be spotted.

Not that there was the slightest chance anyone would recognize him, he told himself in reassuring, rhythmic tones. He had been gone a long time. Men die. Situations change. He had grown up. The Indians had given up their old gods and superstitions to embrace Christianity and placate the army of white invaders.

The name of the ship might be a problem, but there was nothing he could do about that now. He had christened her the *Blue Moon*. That was her name.

For better or worse.

He almost laughed.

He had never thought to marry a boat.

He had never thought to marry anyone.

He was not the only blue moon in the world. Just because someone saw the words or heard the expression, did not mean they would associate the lunar reference with the captain.

If they did, that would be their loss.

He was not in the mood to tolerate any more lies.

Whether or not those lies were true.

Lost in thought, Blue inadvertently struck a half-submerged obstacle with his shoe. Struggling with his balance, he directed a hateful glare at what had tripped him. It was a blanket Scott had used to temporarily patch the hole in the hull before he could affect a permanent wooden one.

Pulling the woolen material out, Blue cursed his crewman to blue blazes. Did they think blankets came cheap? This one had obviously come out of a passenger's stateroom. What would they think if he commandeered one of their blankets to replace the one they stole from an empty bunk?

They would think themselves ill-used. As owner, it was his obligation to room and board the crew.

Let them complain, he thought bitterly. It would serve them right. Lying awake without a blanket, shivering and shaking would teach them a lesson.

Waste not, want not.

Another one of Andy Jackson's wise sayings.

Rinsing out the soiled blanket in river water, Blue had the peculiar feeling he ought to remember something very important. Putting his mind on the problems immediately at hand, he could not recall anything about the hull repairs, the engine leak or the weather which he had overlooked or forgotten.

Why, then, was he suddenly as jumpy as a cat?

When no easy resolution came to him, Blue wrung the blanket dry and returned with it to the boat. His crew gave him surly looks, but that was nothing out of the ordinary. They were coming to the end of the line, literally as well as figuratively, and were not happy about it. It was an awkward time of the season for any of them to get new employment.

Too bad.

His heart was breaking for them.

Try facing the future knowing a five hundred dollar repair bill was staring them in the face. Then they would know trouble.

They might even grow humble.

Taking the blanket with him, he returned to the boat and retired to his stateroom. It was cold and damp. He was lonely though would not admit it. Being lonely was a weakness.

He had enough weaknesses already.

Not that he would admit it.

Admitting weakness was a weakness.

At least he had not sunk that low.

The *Blue Moon* steamed into Natchez exactly one week after *One Third Sally* arrived. Her shingle was set out on the wharf and a lazy looking shipping clerk had already filled half her hold with cargo bound for Saint Louis.

Blue had been correct. Arriving several hours ahead of her would have made a big difference. That cargo, by rights, should have been his.

"Seven hundred and fifty dollars to repair the leak in the engine, chalk the ship and put a better patch over the hole in the hull," the dockside engineer informed him.

More good news.

"How much just to fix the engine?"

"Seven hundred and forty-nine dollars."

Blue's proud shoulders sagged.

"Go ahead," he ordered. As captain and sole owner of the *Blue Moon,* he had anticipated and dreaded the day when this would happen to him. The life expectancy of a Mississippi steamer was three years, maybe four, if she were well built and lucky.

The *Blue Moon* was neither.

She was also ten years old and constructed from salvage.

He had no right to complain.

In Blue's entire existence, not having the right to complain stopped no one.

He was no exception.

"Pretty damn expensive job," he gripped.

"You're welcome to get a second opinion."

It was like asking one undertaker to underbid another.

Or one doctor to go against the diagnosis of another doctor.

Such things simply did not happen.

It was called honor among thieves.

"Go to hell."

"Three weeks. To the day."

Which meant, give-or-take a month.

"I'll be around."

Blue waved a hand by way of sealing the deal and slipped away. He had made four hundred dollars from the salvage of the *Bell Bottom.* That left three hundred and fifty dollars to come up with within the next four weeks.

Asking for a loan from The Bank was out of the question. He could not even bring himself to walk through the door of The Bank, much less speak to a Bank Officer.

He might as well ask Reverent Holly for a loan.

In all the world, Blue knew only one man who had three hundred and fifty dollars. Asking him for that money meant he would have to agree to take the bastard upriver.

Explorers and Bank Officers were added to his list of despised persons.

Whistling to himself, Blue Moon swung down the ramp with an assumed jaunty air and made his way to town. Kress was a man who respected action. Blue could play that game to the hilt. It was certainly better than crawling for the money. Or worse, not getting it at all.

With his personal boilers full of steam, Blue crashed through the double doors of the End of the Line Saloon, full head on.

"Where is Andre Kress?" he bellowed. "That research fellow. I need him. Now!"

Several drunks and a cat scampered out of his way as Blue stomped up to the plank bar. One good shove from underneath and he could send the proprietor's goods to Kingdom Come.

Without benefit of redemption from Original Sin.

"You, there!" he demanded, pointing a finger at the barkeep. "Where has that Kress been hiding out?"

"He's taken a room at the 'Impressed' from what I heard him say."

"Oh. At the Impressed."

The Impressed was Blue's favorite hotel. The large sign outside the establishment had caught his eye and tickled his fancy. It depicted an American naval officer in full regalia knocking a British seaman on the head and dragging him off. Impressing seamen had been a major irritant of the United States when declaring war on England in 1812. The favorable outcome of that conflict and the famous Battle of New Orleans were as alive along the Mississippi in the 1830's as they had been nearly two decades earlier.

Patriotism was always good for business.

While Blue had never actually stayed at the Impressed, he fancied that one day he would rent a suite of rooms and sleep for a week. After which he would hold open house, supplying drinks for the entire city.

Blue Moon was a man with great aspirations.

If not Great Expectations.

Taking the long route through the bustling river town of Natchez, he came out upon the threshold of the Impressed at eleven A.M. Time enough for any self-respecting researcher to be out of bed and dressed.

Time for said Researcher and Trinkets-Exporter to buy his business partner a hearty noontime meal.

Bursting through the doors like a bull in the proverbial china shop, Captain Moon stomped up to the registration desk. He tilted back the cap on his head with the air of one who is wealthy enough not to have to ask the price of a room before reserving it.

"Andre Kress," he stated to the clerk. Then added for his own self-importance, "He's expecting me."

"Your name, sir? I will send a boy up to announce you."

"My name is Captain Blue Moon and I'll announce myself."

Since he was not exactly sure whether Kress would receive him or not, Blue decided to dispense with formalities. Besides, the urgency of his request would not wait until the writer had bathed, dressed and come close to drowning himself in cologne.

Moon was half way to the stairs before he remembered one essential piece of information he had overlooked. Turning back, he gave the clerk a look of disdain.

"What room is Mr. Kress in?"

"Thirty-two."

Blue did not fail to note the landlubber neglected to add the requisite "sir" to the end of his sentence.

When Blue rented the entire top floor of the Impressed, he would see to it that worm served in the kitchen.

At midnight. And was paid off the gratuities.

In company with the broken-down black slaves "impressed" from the cane fields.

Rapping authoritatively on the door to suite number thirty-two, he was immediately rewarded by the offer to "Enter." With a shudder of real dread, Blue opened the door and entered.

Andre Kress looked up at him from under the half-moons of a pair of eye glasses. His look of surprise was evident.

"Yes?" he asked, as though he did not recognize the man standing in his doorway.

Blue stood shock still a moment, then brushed aside his own fears and entered, shutting the door behind him.

"I beg your pardon," Kress began. A look from the captain silenced him.

"I need to talk with you," Blue stated flatly.

"Oh. You are Captain Moon. I was told you had gone on to New Orleans."

"Been there and back. But I haven't forgotten you, much as you seem to have forgotten me."

Despite the fact his heart was sinking into his shoes, Blue refused to back down. There was too much at stake.

"I have entered into an agreement with the captain of another boat to take me upriver," Kress smugly informed him.

"The hell you have." Then, less brashly, "What captain?"

"John Crabbe of the *River Times*. He and I have much in common, it appears."

"Is that a fact?"

"It is. He has read my book. We discussed it together."

Blue's face grew red then purple by degrees. He shifted his weight from one leg to the other, debating how many pieces to tear the researcher into. When his not overly subtle mannerisms made connection with Kress, the author tried a weak smile.

"I really had thought you backed out on me."

"Bull shit. You thought you found a better deal and would be gone before I got back. Well, here I am, so you can welsh out of whatever deal you made with Crabbe."

"Why would I want to do that?"

"Because Captain Crab Apple doesn't know the Upper Mississippi like I do."

"What is there to know? He is an adequate river pilot and he owns a steamboat."

Blue swallowed gall which tasted surprisingly like tears. Biting his lower lip until he drew blood, he held his ground and dealt his ace.

The one he had been saving, even from himself.

The one he had palmed from Life.

"I know the country like the back of my hand." Kress yawned. He began to shake his head in classic dismissal, when Blue interrupted. "I know *Injuns.*"

The professor hesitated, then squinted his eyes. That was a common technique, Blue noted. It enabled men to comprehend better, although it had nothing whatsoever to do with seeing.

"Why does that make you more valuable to me that Captain Crabbe?"

"I speak Injun. I understand their ways. How to deal with 'em. And I'll tell you one more thing that Captain Crab Apple don't know – I know when to run. And how to get away."

Kress paced the room, hands behind his back. He paused once to pick up a book and riffle the pages. The decision he made could affect the rest of his life.

There was one piece to the puzzle which did not fit. Kress fixed his eyes on the captain.

"When I first approached you with my 'scheme,' you weren't too excited about it. You implied to me then – strongly – that your Indian expertise was limited, at best. Explain to me why that's suddenly changed."

Blue swallowed, then took a step forward and looked the man squarely in the eyes.

"I need an advance."

Kress clicked his tongue.

"How much?"

"Three hundred and fifty dollars."

The Famous Author drew back, as though the enormity of the sum frightened him.

"I'll pay you your cut at the end of the voyage."

"I need it now."

"Why?"

Ordinarily, Blue would have lied as a point of honor.

If Kress chose to do some checking, it would not take him long to discover the truth.

The only thing uglier than a spurned women was a thwarted money lender.

"The *Blue Moon* needs repairs. Exactly seven hundred and fifty dollars worth. I have four hundred dollars. I need three-fifty."

"What will you use as security?"

"The boat."

"I don't want to own a steamboat. Have you nothing else?"

Shame crept up Blue's face, reddening his complexion.

"I have my pride, sir."

"That, sir, may have value to you as a riverman, but it means even less to me than does your boat."

There was a long moment of silence. The ticking from Andre Kress' pocket watch filled the void of words and breathing.

Shifting his weight from one foot to the other, the orphan-made-riverboat captain stood on the precipice of pride, then hurtled over.

"I'm begging you," he whispered.

"You're begging me?" queried the cold-hearted man who had never known hunger and experienced humiliation only as a spectator.

"I'm begging you, sir."

"Will you get on your knees for it?"

With a wretched cry of agony, Blue Moon quivered, then wrung his hands. If the man had asked him to take a beating for the loan, he would have submitted to any brutal punishment. If the devil had asked for his soul in exchange for three hundred and fifty dollars, he would have jumped at the offer and considered it a bargain.

If he trusted Kress, if he had one shred of respect for the man, if he believed the Researcher would keep his mouth shut, he might have bent the knee.

He owed that much to the *Blue Moon*. She was his namesake, the only thing in the world he treasured. To abandon her to the auction block was a cruel, cold-hearted Fate, for which he never expected to be forgiven.

For which he could never forgive himself.

Blue Moon had paid his dues. He deserved something for a life of suffering and deprivation. Fate, God, the Devil, Mankind owed him a chance. Nothing more: not a handout, a pat on the head or a favor. Just the ability to survive by the strength of his hands, the intelligence of his brain and the absolute determination of his being.

To lose his honor, his captaincy, his love, for the want of three hundred and fifty dollars was the second worst thing which could happen to him.

The worst was being born alive.

Without a word, Blue turned and left. Walking stiff-legged down the steps of the fancy hotel, he held his head high. He had no one but himself to "Impress."

It was enough.

In truth, it was not enough. For all the world, he was a defeated man. He had no one with which to share his thoughts, his merge triumph.

"Triumph," in a perversion of the common meaning.

But then, he was illiterate, and could be forgiven his misuse of the word.

He returned to the *Blue Moon,* the only thing in the world he owned. She might not be his for long, but while his name remained on the ownership papers, he was captain.

Also, brother, lover, son.

Like him, the *Blue Moon* was an orphan. She had been mishandled, abused, taken for granted. None of her former owners had tread her decks with respect, let alone love. She was a tool to be used, then discarded, worth no more than the money she brought in.

The river boat and the river rat had a lot in common.

Blue did not acknowledge the salute of the crewman on watch. It seemed a cruel irony.

Closing the door to his cabin, he locked it against intruders. Too late. The devils slipped in with him.

He thought to lie down for he was tired, yet his body was too restless for sleep. He poured himself a shot of whisky, then left it untouched. He was hungry, but did not want to admit food into his mouth, so recently soiled by words.

Men were ugly. They created a mean, dirty language. What was the point of learning to read when high-blown sentiments made no difference in the world?

What counted was money.

For the want of three hundred and fifty dollars, Blue Moon had come full circle. He was what he had started out as.

A River Rat.

Blue did not think he was angry, but when his eyes fell on the woolen blanket salvaged from the river bank, his restraint snapped. Grabbing the now dry and decimated rag, he shook it, then wrapped his fingers around a corner and throttled it.

If he could not kill his father, the evil procreator of his own existence; if laws prevented him from murdering the man who could easily have loaned him money but spurned the chance at saving him, he could, at least, destroy this reminder of his failures.

When he did not succeed in ripping the fabric apart, Blue reached into his belt and extracted the long, carefully honed Bowie knife. With the handle cradled in the palm of his right hand in a fit better serving the interlocking of two lover's hands, Blue gutted the woven wool blanket until it was no more than a worthless chard.

Abandoning the lifeless material, he let it slip to the floor, much as Kress would have allowed him to do, had the Writer been less dull.

Looking down at his defeated enemy, Blue noted a pile of sand which had come off the blanket when he first picked it up. His mouth went dry. His eyes widened in shock.

Sand.

Dried, worthless river silt, carried from the Upper Mississippi.

The identification sent a chill down his body. He shook like a calf with the ague.

Sand.

Blue Moon's shoulders squared. The light came back into his hurt brown eyes. Even his freckles, which had paled to near invisibility, stood out on his forehead like beckons of inspiration.

Ashes to ashes, dust to dust.

Blue Moon had just resurrected from a Fate worse than Death.

Clasping his arms around himself, he did a jig on the floor, scattering the sand, scratching the wood as he ground it into the floor with the heels of his shoes.

No matter.

There was more sand where that came from.

He had rediscovered Faith.

The size of a grain of sand and as mighty as the Mississippi.

Far smaller and a great deal longer than a mustard seed.

Balling his fist, Blue took a vicious swipe at his enemies, then leapt up on his bed and jumped on it like a little boy. Never having had the opportunity to be a child, he unknowingly took advantage now.

Then, jumping down with cat grace, he danced to the door of the stateroom and slipped out, an intense expression on his face.

"I'll offer him a bargain even a Famous Explorer can't refuse."

He was going to save the *Blue Moon* and salvage his own pride at the same time.

It was not every day such an opportunity presented itself.

No more frequent than once in a blue moon.

CHAPTER 13

The glint in Blue Moon's eyes should have warned the professor, but he was new to the ways of rivermen and the schemes of schemers.

"What is that?" he asked, staring at what appeared to be the figure of a man wrapped in a blanket that the captain held in his arms.

"This is Hernando DeSoto. The Great Explorer. Don't you recognize him?"

The pronouncement was so outrageous, the spectacles slipped off Kress' nose, falling into his lap where they remained, forgotten and worthless.

"My good man, Hernando DeSoto has been dead for nearly three hundred years."

"I found him."

"You discovered his – remains?"

Kress was aghast, proving that in the scheme of things, he was a Very Little Man, indeed.

"As sure as God saves souls."

"But – this is preposterous. How could you have found –?"

"You said he croaked, they wrapped him in blankets, weighted him down with sand and set him adrift, right?"

"Yes, but –"

"On the Mississippi?"

"Hundreds of miles north of here..."

"He drifted down."

"But surely his body would have disintegrated... by now," Kress lamely finished.

"This is the way I see it," Blue explained. Placing the precious – and valuable – "remains" down, he crossed the room, drawing up a chair so he sat opposite the Great Author and Chronicler of the Even Greater Spanish Explorer. "He floated down the Great River for two hundred miles, then finally got waterlogged and sank. All that sand they put in with him sort of covered him up. He's rested on the bottom until now."

"Preserved?" gasped Kress.

"Not exactly. Not – whole. But there are bones and *trinkets*. And, of course, the sand."

"What trinkets?"

Blue popped up, scanned the room with his greedy brown eyes and saw exactly what he was looking for. With a hop, skip and jump, he snatched a peculiar looking knife of great antiquity from the Author's side table. He held it up. The freckles on his face were as numerous as the grains of sand in Hernando DeSoto's canoe.

"This, for instance."

It all became clear in an instant. Kress stood and tried to grab the artifact from Blue's hands, only succeeding in brushing away the air around it.

"Give that back. Immediately. It is priceless."

"One thing I've learned, Doctor Kress. Everything has a price. And that's exactly what we're gonna do: we're gonna put a price on history."

Kress sat down. Seeing his eye glasses, which had fallen to the floor, he retrieved them and placed them in his pocket, the better to see the scheme his new partner was hatching.

"I think you had better explain."

"I remembered how you described the last trip of our Famous Explorer. It seemed a sad fate, drifting down the river as a corpse, with no one the wiser that inside the canoe was a hero. A sad fate and a waste.

"So I asked myself, what if that body sank somewhere around Natchez and got covered with river silt? Covered and preserved? And what if someone found the body, recognized it – or thought he did – and brought it to you – the man who wrote a book about him. If that author positively identified the body as being that of DeSoto, people would want to see his remains.

He paused for effect. "They would want to *pay* to see his remains."

"But who has heard of Hernando DeSoto in Natchez?"

Kress set himself up for that one.

"Captain Crabbe."

Kress put a hand to his face. He might have wept, had he the capacity for tears.

"Think of it, Andre," Blue continued, adopting the familiar form of address with a partner almost as devious as he. "This discovery could make you famous."

"You think people will pay to see a few bones and a Spanish knife?"

"I paid good money once to see a monkey."

It was a bold lie and an even bolder bluff. Kress bought it.

"What do I get for authenticating the – remains?"

Translated, his sentence ran like this:

What do I get for (unknown foreign word, probably Irish) the – remains?
Or, broken down to its lowest common denominator:
What's in it for me?
Which Blue would have understood in any language.
Even Greek.

"Oh, many things," Blue emphatically shouted, forcing the Author to avert his head. But not far enough away so he could not hear.

"First, you have to prove to me you want to be my partner. And that you can be trusted."

"You question my ver-ass-ity?"

"Yeah; I question your ass," Blue snorted, mistaking the ten dollar word for that found in free usage.

"I resent that."

Blue blew air between teeth and cheek, making an uncouth noise of disdain.

"After you positively identify the remains, you write articles. Send them back east. The newspapers will print them. You'll made money that way. Then there's the book you're going to write. Let's call it, *Great Discoveries on the Great River.* People always read books about Great Things."

Blue's eyes burned with intensity. "We'll put a lot of pictures in it. We can find someone to sketch the bones and the trinkets and the canoe and put them in the book. I know it can be done," he added *authoritatively.*

He had figured it all out. He, himself, was in possession of a Great Book with *illustrations.*

Contemplating life, the destruction of hope, and irretrievable loss had made his mind sharp.

"That would be an abomination to the scientific community," Kress objected.

"Abomination" was another foreign word, but it sounded a lot like "hoax."

"It will make your name famous. Reporters from as far away as Saint Louie will come down here to interview you. While you're telling them about ol' Hernando, you can mention the expedition you're going on up river. They'll be so excited, they'll wet their pants."

Blue was so excited, his nostrils flared.

The rest of him was still safely deflated from the Very Expensive Purging he had so recently undergone.

For thirty dollars, he expected it to last a life time.

Several lifetimes.

If he were Hernando DeSoto suddenly resurrected from the dead, he should still be safe.

Such was the power of money.

And the faith it purchased.

First sand, then mustard seeds. Before he knew it, Blue Moon would take up baptizing.

Andre Kress stroked his chin, a gesture Blue admired. It spoke of breeding. He would have to remember to copy it in future.

Never waste a chance to learn something new.

He had learned Captain Crabbe once read a book and had already used it to advantage.

The power of knowledge could never be underestimated.

When he was rich, he would buy a college degree.

"It might work," Kress conceded. "But – I would expect some sort of remuneration from the – tours, shall we say, of the body?"

Blue nodded. He had every intention of being fair.

He was, by nature, a fair man.

Red-haired men always were.

"You get fifty dollars – *after* the scheme has run its course." He remembered how Kress had promised him payment *after* the *Blue Moon* returned from the Upper Mississippi. "And, you get twenty cents for every dollar taken in."

"Why must I settle for only twenty percent? Without my say-so, no one will believe it is Hernando DeSoto, the Great Spanish Explorer."

Blue held his ground. He was well familiar with that tactic, having recently held ground for a week while his boat was repaired.

To Kress' credit, which was notoriously hard to find in Natchez, he knew he had already obtained all the concessions he was likely to get.

"Agreed. On one condition."

"What condition?"

"You agree here and now to take me upriver, seeking Spanish and Indian *artifacts*. For terms previously agreed upon."

Blue hesitated, torn between his need for a partner and from his youthful vow, made to himself, never to steam the Upper Mississippi. He had reasons. Reasons of his own.

Private reasons.

But in the end, vows made to oneself were the easiest broken.

"All right." Blue turned the chair around so he could lean his sun-bronzed arms over the back. "We've got work to do."

"Hear yea, hear yea, hear yea!" pitchman Blue Moon canted in his best preacher's voice. "Come one, come all. It's the chance of a life time an' God don't give away too many chances."

He was part circus ring master, part Baptist minister, part riverboat gambler, part bear wrassler. Standing on an upturned crate, shirtsleeves rolled to the elbow, captain's hat set back on his head, he was a master craftsman. He spoke with the sincerity of one born to convert the heathens while taking the last penny from their pockets.

"Step up and get in line! No pushing!" he warned, pointing to a ruddy-faced boy he had hired for the occasion.

"But I wanna see the *mummy!*" the child screamed back.

He was definitely worth the five cents a day Blue was paying him.

"Mummy? What's a mummy?" a man in the crowd called to the politician look-alike.

"A mummy is a man that's been dead for three hundred years. A mummy is the remains of a hero!"

Mummy was the word of the hour. While the remains of Hernando DeSoto were not exactly like the mummies of ancient Egypt, which Andre Kress had explained to him, Blue liked the word. It rolled off the tongue, sounding strange, yet familiar at the same time.

It piqued interest.

"Mummy" was the word printed atop the handbills The Great Exposition Company had printed and distributed all over town.

MUMMY
The remains of the Famous Spanish Explorer
Hernando DeSoto
Who died in 1541
Have Just Been Discovered
By the Famous Mississippi Riverboat Captain
Blue Moon.
Viewing and Lectures
Daily
By the Famous Professor and Author
Andre Kress.

Cost ONLY ten cents!

Famous was the second word of the hour.

Professor Kress had been a bit skeptical about its frequent use, but Blue assured him it would impress people.

"Famous," he had decided, was even more impressive than "Great."

"Ex-ca-vated from the bottom of the *Great* Mississippi River, where he was set sail upon almost three hundred years ago."

He still felt an obligation to "great," however. Failing to find a place for it on his poster, Blue incorporated it into his pitch.

"Excavated" was also a new word. Professor Kress explained that "excavated" was not a Spanish word, but it sounded foreign enough to impress the good citizens of Natchez.

"See the actual bones of a Dead Hero! Come in and get a glimpse of his clothing. See the actual blanket he was wrapped up in. Buy a handful of sand the body was preserved in."

Sand was rapidly overtaking salt as the method of preservation in Natchez.

"We're talkin' POSTERITY here, folks."

"Posterity" was a word Blue had learned from the Right Reverend *Holly.*

Which, had he been able to spell, would have noted the reverend's name was only one letter longer than *holy.*

Scotty, the engineer, stood at the entrance of the tent the Great Exposition Company had pitched for the occasion. Holding out a tin can, he collected money as the people rushed to have a look at Posterity.

It was a bargain.

Salvation, as Blue knew only too well, cost a sight more.

When the tent was filled with paying customers, Blue leapt gracefully from his perch and strode inside. Two torches were burning in the middle of the enclosure, one on either side of Hernando.

A battered, cracked and dried canoe was placed on two upended whisky barrels. Inside it was a skull, an arm bone and two leg bones. Surrounding the partial skeleton were Spanish daggers, a dozen gold coins of unfamiliar mint, a pair of black boots and a ring with three flashy stones.

The jewelry was courtesy of Professor Kress, who habitually wore it on the little finger of his right hand. It was well for the Enterprise that few citizens of Natchez had made the acquaintance of the Famous Author before the Exhibit opened.

"Hernando DeSoto was a man of Great Wealth," the professor lectured. "A Spaniard by birth, an intrepid explorer by inclination, he is said to have amassed over one hundred thousand *pesos* of gold in Peru."

Which surely equated to over a million dollars in United States currency.

Being Rich was even more important than being Spanish when it came to being a Dead Hero.

Kress pointed to a hand-colored map he had created for the occasion. Entitled "The World of Hernando DeSoto," it depicted Spain, Peru, Cuba and the eastern coast of the United States. Starting in Florida, a red line was drawn through Arkansas to the Mississippi.

"DeSoto was appointed governor of Cuba and offered a commission to explore what we now call Florida. With the prospect of exploration and wealth before him, he took his army of soldiers and marched northwest, discovering the Mississippi at a point here."

He indicated the "point" on his map.

"Imagine how exciting it was to find the Longest River in the World. Fighting Savage Indians and nearly starving to death on his trek, he ordered barges constructed and crossed the River."

"The Great River," Blue added. It was best not to omit any money words.

"Unfortunately, DeSoto died before he could return with his Great News," Kress continued with a sideways glance at his partner. "In order to do honor to his Remains, he was packed in sand, wrapped in a blanket and set adrift in an Indian canoe the Savages kindly lent for the purpose."

"Lent?" asked a man near the front. "Wonder if they're still waiting to git it back?"

Blue laughed heatedly with the rest. Belief was a wonderful and amusing thing to behold.

Professor Kress cleared his throat and continued.

"From this point, the canoe traveled downstream, guided by the swift river current."

"Great River Current."

"Guided by the Great River Current. The canoe came here," Kress indicated, "and finally sank. It has been preserved by the sand and river – Great River Silt – all these years, only to be discovered by the Famous Captain Moon and brought back here."

That was Blue's cue.

"Call it a miracle," he began, his voice quavering with emotion. He noted with approval a woman wiped a tear from her eye. Nothing sold better than miracles. They were the Road to Salvation. "I was dragging the Great River bottom looking for cargo off the *Bell Bottom* when my eye caught the tip of the canoe. At first I didn't pay it no attention, but something kept nagging at the back of my mind. Then I felt a tugging at my shirt sleeve. It was DeSoto's spirit, no doubt."

"What was ya doing, wearin' a shirt in the river?" a man asked. Blue was certain it was Captain Crabbe's voice.

He always was a sore loser.

"I'm being polite," Blue explained, pausing to tip his hat and wink at one of the ladies. A tittering of amusement ran through the crowd.

Had Blue been an older and more worldly man, he would have known to capitalize on his mistake. As it was, he blushed like a girl.

That did not prevent him from remembering his manners and coming up with a suitable lie.

One he would correct in the future.

The exhibition ran for three weeks, ending on the day the supply of coins in Natchez ran out. It was a Great Success. No one failed to "pay his tuppence," including those who disembarked from steamboats pulled in from upriver. Men who had never even heard of Hernando DeSoto had come to see the Famous Mummy.

Bags of sand from the canoe sold like hotcakes.

There were skeptics, of course. One old wag declared that enough sand had been sold to sink a riverboat. Another had the nerve to speculate on the similarity between "old Hernando's bones" and those belonging to a "gimp Injun" which had once been on display in Gifford's Grub House.

Articles were printed in the *Natchez Weekly*. A sermon on "Resurrection" was preached at the First Christian Church on Sunday. It was well attended. Included were those parishioners who had not been seen for a month of Sundays. They appeared to hear what the Good Book had to say about "Risin' Frum the Dead."

The Mummy Business, it seemed, was good for everyone.

A banner headline appeared in a Saint Louis newspaper, announcing "The Great Fraud of Natchez." This only increased interest in the exhibit. It was well for the editor he capitalized the word "Great," or he most certainly would have heard from the Great Captain Moon.

Who had learned the value of Capitalization from reading his book.

"C" was for coin.

"M" was for money.

"Hoax" and "fraud" were not incluced in his book, and consequently spelled with small letters.

CHAPTER 14

"Two hundred and ninety-nine, three hundred." Blue Moon counted the money and smiled. "Twenty percent of that is sixty dollars."

Blue smiled at his mathematical prowess. Kress was clearly impressed. He had no way of knowing Blue had ascertained the total hours ago when he had gone to his new friend, the bookseller, to calculate the precise figure he owed his partner.

"Not bad for three week's take," Kress agreed. "I have to hand it to you, Captain Moon – you were sure right."

Blue nodded slowly. It *had* been three good weeks. He had earned enough to make the final repairs on the *Blue Moon,* as well as some extra for emergencies. His boat was now seaworthy and he was getting restless. It was time to move out.

"We'll pack Hernando up in his canoe and put him in storage. Maybe when we get back from the Upper Mississippi, we can bring him to New Orleans."

"I was thinking about Saint Louis," Kress said with deliberate slowness.

"No," Blue demurred.

"Why not?"

"Too many people with long noses."

"But we've entertained crowds directly off the boats from that city and never had trouble with any of them."

"They like a good show as well as the rest, but they run too many newspapers. Too many reporters. Besides, after the last interview with that bastard Loretta saying our bones looked like the Gimp Injun, I think we ought to stay in our own hunting ground."

Kress questioned Blue's expression but wisely kept it to himself.

"Have you ever considered New York?"

Kress had been holding back on his sacred dream. Now that a decision on their exploration trip was at hand, he pressed his luck, hoping the red-haired, half-savage riverman would jump at it.

He was mistaken.

"New York? We can't take the *Blue Moon* all the way to New York. She's not capable of making the trip."

"I was thinking of taking 'Hernando' by land. Maybe making a few stops along the way."

"By land? In a wagon?"

"Well, I mean, we could go up river to Saint Louis, do a little business, then continue east by wagon."

"We're goin' to Saint Louie, all right, but not with Hernando. I already told you. And as far as New York? Not me."

"Then let me buy you out."

Blue snorted.

"You don't have enough to buy me out. All you have is enough to go halves with me on the molasses and use what you make to buy whatever it is you're gonna trade to the Indians."

"I have considerably more now, thanks to you. What will it take?"

"Ten thousand dollars. Or the title, free and clear on a new boat. A fancy passenger boat. Low pressure engine."

"Is that what you really want?"

Blue hesitated, then shrugged and spat. It was a good question. One with no ready answer.

The *Blue Moon* was small as steamers went. She was old and in need of constant repair. Old age for a riverboat was five years. She was twice that and not rigged out for the high-paying, first-cabin passenger trade. But she did have her advantages. If push came to shove, and occasionally did, Blue could handle her with a crew of five, maybe four.

She was not only his first command, she was his home. The first he had ever had. He had never worked with a large staff and hated the trouble associated with complaining, whining, seasick passengers, blaming the captain for everything from bad weather to tough meat. He had shipped out as a hand on boats like that, and knew.

What did Blue Moon really want out of life?

That was a question for Authors and Fake Scholars.

All he craved at the moment was to move.

"We set out tomorrow."

"Where are you going to store our friend?"

Blue smiled. It was always easier to work with a man you did not trust. That way, your guard was always up. There were never any surprises.

"Remind me to pick up a load of sand while we're upriver. Might as well make Hernando's burial canoe look as authentic as possible."

"Authentic" was his new favorite word.

Authentic had the ring of money about it.

They had sold nearly four hundred sacks of "authentic sand" from the not-so-final resting place of Hernando DeSoto. At one dollar a sack, that was four hundred dollars clear profit.

In New Orleans, they could jack the price up to two dollars and sell twice as many. But he did not want to use Natchez sand. Patrons in that major river port were more savvy than those residing in Natchez. As long as he was going north anyway, it made good sense to pick some up along the way.

Ten barrels full ought to do it. Blue knew where he could pick up barrels cheap and then "doctor" the bill of sale to make it appear he had paid three times that. His partner would never be the wiser. He would either fork over his share, or forfeit his cut of the "authentic sand" business.

"I'm going for a drink," Blue announced. "Stay at the Impressed tonight if you like, but be dockside at seven tomorrow or I leave you behind."

"How would you fair without me?" Kress asked.

For an Author and Scholar, he was not a Very Bright Man.

"I don't know if I'm interested in trading trinkets to the Injuns, but now that I've got the idee, I'll jest buy some 'authentic antiques' and bring them back down to sell. Maybe I'll even find another dead hero to resurrect."

"Who will write your handbills?"

The accusation stung. Blue rammed his right fist into his left hand, then hurried off. He had two Very Important items of business to take care of before sailing tomorrow.

"I'll write them myself," he called over his shoulder.

He heard Kress laugh and damned the man. As someone who had worked with a Famous Preacher, he knew exactly what words to use.

The Famous Remains of the Great Explorer Hernando DeSoto were wrapped in a waterproof tarpaulin and were waiting for him when he arrived at the tent. A few stragglers were loitering about, hoping to catch a glimpse for free, but Captain Moon shooed them away. He had private business to transact.

Besides, one of them might be on the payroll of a Famous Author.

Waiting for the dark of the moon, Blue rolled the canoe and its Famous Passenger out and hurried along Bleaker Street. With a stocking cap pulled low over his brow to disguise his tell-tale red hair, and several lumps carefully positioned under the wrap to disguise the gender of the corpse he was wheeling, Blue hoped no one would pay him any heed. Dead bodies being taken for interment was a common sight. One more being consigned to the Land of the Lost was of no particular interest to anyone.

Least of all the corpse, who had, so it was said, already gone to his or her "reward."

Spiritually speaking, of course.

The graveyard was situated on the edge of town where all respectable cemeteries resided. This one was not especially notable, boasting no Dead Presidents, War Heroes or Men Of Wealth. The largest crypt was constructed of pink marble, imported, it was reputed, all the way from Italy. A slightly off-color angel perched at the top.

This was the resting place of one Isabel Delgingo. In life, she was diametrically opposite the celestial creature doomed to hover forever over her head. At one time, Isabel had been the town's leading citizen.

If wealth were any indicator.

She was the Madame *Extraordinaire;* the first woman to own property in her own right, the first citizen to own more than one thousand dollars in gold and the only person in Natchez to have blackmail on every trousers-wearing gentleman within one hundred miles.

Isabel had once claimed her blackmail held true for every "gentleman within *two* hundred miles," but she was often known to exaggerate.

As in her repeated use of the term "gentleman."

Her grave was a gathering point for youths as a rite of passage. On almost every moonlit night, a score of young lovers could be seen trying out their new skills for the approval of Madame Isabel.

Hers was the only grave tended to with any regularity and certainly the only mound well supplied with grass.

It was more comfortable that way. Isabel had been known as a friendly hostess.

Her approval for acts committed "above and beyond the requirements of fertility" was said to be a long, sustained groan. Supplied by the wind.

In death, the Great and Famous were often reduced to bags of hot air.

The same could usually be said about them in life. But not to the accompaniment of angles carved in pink marble.

It was commonly believed anything carved in marble to be the Truth.

A conviction begun by the Marble-Cutters Association.

"Here lies Bill Smith, An Honest Man," cost more than, "Here lies Bill Smith," or the frequent "Bill Smith, R.I.P."

Chiselers had much in common with gamblers, politicians, bankers and ladies of the evening.

Some would add riverboat captains to that list.

Blue avoided her grave with the fervor of the uninitiated.

He did not want to be seen.

With or without his trousers.

His destination was at the opposite end of the graveyard at a place he had discovered once, by accident. On the lee side of a small hill, a tomb had been erected for the repository of itinerant or unclaimed bodies. Constructed of thin shale and supported with wooden slats, the site held bodies too poor to afford their own stone houses.

The water table along the lower Mississippi was too high to permit the traditional, in-ground burial of bodies. Therefore, above-the-ground interments were the norm. Unfortunately, for the recently deceased − or more accurately, their heirs − it was also more expensive.

Those who could not afford a mausoleum became a sticky problem to city officials. They could not bury them and the tax base would rise higher than the water levels if they adopted a policy of free crypts. Dumping them in the Mississippi was untidy and posed a threat to navigation.

An ingenious solution was devised. It was never passed by the City Council, and no official vote was ever recorded. The local newspaper never published any articles, pro or con, on the idea. But this resolution was adhered to more closely than the Ten Commandments.

When a man, woman or Indian died without sufficient funds, the body was placed in a large storage crypt at the very edge of town. The next riverboat into Natchez was required to take the coffin upriver and leave it on the levee at Louisville or Saint Louis.

Just leave it. Inconspicuously. Late at night.

No return address.

Problem solved.

What Louisville and Saint Louis did with the bodies did not concern anyone in Natchez.

They reasoned the water tables were lower in those cities.

If the officials of Kentucky and Missouri ever wondered why dead men in cheap coffins kept appearing on their docks, their amazement has been lost to history.

The above-ground, temporary mass-interment scheme was especially appreciated in the winter, when the water froze and no steamboats ran.

Without the wherewithal to dispose of their dead bodies, the large crypt became a godsend.

It was, after all, better than leaving the coffins stacked up beside the church, for obvious reasons. No one attending services cared to be reminded, in so graphic a way, of their common end. After all, it was difficult for even the most pious to imagine sitting on a cloud with the stench of rotting flesh stinging their nostrils.

No one without specific deposit business ever went near this crypt. The rumor of a ghost haunting the tomb had done much to promote its isolation.

It was said, and printed in the newspaper, making it true, that a foreigner from one of the far eastern nations, New York or Vermont, perhaps, had come south, seeking his fortune. He bought a sugar plantation outside New Orleans and did well the first few years. However, during a protracted drought, when tempers were short and slaves had nothing better to do, they rebelled and overran his house.

When the master was caught with a black woman in his bed, without benefit of her permission, he was decapitated, the larger of his two heads being unceremoniously tossed into the cistern. What happened to the other head was long a matter of conjecture.

The skull was later discovered on the wharf at Natchez. The other remained absent without leave.

Unfortunately, the first head was not recovered until the body had been Shipped East. That made it impossible to reunite the corpse with its missing items. The skull, now devoid of flesh, was sold to an Indian agent. As luck would have it, he was fallen on by thieves, beaten and killed.

With opportunity knocking, the agent was temporarily interred with both heads – three actually, but nobody was counting – in the holding area. As it was then winter, he was doomed to a long wait before traveling up the Mighty Mississippi to his last port o' call.

Soon afterwards, a two-headed spirit was seen walking about the kirk-yard. Its night-time visitations so unnerved the visitors to Madame Isabel's grave, it was determined to be rid of the agent the moment the river unfroze. The word "unfroze" having as many meanings as the poor agent had heads.

With the opening of the spring season, the agent's coffin was shipped to Saint Louis, where it was dumped on the wharf, its fare having been paid only that far. No one in Natchez knew what became of it. Thereafter, the vision of a head without benefit of body was seem fluttering over the lee side of the hill.

The final result was, no itinerant or penny-pinching citizen of Natchez died during the winter, for fear of being laid out with only the floating skull for company. This caused an unusually large number of deaths in early spring, coinciding exactly with the melting of the river and the start of steamboat traffic. This being the busy season, attendance at funerals was noticeably lax. It was therefore determined not to use the old, temporary interment area, but to construct a new one. This crypt held six coffins, but gave peace of mind to those ready to depart the world.

It promised a good turn-out at their obsequies.

It also gave rise to the very lucrative betting scheme of trying to guess who would be one of the six individuals to die during the winter. When the number was reduced to three, the physicians in town did a lively business dispensing nostrums and notions. Men who would otherwise shun the professional services of a "sawbones" could be seen visiting that worthy's office in an attempt to postpone death.

The higher the betting ran on specific individuals, the more often they went.

It was the greatest boon to the practice of medicine in the annuls of Natchez. Two riverboat captains, laying over during the dull season, put out shingles advertising their prowess with the Healing Arts.

Lying was a skill they had learned plying their trade on the river. It carried over nicely into private medical practice. One captain even had a ship's bell installed outside his door. When business was slow, he was heard to ring it continuously, in a sort of warning that someone was about to depart. Those patients feeling "under the weather" were thus advised to see him before their "boat left one port for another."

Blue prided himself on the fact he was not a superstitious man. He was a realist, however. Needing a place to store Hernando DeSoto, he knew he could not trust a living soul. Leaving the Famous Spanish Explorer with the ghost of a Famous Head seemed the best solution. No one would go near the haunted crypt. The Headless Foreigner would be a silent partner.

Pulling back the dead tree limbs, as opposed to the limbs of Natchez's citizens, Blue kicked away the accumulated wind-blown trash around the entrance and deposited his corpse. The vault was better than The Bank for it charged no holding fee and did not suffer the occasional failure common to all men and financial institutions. There would be no "run" on the grave, nor would the skeleton come up empty-handed.

No mortal eyes would inspect the bones for a supposed resemblance to a "gimp Injun" and no enterprising clerk would scoop away a handful of Burial Sand for his private, "never to be sold unless the price was right," collection.

Squatting on his haunches, Blue pulled back a loose slab of shale. Hidden beneath it, he unearthed a small metal coffin, just large enough to hold the body of an actual river rodent. Opening it with more reverence than he would have accorded the remains of a dead saint, Blue lit a match and stared at the object interred within.

It was not a river rat nor did it contain anything which could rightful be said to have lived. Yet what the look-alike coffin held was life itself to Blue Moon, for it held all his worldly treasure.

He hated The Bank and did not trust Bankers. Keeping his fortune aboard the *Blue Moon* was risky, for although she doubled as his home, she could be sunk and lost, leaving him totally destitute.

Blue was not alone in his fear but he was alone in other things men took for granted. Where others had parents, Blue was an orphan. Where others had brothers, sisters, he was an only child. Where the vast majority of Mankind had at least one boon companion on whom they could trust, he was utterly friendless.

If Blue Moon needed to cry on a shoulder, he would be in little better position than if he were advised to perform that act which is generally thought to be anatomically impossible.

He had lived alone since boyhood and had not learned the social skills requisite to survive in a community of people. He was better adapted for solitary pursuits, lonely vigils, communication with the stars. When forced to travel a well-worn road, he was as alien to his environment as the *Blue Moon* was out of water.

It was no surprise to anyone when, after winning the boat, he had renamed her after himself. Why not, they argued without pity. He was his own best friend. The first anyone on the lower Mississippi ever heard of Blue Moon had been on an island without a name, offering to chop wood for "the going rate." As far as they, or anyone else knew, Blue might as well have been a tree come to life in the guise of a boy.

Perhaps someone had put a *spell* on that tree.

It was as well they had not suggested that theory to Blue, or it would have meant another trip to New Orleans and the infamous gypsy.

At that rate, he would be broke within the year.

Not that that anyone cared. If he disappeared tomorrow, no one would look for him. He rubbed people the wrong way. Those who had tried, once upon a time, to help him, lived to regret their generosity....

"Are you the wild boy of No Name Island?"

The question was kindly meant, but Blue would not have known an act of kindness if it had hit him in the face.

"What's it to ya?" he demanded, eyes darkening with suspicion.

"He's a white boy, all right," the tall questioner with deep, dark, black eyes replied, turning to his companion. "No doubt about it." Then, regaling the boy with a smile, he tried again. "Where are your parents, boy?"

"I ain't a boy!"

"Where are your parents, son?"

The man rephrased his interrogative. His effort went unappreciated.

"I ain't yer son!"

"Whose son are you?"

"Who's askin'?"

"My name is Mr. Canfield. I have just come from Indian Country. Up river."

"Then go back there. We don't need no Injuns down here."

"The natives spoke of a boy with red hair – like yours. I wondered if you were the –" Rather than repeat his mistake a third time, he finished quickly, "fellow."

"No. I ain't."

"Where'd you come from?"

Blue waved his arm in a vague direction, then shrugged.

"I been around."

"Come from the Upper Mississippi?"

"Yeah," he spat, narrowly missing the man's boots. "I cum frum the Uprivers. Ma and Pa Upriver. How'd ya know?"

"He's clever. Has a good mind," Canfield said to his partner.

"Who taught you how to speak English?" the other man asked.

"What's English?"

"Who taught you how to speak?"

"Mr. Tongue."

The men smiled. The tall man held out his hand. Blue stepped back.

"How would you like to come with us?"

"How would you like a rock hittin' yer head?"

"We'd like to take you back."

If he had been older, Blue would have replied, "Back where?" But he was only a boy.

"I ain't goin' nowhere."

"We'll feed you proper and give you warm clothes to wear. We'll take you back upriver. Where you belong. Where they're waiting for you."

"Touch me an' yer dead."

The second man made a move. Before he took a second step, Blue whipped out a knife and stood, weapon out, ready to defend himself to the death.

"All right."

Canfield held up his hands in a consolatory gesture.

"We understand. We'll leave you alone."

They went back aboard the boat they had come from and did not reappear while the crew loaded the wood Blue had chopped. He did not breathe easy, however, until he heard the bell ring, announcing departure.

Had he been more suspicious, he would not have relaxed his guard. Had be been less hungry, he would not have gone back to camp to prepare his meal, until he had seen the steamboat pull away.

They came upon him when his back was turned and he was whistling to himself. Not caring to do battle with a wild boy and a knife, they brought a fishing net and threw it over his shoulders.

The contest was over before it started. They took their prize, trussed up like a holiday present, back to the boat.

"Thank you, Captain," Canfield replied. "You were right. Not knowing the ways of the river, it never occurred to us to deceive the child into thinking your vessel had pulled away by ringing the bell."

The Captain pursed his lips. It was a dirty trick to play and he was not proud of himself. But times were hard and he had sailed without a full load of cargo. If he had not made it up by the fee the two men paid him, he would face the prospect of angry creditors at the end of the line.

Even stowed away in the hold, the captain could hear the yells and screams of his small, red-haired cargo. He hoped the boy would not keep it up all the way to port.

The captain hoped in vain. For three days and two nights the wild captive kept up an incessant wailing, half anger, half sobs. When, on the third night the noise stopped, he heaved a sigh of relief.

It was short lived.

Just after midnight, when the captain left the pilot house, he saw a trail of blood leading down the corridor. The hair on the back of his head rose in dread. Following the red path, he came to the cabin door of his two passengers. Knocking elicited no response. He tried the knob. Unlocked.

Upon entering, he realized the blood had not come from an occupant leaving the cabin, but had been dropped from a bleeding wound of someone going into the stateroom.

Someone who had come up from the hold.

Someone who had cut himself free of restraining ropes and injured himself in the process.

Badly, from the looks of the trail he left behind.

Canfield and his partner were lying on their bunks. Neither were easily aroused, though neither were drunk. Canfield's arm had been stabbed with a knife. He was nearly dead from loss of blood. The other man, whose name the captain had not ascertained, had a wound in his belly. The room reeked of blood and bowels.

Shaking Canfield, the captain was relieved to see a flicker of light in his eyes.

"What happened?" he demanded.

"That – bastard. That *boy,"* he whispered with a hate-filled tone.

"He did this to you?" Canfield nodded. "In God's name, why?"

"Jonas was fooling with him – kept dunking his head in a bucket of water and holding him under. Wanted to make him shut up. That screaming was getting on our nerves. Wanted to make him talk. I told him it was no good. The damn boy's no better'n an Indian. You had the right idea. Fool him. But Jonas wanted to know if he was the right boy. The one we come after."

"Was he?" the captain whispered, feeling shamed for his complicity in the deed.

"Don't know. He never said a word. Not a word in English. Cussed us in some other language. Damn bastard. I told Jonas to leave him alone. We'd take him back and see. He damn near drown the rat before I pulled him off. Got cute then with a knife. Left it there, in front of that damn boy. Just to remind him he could be made to talk. He's only a boy, damn it!"

"What happened?"

"I don't know. He stopped yelping, anyway, so we left him tied up in the net. Must have gotten that knife, somehow. Cut himself out. Done some goddamn damage, doing it. He was bleeding like the devil when he slipped in. Had the knife with him. Quiet as an Indian. Stuck Jonas, then came at me. Bad business."

"Bad business," the captain agreed.

He gave Jonas a rough prod with his hand, taking care not to get blood on his uniform. The man groaned, nothing more.

"He'll be dead before we get to port," the captain said. Canfield shuddered. "Who the hell is that boy?"

"Just a boy. Nobody. Nobody special."

"Then why'd you come after him?"

"Heard a story. That's all. Thought we could sell him back. Bad business." Canfield raised himself enough to stare over at his partner. "What are you going to do with him?"

"I'm gonna set you both off on shore, soon as it's light."

"Where'd that damn boy get to?"

The captain shrugged. It was no longer any of his business. He would wash his hands of the whole affair.

Never should have helped. Fooling the boy: bad business.

Maybe the boy had slipped over the side and swam to shore. Maybe he had downed.

One thing was certain. The captain would never stop on that island again for wood.

Nor did he ever stop at any other island called "No Name."

Just to be on the safe side....

Blue Moon cradled his money in his arms as though the coins constituted a body and not a treasure. A man with money did not need a past.

As he replaced his worldly status, a small trinket slipped out from between his fingers. He made a low moan, picked it up quickly and buried it in his hand. He did not look at it. He did not have to. He knew what it looked like.

When he finally emptied his hands he saw a small indentation in his flesh.

It had the shape of a cameo.

There was one more piece of business Captain Moon wished to transact before returning to his boat. Not exactly sure where to go, he made inquiry, and was directed to a dry goods shop toward the middle of town.

When Blue did not see what he was looking for, he was compelled to ask.

"A pair of eye glasses? No. I ain't got any spectacles in stock jest now." Seeing the look of disappointment on Blue's face, he added quickly. "But I kin tell you where to get a pair. Ask the parson. He's got half a dozen. He'll sell you one."

Blue nodded. He disappeared as fast as a river rat upon discovering no meat on a pile of bones.

Applying at the house of the parson, he explained what he sought. The man gladly showed him his collection.

"Never saw no need to bury eye glasses with a dead body. Always take 'em off, unless the deceased specifically asked to have 'em buried with 'em."

"How much?"

The parson considered, then rubbed his fingers together.

Unlike a riverboat captain, he was not in a lucrative business.

"Two dollars?"

Blue eyed the collection, then selected a pair at random, having no idea what, if any difference, there was between them.

"This will do."

"Try 'em on, if you want."

"They're not for me."

He paid the finder's fee and went away with the wire-frame spectacles.

Reading glasses. He had seen Professor Kress read with a pair of such lenses on his nose.

Now he had a book *and* a pair of eye glasses.

A new world was before him.

It had to be better than the old world.

CHAPTER 15

Saint Louis was a bustling town of noise and activity. Steamboats crowded the wharfs, while the odd barge and flat-bottomed keelboats vied for attention. Commerce was the name of the game. Being the "Gateway to the West," there was much to be had.

As Captain Moon disembarked, he was immediately accosted by boys from two rival supply houses. One tugged his arm, while the other danced in front of him.

"Wares fer yer boat, Captain!" pleaded one. "We has the best prices around."

To compliment his patter, he interlocked his fingers and made a large "O" with his arms, to symbolize *around.*

The other boy, half Indian, half white, rolled his eyes and made little war-dance steps as he attempted to drag Blue off.

"Come with me, General," he demanded. 'I got all you need."

"I doubt it," Blue muttered beneath his breath. He had heard another man mutter those same words and been impressed with the way his listeners nodded wisely. Blue was constantly on the alert for expressions and words which would make him sound educated. When he saw a man get a reaction, he remembered the circumstances and practiced saying the sentence in exactly the same tone of voice.

It made him feel worldly and fancied others respected him more because of it.

Immediately after Money on his list of things to accumulate, was Respect.

He had heard it said once that money cou d not buy respect.

He often repeated that joke after spending an hour or more in a tavern.

His words failed to impress the huckster-boys, a fact Blue ascribed to their tender age. Boys simply did not have the same knowledge or appreciation as men.

"Leave off!" he growled. He was not in the market for supplies. Not now. Not until he and his partner sold their cargo and made of a list of what was needed for the coming journey.

And discussed exactly how such items were to be paid.

He would not have gone to the chandler's which employed the half-breed, in any case. He did not do business with Indians, half-Indians or men who employed Indians.

It was a matter of principle.

Call it a memory.

He did want to buy barrels, however, and accomplished that task readily, even surprising the seller by his insistence on paying a full three dollars for each, rather than the asking price of two dollars, two bits. Putting the number "1" in front of the figures "$3.00" on the invoice made his purchases worth thirteen dollars, rather than two dollars and twenty-five cents.

He would therefore make a clear profit of ten dollars and seventy-five on each barrel he purchased. His partner would never be the wiser and he would have more reason to look forward to the coming trip.

Leaving his supplier bewildered by his unexpected generosity, Blue gave orders for the barrels to be delivered to the *Blue Moon* that afternoon and went in search of a good dinner and a drink.

He owed it to himself.

He was stopped a dozen times by women plying their trade. While most opted to walk the streets in the evening, whenever a ship pulled into port, a select group made their appearance, hoping to grab rivermen who had just gotten paid. Their presence reminded him of Mrs. Lang, causing him to break out into a sweat.

Making him regret the fact he hadn't purchased an extra bottle of magic potent from the Medicine Woman. He had a sick feeling he was going to need it.

Damn those Irish, anyway. They had the power. "Lang," he supposed, was an Irish name.

Whenever any person got the better of Blue in a deal, eyed him with suspicion or held some mysterious threat over him, he always identified them as "Irish."

What, exactly "Irish" was, he could not say. He knew only to avoid them.

They always recognized him.

It was something, he suspected, connected with his red hair.

Which reminded him of another task he wished to have performed before going upriver. One that could not be put off.

Turning abruptly away from a woman standing outside the "Unbuttoned," a popular boarding house where no man ever stayed the night, he ducked down a side alley. Nearly at a run, he came out on what was commonly known as "Wench Street."

Someone had explained to him once "wench" was an Indian word, meaning "high times." He knew that to be an untruth and suspected it was an Irish word.

No matter the language, he had learned "high times," meant "women."

He was not as naive as they thought.

He kept going.

Fast.

On the next street he saw what he wanted. With a sigh of relief, Blue entered the tonsorial and took a seat by the door. There were two men ahead of him, both hardly in need of the barber's services.

He supposed they were Famous Authors, like the Professor. No one but that type ever bothered to have a shave and haircut more than once a week.

To pass the time, Blue picked up a periodical and flipped through the pages, amusing himself by identifying the letters he had learned. Each time he discovered an "A," "B" or "C" he patted himself on the back. Had he remembered, he would have brought his spectacles and tried them out. But he had left them in his cabin.

Too bad. Here he could take advantage of free reading material.

Tiring of the first magazine, he tossed it down and selected a second. This one had line illustrations of steamboats. Sticking his nose deep within the pages, he studied the drawings. Beside them were columns of figures, then a series of words describing what the tables meant. He could not make sense out the article because there were not enough a's, b's and c's. He tossed that down, as well.

His third choice was a yellow-jacketed pamphlet. There was a sketch of a riverboat captain on the cover, standing on a wharf he did not recognize, a wad of paper money in one hand, the other arm bared, displaying an overabundance of muscle. The man's jacket was unbuttoned and his shirt, secured by latigo lacing at the top, was much like Blue's own. His interest aroused, he turned the page.

There was much incomprehensible writing, but the text was lavishly garnished with illustrations. This captain, whoever he was, apparently had prodigious strength, for he was depicted holding the wheel during a terrible storm, drawing the boat to shore with a thick rope and defeating any number of would-be assassins in a barroom brawl.

Likening himself to the mythical character, Blue enjoyed himself thoroughly. Not only could he picture himself performing those daring feats of strength, he found a great many letters he recognized. It would not be long before, he, too, was the subject of a book.

The last chapter ruined everything. The captain, after having run through a storm, single-handedly shoved his boat off a sandbar and beaten a tavern-full of enemies, was rewarded by having six ladies, all dressed in extremely revealing costumes, falling at his feet.

There was no mention whatsoever of all the money he had earned. The cover, therefore, had been a lie.

Blue tossed the periodical down in disgust.

"Irish," he muttered.

"Yer next," the barber invited.

Not a minute too soon, for he had been close to losing a customer.

Blue hopped up, crossed to the chair and settled himself down. Rubbing a hand over his well-stubbled cheeks, he nodded to the man.

"Shave and a haircut. Crop it close."

With his captain's cap removed and his hair brushed down, the red locks spilled well over his collar. The barber clucked his tongue, then grinned.

"Going courtin'?" he slyly inquired.

"No," came the sharp, sullen reply. The barber took it for an affirmative.

He placed a steaming hot towel over Blue's face, then went about snipping his hair. By the time his customer's whiskers were soft enough to attack with a well-honed razor, he was bathed in a red glow of fine, delicate hair.

Unlike the hair on his head, Blue's facial hair was tough and prickly, compelling the barber to strop the razor twice before completing the job. When he was finished, he held a bottle under Blue's nose for his approval. The riverman sniffed the contents then looked up quizzically.

"What is it?"

"Witch hazel."

"Smells all right," Blue allowed. "What's it fer?"

It was too late to stop the barber, as he replied, "Sparkin' the ladies," compelling the customer to endure the application with disgust.

This evil deception cost the barber his five cent tip.

"You look like a new man," the clipper announced, drawing back the drapery covering his patron.

Blue stared at himself in the mirror. What he saw was a young face covered with freckles. Not what he had been hoping for. He did not look wise and mature. He appeared more like a cabin boy than a ship's master.

"Don't you have something for these?" he asked, pointing to the countless red freckles on his face. If only he could rid himself of those telltale spots, he was sure no one would ever call him "Irish" again.

Or, "boy."

The barber laughed.

Which was a greater sin that sprinkling him with the witch hazel.

"No, sir. Afraid I ain't. You got them frum yer daddy or yer mommy and they're yer brand for life."

"I never had a daddy or a mommy!"

Blue jumped from the chair and angrily tossed the man his due. Had he the time, he would have stiffed him completely and spent the night in jail.

Considerably flustered, he stomped away, hands stuffed into the pockets of his coat. What had started out to be a simple excursion had turned sour in a hurry.

It did not bode well for the journey upstream.

Professor Kress paid Blue his share for the barrels, then checked his cash, which he secured in a small box with a Very Large Lock.

"What next?" he asked.

"I've a flyer out on the molasses. I expect we'll be able to sell it at a decent profit."

He had already planned on what he would get for the sugar and how much he would tell his partner he got for it.

"Good. Now, what about the gifts for the Indians?"

"I thought you knew what you wanted," Blue smugly replied. He had learned a great deal about Andre Kress in the month he had known him.

His opinion had lowered considerably.

There was a fine point between education and intelligence, he had learned.

It was a valuable piece of information to possess.

Especially now that he could read three letters and owned a pair of spectacles.

"Yes... but seeing as how you are an authority on Indians... I thought you would have some suggestions."

"I never traded fer artifacts." His words were guarded.

"But you did say you had been to the head waters of the Mississippi."

"Not that far."

"How far have you been?"

Blue hesitated. To say too much was worse than saying too little.

"Hard to say. Names change. The river's the same, I expect. How far did you want to go?"

Kress raised an eyebrow.

"As far as it takes for me to get what I want."

Blue paused to contemplate the ceiling of the riverboat cabin, then picked at a hangnail with the point of his knife. It was, by all appearances, an Indian knife.

"Where'd you get that?" Kress asked, indicating the ugly looking weapon. It was not Moon's accustomed Bowie knife, but one he had not seen before.

Blue shrugged.

"Traded for it."

Kress hesitated, clearly uncomfortable. Like Moon, he had learned a lot about his partner in the past four weeks. He liked none of it. The captain was too moody, too greedy, too vague. He was also too young, a sin which Blue could only correct with time. Time Kress did not have to give him.

"If you cannot tell me –" he began. Moon cut him off by abruptly sticking the knife into the table around which they sat. The blade penetrated a quarter inch and remained upright.

"Tobacco. We'll need tobacco and pipes. Clay ones ought to be good enough. Nothing too fancy. Well, mebbe a dozen briars. With long stems. They like the ones with long stems. They affix feathers to 'em. Makes the chiefs and the medicine men look important. Looks is very important to an Injun. A lot of his status depends on how he presents himself. He's part bluster, part savage, part bear. Take away one part and the rest don't work.

"And then there's tradition." Blue leaned across the table, resting his chin in his hands. "Injuns are keen on their ancestors. They hold 'em in reverence."

"I see."

"Now, let's get down to it," Blue suggested, his brown eyes intense. The light from the lamp reflected in his pupils, making them appear lupine. "You tell me what you're really lookin' fer and I'll tell you what kind of 'trinkets' you need to trade with."

"I – I have already told you," Kress began. Blue shook him off.

"I believed you once, but not twiced."

"What do you mean?"

"Mebbe you wrote a book and mebbe you really are a professor. But you sure as hell ain't going into Injun Territory looking to barter fer beads and rattles."

"Well, not exactly beads and rattles," Kress admitted. "But I fail to see how I have misrepresented myself."

"You went along with my scheme to make money on the fake corpse of a man who you made out to be a hero. That was your word – hero. If you was a real Famous Author, you would have told me off; exposed me for a *fraud*. You didn't. You were real glad to go in on it with me. Now, you better tell me who you are, and what 'exactly' means."

"I *am* looking for artifacts; for precious items."

"What do you mean by 'precious items'?"

Kress withdrew from the table and stared at the youth before him. The professor's face was troubled. He had made discrete inquiry in New Orleans, asking for the names of any riverboat captains with experience on the Upper Mississippi. From that list, he had made further investigation, seeking one with a questionable, or corruptible reputation.

The name Blue Moon had come up more often than anyone else's. He had taken that information on face value.

Now, he realized he had made a mistake.

It was a disquieting thought for someone who prided himself on his Infallible Judgment.

He should have passed on the Herrando DeSoto scheme and played it himself at some later date.

Now, Kress was stuck with a man who knew too much. He was left with the option of saying more than he wanted, or delaying the enterprise.

He twisted in his chair, finding his eyes inextricably drawn to the knife in the table.

"Furs," he said finally. "I want furs. Beaver. Mink. Well-tanned hides. Pelts of rare animals. The Indians, I am led to believe, have a wealth of such items."

"Yeah," Blue agreed. "They take them from the white trappers they catch."

"That is not my affair."

"There's government trading posts – United States forts they trade with. There's soldiers stationed along the river."

"I know. I was planning on avoiding them."

"How?"

"With your help."

"You won't get furs with tobacco and pipes. Not even with barrels of salt pork or flour."

"What will it take?"

"Whisky. Guns."

"If we get caught trading those items –"

"There will be the devil to pay," Blue agreed. "Not just with the Union boys. With the neighboring tribes. There's a half dozen tribes upriver. They make treaties and those treaties don't mean a damn. Not when they have guns. What you're proposing, Professor, is to trade for furs and start a series of Injun wars."

"Nothing else will do?"

"I told you – whisky. Course, we'll water it down – half whisky, half river water. There never was an Injun alive who could hold his licker. Not even watered-down licker. But that's what they'll want."

"How dangerous is it?"

"That depends on how careful we are; and how lucky. And how watchful them soldier boys are. We get caught with a cargo of guns and licker and we're dead men. Then, of course, if the Sioux catch us trading guns to the Fox, we'll have the Sioux after us, as well."

"What do you suggest?"

"Two things. Tradin' fer beads and rattles is a good cover. We'll keep it. Which means we'll have to do some tradin' in them commodities. Second, you pay me five hundred dollars up front, before we leave Saint Louie. An' then half the profits from whatever we take out."

"Why should I do that?"

"Because all you're riskin' is yer skin. I'm riskin' my skin and my steamboat."

Kress hesitated, clearly torn.

"I'll think about it."

"Not too hard. Because if you don't meet my terms and you think about hiring another partner, I'll go to the authorities and tell 'em what you're up to."

There was no doubt he meant what he said.

Blue had Andre Kress right where he wanted him – between a hogshead of tobacco and a barrel of gunpowder.

"Deal," the professor agreed.

"Deal," Blue acknowledged.

They shook hands.

Which was worth no more than the promise either would cheat the other at the first opportunity.

Just the way Captain Moon had it figured.

Those men who had spoken so deprecatingly of him in New Orleans would have been amazed.

But then, life was full of amazing things.

That was what made it interesting.

That, and the potential for profit.

CHAPTER 16

Captain Blue Moon had a dilemma. He needed money. Running a transient riverboat – being a river rat – was an expensive business. He had wharf and dock fees to pay at every stop, the cost of handbills announcing date and time of departure before any major trip, and the added, under-the-table expenses of doing business with merchants. During high water, when there were several boats in dock, it required more than a little haggling to secure a full load of cargo.

Then, there was the crew to pay. Stiff one of them and there was a devil's row. An owner could get away with docking them five cents here and there but if he were to pull short on their due at the end of the season, he would find kindling wood where once a riverboat floated.

Not that he blamed them in the abstract.

In the tangible, however, he would chase them to the *Atlantic Ocean* to inflict revenge. He could use that expression now, for now he knew where it was.

Then there was insurance. At one dollar per foot of boat, he could have managed to protect himself from calamity, but had never availed himself of that safety net. Owning his own boat outright, he was not compelled to do so, and therefore, did not. A penny saved was a penny earned.

General Andrew Jackson was reputed to have said that.

The cargo was insured by the shipper. If the *Blue Moon* sunk, the insurance company and not the boat's owner was liable. Which never stopped anyone from suing. He had sat in on a trial once and had learned a great deal.

Lawyers and judges were like merchants. All required a little "above board" for the business to come out favorably.

His biggest expense and in truth, his greatest fear, was the constant need for repairs. The hull of a boat, exposed to rough currents, abrasive sandbars and the frequency of striking floating bodies, wore away the wooden structure with the certainty of death. Laying over to have the hull replaced was not only costly, it prevented the captain from taking on cargo.

As he knew from experience.

The hull he had replaced was good for a year, sixteen months if he were lucky. Then he would have to go through the procedure all over again.

There were no guarantees in life.

At least, not the kind which promised Good Fortune.

If it were not the wooden hull, then it was the boilers. Exposed to great temperatures, they were the biggest treat cf fire on a boat. If a valve corroded, a pipe exploded or a door blew off, fire spread like melting butter. If the boat were heavily insured, the crew let it burn, saving themselves without regard for passengers.

If the boat were uninsured, the captain, who was probably also the owner, saw to it, with everything in his power, including a musket to back his demands, that the boat be saved.

Rivermen naturally preferred to ship on insured boats.

Blue made it a policy to post his Insurance Form in the wheelhouse. When he thought of it, or was reminded by a worried crewman, he altered the date to make it appear the policy was current.

The form itself had cost him fifteen cents. It was the best investment he had ever made.

Money was the reason Blue Moon was steaming up the Mississippi. Nothing else would have tempted him. Thus his dilemma, which was actually no dilemma.

Rather, it was buckshot in the backside.

Known, in less polite society, as a pain in the ass.

He did not *want* to go upriver. He had to.

The point was moot.

With the trinkets and the foodstuffs for the Indians carefully stowed aboard and sixteen cases of guns, marked "Heavy Machinery: Lead Mining Equipment," placed below, the *Blue Moon* left Saint Louis. Whisky could be picked up along the route. Buying guns and alcohol together was not a wise move. A man might as well write on his shingle that he was off to bribe the Indians.

While not a bad business venture, the government frowned upon such activity.

They preferred to keep the business to themselves.

It was never smart to flaunt one's intentions to the army. That had what was called "A Bottomless Exchequer."

When Blue had first heard the expression, he thought it meant "ex-checker," referring to a man who formally played checkers, a game even he knew how to play. Blue had not been able to reason out why such a man, on the payroll of the army, would be of much use, but men spoke of this fellow with fear. Being a prudent man himself, Moon thought it best to avoid checkers all together.

It made for a dull winter.

It was not until he sat in on a trial of a riverboat captain being sued by the government that someone explained "exchequer" meant purse. An unlimited purse meant the outcome of the trial was a foregone conclusion.

That knowledge did nothing to improve his opinion of the game, but taught him a new respect for government rules and regulations.

Out of respect grew wisdom.

It was very wise not to get caught doing anything the army deemed illegal.

The *Blue Moon* set steam at dawn. Several miles upriver, Blue felt a tugging beneath his feet and peered over the lee side of the boat. Without any experience at all, he could have detected the increased flow of current.

But he was not inexperienced. In fact, he knew far more about the Upper Mississippi than he cared to.

There was, in his denial, a form of self-deception, although the captain would have passed it off without a second thought..

If pressed to explain why he had lied, Blue might had said, "For reasons of my own," or "For good reasons." He would likely have added, "Because I don't want nobody to know too much about me."

Which was closer to the truth.

Had he added, "And I don't want to know anymore, myself," he would have been closer, still.

In truth, he gave away more than he concealed.

Eleven miles upriver, the *Blue Moon* steamed past Chain of Rocks, a huge series of walls jutting upward with ominous intent. Just beyond, he pointed out a peculiar – in this case "peculiar" meaning "welcome" – phenomenon.

"Look there," he indicated to Kress. "That is the Missouri River. She feeds out into the Mississippi. If a riverman didn't know where he was and he saw that water, he'd be able to get himself square."

"Why is that?"

"Look into the water. If you can't tell, then cast yer eyes about on the banks." He waited a moment in polite silence to give the Scholar time to reason out the problem.

"Tell me," the professor finally demanded.

"Two words. Yellow silt. Now that I tolt you, you'll be able to see it fer yerself."

Kress was more interested in the fact Blue's carefully structured speech patterns had disintegrated than in yellow silt, but refocused his eyes as ordered. As if by magic, he saw what, only a moment ago, had been invisible.

"What does it mean?"

He had a two-way curiosity. One, to discover the extent of Blue's knowledge; the second to have an answer.

"The Missouri is a muddy river; with its fast current, it wears away the sides o' the banks at a good clip. That river water's traveled nearly three-thousand miles."

"Where does it originate?"

"The Rocky Mountains."

Not only did his speech alter with each answer, Kress detected more than subtle traces of a dialect in Blue's voice. Pausing to listen, he found he could not be certain whether that regional accent had been there all along and he had simply failed to note it, or if passage up the Mississippi had somehow brought it into sharper clarity.

Blue broke into his thoughts.

"Ever been up this way?"

"I've heard the Missouri is nearly impassable."

"She has a strong current. Comin' n as fast as she does would ordinarily make this *confluence* a nightmare to navigate." The riverman made a point of pronouncing the ten dollar word correctly, a fact not lost on his listener. "But that island there diverts the current; breaks it up, so's a boat kin git past."

"I see. Very exciting."

Exciting was not the word Blue would have chosen.

"When shall we pick up the whisky?" Kress inquired, changing the subject. Captain Moon was an interesting study, but there were more pressing issues.

Blue quieted him with a warning look.

"I don't want ta hear that word outta yer mouth. The crew don't know what we'll be taking aboard an' I don't want 'em to suspect. Iffn they do, they'll be jumpin' overboard first chance they git. Or worse, demandin' more money for the risks they're being made ta take. You're a partner in this venture. You want that?"

Kress shook his head but he was not thinking along the same lines.

"The crew is your affair. I have contracted you to take me upriver. If there is a problem with this boat or with the men handling her, that is your affair."

Captain Moon shrugged.

"Comes to it, I'll throw you overboard after 'em."

Andre Kress decided he did not like Blue Moon.

Come to it, Kress was not above making a separate deal with the steamboaters and throwing Captain Moon "overboard."

A bit of forgery on a partnership agreement would be a simple matter, enabling him to file claim on the steamboat when they returned to Saint Louis. Being the "surviving partner," everything the late, unlamented captain owned would belong to him.

The first thing he would do would be to change the name of the boat.

The second thing would be to sell her at auction.

In the Field of Academia, it was well to have Contingency Plans.

Call it a form of tenure.

"I have made note of your warning, Master Moon."

Blue, who had been turning away, stopped abruptly and shoved the professor back with such force he nearly lost his balance and made good Blue's threat.

"Captain Moon," he was corrected. "My apologies. In many states of this magnificent country, the word 'master' is considered a compliment."

"That depends on what color yer skin is. I wouldn't use it where we're goin' iffn I was you. There's some might take it wrong."

Again, that veiled suspicion nagged at Kress' mind. But it was impossible. Moon's skin was the product of two whites, not a Caucasian and a Negro. Not even the result of a white mating with a red Indian. What he had heard about Blue Moon in New Orleans had to be exactly what he thought it was: a rumor. That the man was odd was certainly true. That he had a taste for money was beyond question. But that he was a "breed" did not fit the picture of the youth standing before him.

Not impossible, he conceded, but highly unlikely. The proof of the pudding would either come with age or be made plain, were Moon to father a child. What was hidden in his own features would come out in those of his progeny.

The thought disgusted Master Kress.

He decided, ultimately, this part of the country would never be civilized. He was glad he did not plan on staying longer than his scheme required. With money, he would return East, where he Belonged.

Leaving the "Louisiana Purchase" to the savages.

Whatever their skin color.

When the *Blue Moon* reduced speed and rang her bell, Kress returned to deck.

"Are we stopping?" he asked the captain.

"That's right."

"To pick up cargo?"

"You might say that."

"Good."

"Not that kind."

"What kind, then?" There was obvious annoyance in the man's voice.

"The walkin', squalkin' kind."

Blue adjusted his cap than rang the bell again.

"Poultry? I thought you said Indians preferred pork."

"Who's talkin' aboot Injuns?"

"I am."

The captain stepped away from the wheelhouse and leaned over the railing. The small, riverside town of Alton, Illinois, was just coming into view.

"You don't own this boat an' you don't give orders. I'm stoppin' to take on passengers."

"What do you mean? I don't want any passengers aboard. My dealings are with the Indians. I want as few witnesses as possible."

There was a strong hint of antagonism in the statement.

"I don't give a damn about what you want. It's what I want that counts. An' I'm stopping to pick up payin' passengers."

"How do you know there will be any?"

"Heard about 'em in Saint Louie."

"Let some other boat stop. We have important business –"

Blue jerked angrily around and puffed out his chest. Though a head shorter than Kress, the redhead was a match for a grizzly bear.

"I never pass up a chance to make some easy money. Never. Got it? This is my boat an' I'll stop when an' where I please. Got it?"

The Famous Author backed down.

You get what you pay for.

No reputable captain would have accepted his commission. It was a bitter tonic to swallow. He was accustomed to working with honorable men.

Opposites, so a student of natural and experimental philosophy would explain, attracted.

A crowd had already gathered as the *Blue Moon* sailed into harbor and her ropes were thrown shore-side. Walking to the ramp leading to the wharf, the captain shaded his eyes with his hand and stared out into the sea of faces.

Blue's gesture had all the appearance of a man looking for someone or something specific; a familiar face, a wave of welcome, a friendly shouted "Hello!" His eyes roved over the faces, then adjusted to stare beyond them into town. His expression remained unchanged. When he finally dropped his hand, he gave the impression of being disappointed.

Another bit of play acting, for he was not disappointed. In fact, he was pleased.

Although, perhaps, relieved might be a better word.

Moon did not want to see any faces he knew, did not wish to recognize or be recognized. Had he a price on his head, these sentiments might be understandable. The fact he was not a wanted man made his actions stand out. Another peculiarity of Blue Moon's.

Part of the legend.

"Leaving in an hour!" he called to the waiting passengers. "Step up and buy your tickets now or wait until the next boat comes by." So saying, he turned to his mate and asked in a louder, though slightly conspiratorial tone, "What did they say in Saint Louie? The *How Come* was due up this way next month?"

"If then," the officer agreed, shrugging his shoulders. "I heard her boiler was on its last legs. If that goes, she may never get this far."

"No problem." Blue brushed aside the carefully staged objection. "She's well insured. I hear."

The men on shore pressed closer in on one another. No one wanted to wait a month for a boat ready to explode beneath their feet.

Fifteen men pushed and shoved their way aboard, pressing their coins into the mate's hands. Blue stood aside, watching the proceedings with a wary eye. Giving the appearance of a man disinterested, he was anything but that. In truth, he was acutely interested in who came aboard the *Blue Moon.*

"Hold it!" he yelled, startling the tall, gaunt man dressed in buckskin. Next in line, this stranger had his money out, when the shout arrested him. Turning only a pair of black eyes toward the speaker, he hesitated.

"Not you," the captain said, dismissing him. "The fella behind you."

In truth, there was a woman immediately behind the tall man. She raised her head and stared at the boat owner. It was only this movement which finally caught his eyes, for she was diminutive in stature, completely dwarfed by he who stood before her.

"This is my servant," the tall man explained. His voice was deep, marked with a dialect Blue did not immediately place. "She will be no trouble. She can sleep below," he added, if he had in some manner offended the captain's morality.

Momentarily startled, Blue drew back his head. The man seemed vaguely familiar to him but he could not place when or if he had actually met him before.

Nor could he identify the woman's nationality. In that more pressing puzzle, he put aside the first. Her complexion was neither white, nor red, though her hair was jet black and her features finely chiseled. Her age was un-guessable, though she was not old.

"Where are you from?" Blue demanded.

He had never seen a woman like her. Dressed in a dirty yellow shirt which hung to her knees, she wore black trousers and what he guessed were   slippers.

"She's a Chinese," her master informed the captain.

"What's that?"

"From China."

"China," he knew, meant expensive table settings. He frowned, suspecting the man of mocking him.

"Off you go," he ordered. The tall man with black eyes squared his shoulders, then reached into his pocket and removed several more gold coins.

"I will pay twice her fare."

"Don't want no Injuns aboard."

When his objection became clear, the master shook his head.

"She is not an Injun."

"She looks like an Injun."

The woman took a step forward and made a slight bow to the captain.

"China, sir" she spoke in perfect English, "Is a country beyond the sea. I was born there and brought to this country many years ago. I have no Indian blood."

He squinted, taking in the slant of her eyes, the female figure just discernible beneath the loose-fitting shirt. She did not sound like an Indian.

"Fine. Fine." He dismissed them both with a curt, axe-like jab of his hand. "You," he continued, pointing to the man standing behind her. "You're an Injun. Off the boat. I don't give passage to Injuns."

"He's tame enough," protested the man with black eyes.

"There's no such thing as a tame Injun. Off."

The Indian gave Blue a cutting glance, then moved out of line. No further passengers were taken aboard until he had stepped onto the ramp and walked back to solid earth. With his departure, the rest paid their fee and crowded aboard.

Within the requisite hour, the *Blue Moon* took aboard twenty-three men and one "China." When no one else remained in line, the bell was rung and the boat pulled away.

Not until the riverboat was well distant from shore did Blue's partner approach.

"What's wrong with Indians?" he inquired.

"Don't want any aboard."

"We're going upstream to deal with them. Your attitude may prove dangerous."

Blue made an obscene gesture with his hand then shook his head.

"Don't worry aboot me. You do all the tradin' you want. Sell 'em guns and licker. I don't care. Just don't invite 'em aboard."

"Will you go on shore with me to deal with them?"

"The hell I will. That weren't part of the deal. My job, as you so recently reminded me, was to git you upriver with cargo intact. What you do or don't do with them damn Injuns if your affair."

"What do you have against Indians?"

"Nothin' I don't have against the rest of mankind."

Kress picked at a mosquito bite, debating whether or not to pursue the subject.

"You are – known – where we are going?" he finally asked. Blue gave him a hard stare.

"I told you. Never been up this way before."

The story, it appeared, changed with the wind.

"Then how will you navigate?"

"With my eyes. And my maps."

It was all the answer he was going to get. Kress nodded and moved away, disturbed and annoyed.

He was not sure who he despised more – liars or cheats.

Unfortunately for him, the man he hired and upon whom his life depended, appeared to be both.

CHAPTER 17

Blue spent a restless night in his cabin. Memories disturbed his sleep and he did not fall into a slumber until near dawn.

Dawn was the time men died and hearts broke, which were not necessarily the same thing.

He dreamed he was a boy. Blue could not see his body, but knew his age to be under ten years, by the feel of his hair on his naked shoulders. Worn Indian-style, the locks caught the sunlight, casting a red glow around his face, like an aura.

He remembered, now. It was his birthday, because Hatchet Nose, chief of the Fox, had told him so. There had been great excitement building for weeks around this event. There would be a celebration. Food. Dance. A gathering of the clans.

Once mortal enemies, the Fox, Sauk and Chickasaw had learned that fighting each other only made them weaker when it came to fighting their real enemies: the white man.

This new enemy was insidious. He came with weapons which killed with invisible arrows, boats which belched fire, and whistles which scared the game away within a ten mile radius.

This enemy spoke in a strange tongue, pantomimed promises of great treasure and smiled when stealing furs and land away from those who should have had first and last claim to it.

"Sell us the rights to your hunting grounds," these pale-skinned men demanded. "We will give you food to feed the hungry; we will provide tobacco weed and fire water for the braves and beads and sewing needles for the squaws."

"Trust us or we will kill you," they meant.

That kind of threat required an army of blue-uniformed soldiers to back it up.

To hope for victory against such odds, the natives placed their faith in ineffectual arrows, purloined guns and a Boy of Legend to lead the Red Men in triumph against the White.

The Medicine Man, an old, withered, skeletal man, held out a bony hand and placed it atop Blue's head. Appearances to the contrary, it felt as though it weighed twenty pounds. Blue held still, for so he had been taught.

When the Medicine Man read prophesy, all braves, young and old, remained motionless.

Easier for them. They were in a circle around the old man and the young boy. Easy for them, for it was not their eyes the Teller of Tales was looking into.

"It has been foretold," the Ancient One began. His voice quivered with righteousness. "That a boy would come to us. A boy not of our blood. A boy with red hair.

"A boy with the pattern of stars imprinted on his face."

The Medicine Man pointed to Blue's freckles. His fingernails were long and sharp. There was no love, no affection in his words or in his gestures. He did not speak directly to Blue. That was forbidden. The boy was treated as though he were a captive wolf cub or a lucky stone. Blue understood well, for he had been treated as an outsider, as something not human, not Indian, for as long as he could remember.

Other boys had mothers to soothe their hurts; fathers to teach them hunting; brothers and friends before whom they could display courage. Blue had no one. Before he knew his name, he understood he was an outcast. He alone, of all the people in his limited universe, had no one.

And no one had him. He was passed from tribe to tribe, each feeding and sheltering the boy, yet none caring for him, none speaking to him. Not once in his life had an Indian question put to him, or directed a kind word his way. He was not even verbally chastised for bad behavior. A cuff to the ears, a blow with the back of the hand, served as communication enough.

As he grew, Blue learned language. No one taught him. He picked it up by observing others. When still a baby, he had tried to practice his new-found skills as he saw the other children doing. They were praised, encouraged He was ignored. He might not have existed, save for the ever-present eye of a warrior following him like a second shadow.

Do not speak to the red-haired boy, do not love him, do not include him in your games, your family circle. But do not lose him. Keep him close.

He was a valuable cur on an invisible tether.

As a child, Blue Moon cried himself to sleep with no one to hold his thin, shaking limbs. He called piteously in his sleep and none came to chase away the nighttime frights. He whispered and no one heard. He shouted and everyone ignored.

He threatened to escape and the invisible tether tightened.

And so he learned. Cruelty and violence were his tutors. Earthquake and comet his inhuman, unloving family.

He came to know hatred. It was his substitute for love.

He developed a craving for freedom. It was his chance at life.

Blue Moon did not know what "freedom" was, or where to find it. He would look. To seek was in his nature. If it meant going "downriver," by following the current, that is what he would do.

As he aged from timid toddler to brave walker, he made his plans. He hoarded bits of dried beef. He found a knife and kept it. Over the course of long, lonely days, he taught himself to throw that knife until he possessed the skill to put it in an enemy's throat at thirty paces.

An Enemy became anyone who tried to prevent him from finding Freedom.

He did not care whether or not the Indians were saved. His understanding was, at best, confusing. They needed him, yet saw to it he did not need them. He could have loved them, for Blue had a big heart. He needed affection; craved the comfort of a kind word and did not get it, until he would have settled for an approving nod of the head.

Even that was deprived him. So he was not even a wolf cub, for the Indian respected nature and would not have held such an animal, born of wild and wilderness, against its will. The Indian revered strength, courage, loyalty, cunning. Blue had all those traits. In his nearly ten years, he cultivated the wisdom of age and that was not enough.

It was an oversight. The gods had forgotten to tell the mortals the entire story. Or perhaps they did and no one understood. It was ironic. The Indians prayed to gods who did not hear. Blue pleaded to his Indian family and did not receive.

Give a dog a bad name, you might as well shoot him. Raise a child without love, do not look for redemption from that tortured spirit.

The Medicine Man was still chanting. Blue did not bother listening. It was nothing to him. He was biding his time.

"Freedom," he whispered to himself. "I will have freedom." The time was near. He could feel it in his bones. The same kind of bones the Medicine Men kept in bags and tossed on the ground to read fortunes.

One of the chiefs was speaking. It was part of the celebration.

"The gods have told the Old Ones and the Old Ones have whispered to us. When the Red Man has lost his way; when he has lost his hunting grounds to a great and powerful enemy, a child will come to lead us in great battle."

The red universe of the Upper Mississippi held its breath while the chief made his pronouncement.

"This is the child. The boy of earthquake and comet. The boy without earthly parents. The boy who shall be friends to no man and no man shall be a friend to this boy. He is alone. Destined to walk the earth in a solitary path. Waiting for his time. His time is soon."

The Old One turned and faced the gathering.

"Has the girl child been found?"

There was a moment of profound silence before a Chickasaw chief spoke.

"She has been found."

The Chief nodded and turned to the Medicine Man. The Old Ones had told of a red-haired boy and a dark-skinned girl. The boy would lead the warriors of the Fox and Chickasaw and Sauk in battle. The great war would take years. Many would die. The boy would grow to manhood. He would receive a terrible wound; a wound of death. Before his spirit passed from earth, he and the girl, who was not a squaw, would be united. As a parting gift from the gods.

Blue, the child, did not comprehend the enormity of his situation. He saw only that he was unloved, an outcast. It would do him no good, and do great harm to this girl, if they were "united."

He therefore resolved, for the five-hundredth time in his young life, to escape.

Always before he had been tracked down like a dog, or a captive wolf cub, and brought back.

Each time, the collar had tightened.

He did not think it would be long before that collar choked him to death. He did not want to die, nor could he endure his life. Without an Old One to ask, without even one ear attuned to his cries, he consulted his bones. They were itching for action, not rightfully called adventure.

He would stand free or he would perish in the attempt.

One chance to live the life someone who was not of earthquake and comet had wanted for him.

That was Blue's terrible secret; the mystery which had been revealed to him and which sustained him. It was a mystery cloaked in the hard, cold stone of a cameo broach.

Blue Moon did not know the word "cameo" and he did not know the meaning of "broach." He did, however, have a strong sense of need for the word "mother." He never had a flesh and blood mother; at least none he remembered. It was a trapper who had told him. More words. But these words were chiseled in his heart. A heart now quite as cold and hard as that stone from which the cameo had been carved.

"She's yer mother, boy," the trapper had said. The news was so revelatory, Blue had nearly caved under the enormity of it.

"My mother? My mother was a comet."

It was a weak protest, at best. It was all he knew to say.

"That's Injun talk, Red. Ain't no man which got a comet fer a mother an' an earthquake fer a pappy. Yer a boy and a boy's got flesh an' blood parents. You was made by a man an' a woman."

Blue shook his head slowly, afraid to believe. Belief was such a precious thing. Once shattered, the bits and pieces of the believer were scattered to the four winds, never to be resurrected into one whole human being again.

Blue did not know whether to lend credence to what the said trapper or not. It was difficult enough to comprehend a human being speaking to him, let alone speaking truth about his mother. Had the trapper been caught in the act, he would have left the encampment without a tongue. And without that other appendage which separates man from half the other beasts of the forest and all the cooking fires.

"That there is yer ma," the lanky, bearded man explained. "I know some of her story; don't know it all. She and yer pa came on a great big steamboat; you know the kind. You seen 'em on the river. The kind what has a fire in its belly."

Blue Moon did indeed know the kind. Steamboats were a great source of power. They floated upon the Great River, bringing food and strange-looking men. Men the Indians feared. Steamboats, therefore, were wondrous monsters.

"They was the first to bring riverboats to the Mississip'. You was born on that riverboat. It were called the *New Orleans*. The Injuns, they snuck aboard and took you frum 'em. You know what a 'prophesy' is, Moon?"

Moon shook his head. The locks of his fire-red hair rustled from the slight movement.

"I shouldn't be tellin' you this, I guess. But it ain't right, the way they treat you."

The trapper was speaking in the language of the Fox. His command of the vocabulary was no better than fair, and the boy understood only little of what he said.

Little was enough.

"They'd been waitin' a long time." He counted on his fingers. "They was lookin' fer three signs: the first bein' the second full moon in a month. That didn't make no sense to them 'cause they dicn't keep time like the whites. It was one of them holy rollers what explained it an' after that, they kept track. The second was fer the earth to shake like it was gonna bust apart an' the third was fer a star to fly across the neavens. That'd announce the birth of a boy. A savior, you might say. A boy with red hair who cume from afar."

He spit out a stream of tobaccee juice and wiped his mouth with the back of his hand before continuing.

"Them Injuns – those frum all the tribes, each one knowin' the story – was watching that great monster what belched the black smoke an' when the saw the last sign, they swum aboard. An' there they found you." He signed at the heathen prophesy but it was clear he was more frightened than his disbelief would indicate. "You're to grow up and save them from yer own kind. What do you think of that, Red?"

The white boy called "Red" did not have an answer. He did not know what to think.

"I reckon," the trapper continued, "that if I was you, I'd hightail it outta here."

"Take me with you."

It was as close to begging as the boy baptized Blue Moon knew how to come. He was unused to expressing his sentiments with speech. It was, perhaps, his unfamiliarity with pleading that caused the trapper to refuse his request.

"Can't be done, son. Them Injun's 'id come after us. They'd find us an' take you back. Ain't no man on the river brave enough to take you away."

The sentence was long and confusing. But even a child without language understood a denial when he heard one. Tears came to his eyes.

"Don't cry, boy. Don't never show no weakness. Not to them Injuns. Not to no man. You remember that."

The trapper left the next morning. Blue never saw him again. But the damage, if such it was, had been done.

Damage was a lot like Belief.

Blue Moon's chance had come after the celebration of his tenth birthday. Because no one ever spoke to him and because he was not allowed to speak, the slight, red-headed boy was easily overlooked. While the braves danced and the Medicine Men prayed, he slipped away. As integral as he was to their plans for the future, his present was inconsequential.

It was a concept, if not a word, with which he was well familiar. On the night of his birthday, it served him in good stead.

He went to the river, to the waters of the Mighty Mississippi. He knew that if he entered the rapidly swirling river, he would leave no tracks for the warriors to follow. He was a keen observer. No one had taught him to swim, but he possessed the skill. An unknown gift from his captors.

It was late October and the water was cold. It chilled him to the bone, yet he dared not leave its comforting protection. If a riverboat could float on the water, so, too, could a boy born on one.

His association between "riverboat" and "boy" was not clear. While a vessel was built of wood and metal, he was constructed flesh and bone. It made no difference. He was afloat, he was away.

With starvation came fire in his belly.

Blue Moon did not complain. It was a link. A tie to something. A boat, he believed, could love. An Indian, he knew, could not.

Blue Moon swam and came close to drowning as his tiny boy's body was whipped cruelly in the freezing, swirling water. His senses numbed and he thought this was good. He did not cry, remembering the trapper's words.

On the morning of the third day, his head was struck by a partially submerged tree branch. His world went dark and his head went under the water. When he tried to breathe, water filled his lungs. He struggled, flailed his useless limbs, submerged again. His world became water and the water frightened him. It drew him toward the bottom, held him down.

It was death come calling. Like the visiting Medicine Men; like the tribes who passed him from unfeeling hand to hand. Like the trapper. Another type of invisible collar was placed around his throat. This one, like the others, choked him. He fought. He was a fighter.

His small, strong fingers grasped hold of the tree trunk and threw themselves around it. There was no warmth there, only solid wood. It was a familiar sensation. He clung to the tree for dear life. He held his heavy head above water. The Mighty River carried him away.

He held onto the tree and hid in the water. The braves came. He saw them on shore. They did not see him. He was a boy of the river. It was a lesson.

Blue Moon was a fast learner.

When the tree trunk finally snagged on a sandbar, Blue did not have the strength to crawl away. He curled up to the dead tree, his arms wrapped tightly around the rough bark.

He knew no more.

"It's a white boy!"

The voice was foreign, speaking in a language Blue Moon did not know. He struggled when his arms were pried loose from his protector, the tree.

"He's half drowned, half starved!"

"God be praised."

It was as well Blue did not comprehend what they were saying.

The men wrapped him in a dark blue blanket and took him away. When he awoke again, he was inside a soldier's fort. A man in a dark blue uniform was staring at him. He spoke. The wonder was, he spoke *to* Blue. Blue did not respond. He thought he was being fooled with.

He was well familiar with that kind of torture.

A cup of something hot was pressed to his lips. He did not want to drink. He had enough river water in him to float a riverboat. The broth dripped from his clamped lips. The man's hand struck him in the face. Blue's jaws sprung open and the soup was dribbled into his mouth.

He swallowed it and vomited. He was beaten for his trouble.

When Blue was strong enough to work, the soldiers taught him English and how to chop wood. He earned his keep and kept his tongue. They were rough men who did not understand silent boys. They had never been boys themselves.

He stayed in the fort for the winter and never spoke a word. In spring, he was sold to missionaries. He was used to being sold. He did not complain.

The men of God educated him in the ways of civilization. They, too, were rough men, cut from a different cloth.

What they taught him was cruelty of a different sort. They were lonely men and he was a boy. Blue Moon learned well the ways and passions of beasts. Without knowing the word, he was a walking encyclopedia of knowledge.

The missionaries knew of a red-haired boy who had escaped from the savages. He was their ticket to converting the heathens. Blue Moon stayed with them for the summer and fall. When he heard them talk of bringing him back "upriver," he took his Indian knife and stabbed the point of the carefully honed blade into one of the men's throats.

As Moon escaped into the night, he spoke the only sentence he ever uttered during his captivity.

"Go to hell."

They had succeeded in making him a Christian.

"Captain."

Captain Blue Moon broke from his keen observation of the shore and scowled at his crewman. Hansen touched hand to cap in an apologetic manner.

"What is it?"

Whether the owner of the *Blue Moon* was informed the aft cabin was on fire, or a chest containing treasure had been found on the river bed, Hansen would have gotten the exact same response, in exactly the same tone of voice.

Silence spoke louder than words. It was a lesson learned in childhood.

"The men below are complaining," Hansen continued. He was used to his captain's quiet ways.

Blue shrugged. It was an effort to speak. Had he not been on the deck of his own boat, he would not have uttered one word. But he was on the deck of his own boat, and that gave him cause.

"The sun comes up, men complain. The sun goes down, men complain. Complaining is human nature. What do you expect me to do about it?"

The lieutenant shifted his weight from one leg to the other. He stood at so lopsided an angle, he appeared to live in a continual storm, where one side of his body was buffeted by wind, the other unaffected.

"They don't like the Injun."

Sun rising and setting not withstanding, the word "Injun" caught his attention. Blue's eyes narrowed into slits and his hands clenched.

"What Injun? Didn't know there was one aboard."

"That female – the one in the long shirt and trousers."

The tension sapped out of the captain, although his hands remained clenched.

"She's not an Injun. She's a China."

"She looks like an Injun."

Blue shrugged.

"What do they want me to do aboot it? Paint her face white?"

His words were guarded, however and his suspicions aroused. She *did* look like an Injun. He silently cursed himself for allowing her to board. First instincts were always right.

"It ain't that..."

"Then what is it?"

"She's... doing things."

Blue blinked at the absurdity of the statement. When the season was over, he reminded himself, he would dismiss the entire crew, Hansen included.

"Doing what?"

"She smells."

"Justifiable homicide" were the words running through his mind.

"So do you. So do I, for that matter. Do you hear me complain?"

"No, sir."

"Breathe through your mouth."

He turned away as the man spoke once more.

"She's burnin' somethin' down there in the hold. That's what smells."

"Dog meat," Blue scoffed.

"It ain't somethin' to eat. She's workin' magic."

The last words were spoken in a whisper. Captain Moon bit his lower lip, then nodded stiffly.

"I'll look into it."

"Thank you, sir." Then, afraid the captain would not keep his word, Hansen added, "Wouldn't want her to conjure no spirits ag'in you."

The tactic worked. Blue left his post and descended the companionway, hopping the last three steps to the bottom.

It did not take more than one deep breath through his nose to confirm Hansen's statement. Something *was* burning. The odor was sharp and vaguely familiar, bringing to mind the New Orleans gypsy and her "cure." By the time he located the "China" and had made his way past mislabeled crates and stray trunks belonging to passengers, Blue was sweating profusely.

Not from physical exercise.

"What are you doing?" he demanded. She was hunched over a small figure, apparently tending a fire of some sort within a cavity of the doll.

The woman looked up and smiled. Her reaction was not what he expected, causing him to recoil.

"Hello," she greeted him.

"Never mind, 'hello.' What are you doing?"

"Praying."

He would rather she had said, "Throwing a curse." That, at least, he would have understood.

"Well, don't burn anything while you're saying yer prayers. You might set the boat on fire."

"There is no chance of that. See?"

She withdrew slightly, giving him a better look at the figure carved in stone.

"There is no flame. This is incense."

"In-sense, or outta-sense, it smells. The men don't like it."

"I am sorry. I did not mean to offend."

"Well, you are."

"Would it be all right if I move? Continue my prayers somewhere they would not be disturbed? Outside, perhaps?"

"Not on deck. You'll have the whole damn boat in arms." He looked around, then shrugged. "Past there you can get to an open area. Go there, if you want. And don't be makin' any noise, either," he warned. "I don't want any chanting or yellin' going on. Makes people nervous."

"I pray silently."

"You'll never git to heaven that way," he scoffed, watching with interest as she gathered the stone figure in her hands, cradling it lovingly. "What is it, anyway? I've known enough preachers to tell that ain't Jesus."

"It is Buddha."

"Buddha? Never heard of him. He ain't no Injun god, is he?"

She turned her back on him before answering.

"You know he is not."

Instantly rankled, Blue followed her, stiff-legged, as she made her way toward the back.

"Why would I know any such thing?"

"You have never heard of an Indian god named Buddha."

She spoke with a statement, rather than a question, further annoying him.

"I am hardly an expert on Injun gods." She made no reply. He tried again. "The only thing I know about Injuns is that I don't like them."

Reaching the open space looking out upon the river, the woman set the figure down and turned back. She was smiling. It was not a sarcastic smile, nor was it superior. Instead, her expression was one of compassion and gentle wisdom.

"There is a legend," she began, choosing her words carefully. "That if anyone touches a piece of straw or prairie grass to the head of a man with red hair, it will burn. Is that true?"

"Never heard it." He lied badly.

"There is a legend —"

"I do not want to hear it!"

The horrors of his youth were being resurrected, word by word, into a powerful fear.

"The Indians whisper among themselves of a prophesy. Of a boy with red hair who has come to get back the lands they so foolishly sold away. A boy grown to manhood who will defeat their enemies."

"I never knew no Injun with red hair," he stubbornly replied. "I guess they'll have a long wait."

"I did not say the boy was an Indian."

"Why would anyone want to save the Injuns?"

"I did not say he *wanted* to save the Indians."

Blue's world grew small and confined. His head swam with memories. Forgetting to breathe, a wave of dizziness overwhelmed him, causing him to topple, suddenly, against a bulkhead. The woman made no move to help. He cursed as he straightened.

"You *are* an Injun!" he cried in agonized desperation.

Before the plan was half formed in his mind, Blue reached out and grabbed the woman by the loose clothing of her tunic. Shaking her with all the strength he possessed, he cast her back with one hand, while retaining a grip with the other around her neck.

"I'll throw you overboard." She made no effort to extricate herself. "I ain't that boy. Do you hear me? I never heard that legend. I don't believe it! Why are you telling me this? Explain yourself!"

She could not talk while he held his fingers pressed into her larynx, finally compelling him to loosen his grasp.

"I thought you might be interested," she replied with unruffled demeanor.

Her tone of voice implied more than her words.

"I ain't interested. I don't want to hear no more about it. I ain't that boy. I'm a man; a riverboat skipper. I don't know nuthin' aboot Injuns, legends or China, neither!"

"But you do know about blue moons," she replied softly.

He groaned and put his hands to his face.

"Leave me alone."

It was not an order, but a plea.

"You must not sell guns to the Indians."

This aroused a different type of emotion in his breast. His head snapped up. Baring his teeth, Blue recovered his equilibrium.

"I'm not on a trip to sell guns. I'm takin' an Explorer upriver to trade trinkets for beads and rattles. He's gonna write a book."

"Then why do you have two dozen crates filled with muskets?"

Startled, Blue swallowed the lump in his throat, dumbly shaking his head.

"That's not true. There are no muskets aboard."

She pointed to the crates.

"What is in those?"

"Pipes. Tobacco. Trading items."

"That man you speak of is a bad man. You know that. You should not be taking him upriver."

Blue cleared his throat and spat on the deck. It was past time to regain control of the situation. She had confused him with words and legends.

"I go where I please. I take whoever pays me. I bring cargo to trade." No answer.

"What is your name?" he suddenly demanded.

"Ching Lee."

"Miss Lee –"

"No," she said, correcting him. "Like you, Captain Blue Moon, I have no last name. Like you, I go by two names, neither of which is a family name."

"Why?"

"Because I am owned."

"By that man who brought you aboard?"

She nodded with a nearly imperceptible movement of her head.

"You be a slave?"

"Call it what you will. I would not argue with the word."

"How is it he came to own you?"

"He bought me from missionaries."

The word froze Blue. He remembered missionaries. It took effort to speak without thinking.

"Why?"

"I have many talents."

He blushed to the roots of his hair and did not understand why. She was nothing to him, be she slave or free.

"That is your affair, Ching Lee. This is my boat. Do not make your fires where men will be disturbed. Do not speak to me again. And hold your tongue," he added with emphasis. "I do not wish to hear you speak of muskets and Injuns. There is danger in your words."

"I understand what it is like not to speak. Or be spoken to. I will remember the warning – Blue Moon."

His lips curled into a sneer but the facial gesture did not reflect what was stirring in his heart. With a curt good bye, he turned and walked away, more confused than he had ever been in his life.

CHAPTER 18

Discharging and taking on passengers along the route, the *Blue Moon* diverted off the Mississippi, steaming down the well-traveled Fever River to Galena, four hundred miles above Saint Louis. Cursing the authorities for their high, unfavorable tariff which he paid with coin and complaint, Blue pulled Kress aside.

"This is where we buy the whisky," he said in an undertone. "There's upwards of forty stores here an' business has been off since the bastards messed with the riverboat fees. They need supplies as much as the Injuns do. If we have to, we'll trade some of the foodstuffs for what we want."

Kress nodded, only too glad to leave the bargaining to his not-so-silent partner.

"Be sure you get a good exchange."

Blue squinted at him from under red eyebrows.

"This is the last I do fer you. I said I'd get the whisky an' I will. After this, I'm not going ashore."

"Why not?"

"I have my reasons. An' one more thing," he warned in a voice not to be ignored. "There's nothin' I can do aboot the name of the boat, but once we git rid of these passengers, I don't want you callin' me 'Blue Moon' anymore."

Kress took an added interest in the conversation.

"Whatever you say," he agreed. The captain's words stirred the possibilities of blackmail in the Explorer's mind. If not that, then at least a bargaining tool. One he had an inkling he would need. "What shall I call you?"

"'Captain' will do."

"And your crew?"

"They will be told the same thing."

"How many passengers are remaining with us for the trip to Saint Paul?"

"We're not goin' nearly that far. Not fer what you want. There's Injuns aplenty who want whisky and guns long before we ever reach that city. Those from Black Hawk's War that don't appreciate havin' their homeland traded away. They'll give you what you want. And more you don't want, if you're not careful."

"How will we contact them?"

"They'll contact us. There's Injuns all aboot these waters. They see a steamboat, they'll follow it like a shadow."

"Is there danger they might use violence against us?"

Blue laughed.

"Does the Irish cause trouble? I thought you understood what you was askin' for."

"I – want to trade, fair and square."

Blue snorted, then wiped his nose with the back of his hand.

"Mister, there ain't no 'fair and square' when it comes to dealing with Injuns. Not now. Mebbe never. They know the white man fer what he is – a low-down liar and a cheat. They know you're out to steal them, and they know they're out to cheat you."

There was an awkward silence before Kress spoke again.

"You didn't answer my question. How many passengers are going north with us?"

"That tall man and the China. I may take a few on board here."

"Why?"

"As cover. If I say I'm goin' to Saint Paul and I got room, the authorities will wonder why I ain't taking on passengers."

"What will you do with them?"

If Blue did not know better, he would suspect Kress of having been born yesterday.

"Let 'em off."

"You mean – abandon them?"

"It's common practice. I'll say there's something wrong with the engine and it's too dangerous fer them to go farther with us. We drop 'em on the bank and go on our way. You do the tradin' you want and we come back. If they're still alive, we pick 'em back up. For a fee, of course."

"I see."

"I thought you might."

Pushing his way past the Great Indian Trader, Blue swung his lithe frame gracefully down the wooden planks and stepped into the lead mining town of Galena. With a growing population exceeding 10,000, this city on the Fever River catered to the lead mining trade.

Lead was the cash crop of the Upper Mississippi. The Indians had mined it first, long before white settlers knew the riches the land contained. As early as 1818, the Fox tribe was melting 400,000 pounds of the mineral annually.

By 1828, however, the rights to the lead district were purchased from the Indians for a cash price of $20,000. Continuing the traditions of the past, the United States government leased parcels of land in 160 acres increments, retaining one-tenth of all lead mined as their "share."

After the Black Hawk War of 1829, the losing Indians signed a treaty at Prairie du Chien, giving up the entire territory east of the Mississippi between the Rock and Wisconsin Rivers. This made overland travel safer and reopened the Mississippi to river trade.

Which was not to say the Indians had gone peacefully. They continued to lurk deep within the forests and along the river banks, hurting, trapping and occasionally fishing for Big Game.

Considered more of an economic nuisance, if not more dangerous to riverboat captains, were the high tariffs put in place after the War. A boat could not pull into any of the lead mining towns without paying for the privilege. Wharf taxes were common along western waterways, but these fees staggered even the most easygoing skippers.

The skippers threatened to bypass the lead towns altogether, but business was just too good. A boat bringing in supplies could return downriver filled to bursting with heavy lead cargo.

On the levees of Saint Louis, he could then sell it for almost any asking price.

Times changed fast and furiously. As more infantry and mounted dragoon soldiers were brought into the territories by the Great White Father in Washington, natives were forced further and further west. Steaming the river became less risky. Improvements in engines and navigation, and steamboat construction designed especially for the upriver trade, promised increased expansion.

With immigrants pouring in from the eastern states, Illinois, Wisconsin and Minnesota filled up. Land was cleared, crops planted, trapping and mining expanded. Without the constant threat of Indian attack, the United States fleshed out its boarders, drawing closer and closer to the elusive, "coast to coast" manifest destiny.

Blue had not been through Galena in years, though he had spoken to skippers who had. Forearmed with the names of several traders eager to do business, he worked his way through the inevitable throng of people coming to the wharf to see the newly arrived boat.

Gaping with wonder at the vast expanse of newly constructed shops, grog houses, warehouses, dry-goods stores and dwellings, the captain of the *Blue Moon* tarried only briefly to cover his tracks before getting on with business.

His initial fear of being recognized somewhat allayed by the newness of the town, Blue stepped into the two-story trading establishment of Cutter and Coulter. The store smelled of pickles, leather and hides.

"I'd like to speak to Mr. Coulter," he announced. "On a private matter."

This not being an unusual demand, the clerk directed the inquirer toward the back. He found the shop owner stacking crates.

"Mister Coulter, I was put onto you by a man in Saint Louie named Jack Dice."

Coulter, a rough-looking individual with a scar down his right cheek, paused from his labor to stare at the speaker.

"You come in off the steamboat?"

"That's right. I'm the skipper."

Coulter extended his hand and they shook.

"What can I do for you?"

Blue indicated with his head. They waked out a back door into a narrow alley.

"I want whisky."

"By it at a saloon."

"Barrels of it. As much as you can get me in a week."

"What for?"

"I'm opening up a drinkin' parlor."

"Where?"

"Upriver."

"I see. Might be a dangerous venture."

"So I've been told."

"The Salk are restless," the proprietor said, scratching his chin.

"Don't intend to stay long."

"Guess that's your business."

"Guess it is."

"I can git you fifty barrels at fifty dollars a barrel."

Two hundred and fifty dollars.

"Deal."

"Dilute the whisky with river water gives you one hundred barrels to sell."

Blue laughed and they shook hands, signifying acceptance of the deal.

"Bought them in Saint Louie."

"Just asking. No harm meant."

"No harm done."

Kress was pleased with the deal. He gladly gave Blue the three hundred dollars he demanded for the cost of the whisky, making it a good exchange all around.

CHAPTER 19

The Sauk Indians were restless.

That was the news the whisky dealer gave Blue.

Restless.

They were not the only ones.

Blue was restless to leave Galena, steam back down the Fever River and return to the Mississippi. While the project was progressing smoothly, Blue was jumpy. If they were to steam as far north as Kress wanted, the *Blue Moon* would have to pass by Prairie du Chien, where Black Hawk, the defeated Sauk leader, was brought by his captors, the Winnebago Indians.

Blue knew the Sauk tribe.

He knew the Fox tribe.

He even knew the Winnebago, who had sided with the other two tribes in 1831 to cause disturbances at Rock Island.

He could speak Chickasaw and Sioux, in addition to the aforementioned languages.

His English was not bad, either, considering how and where he had acquired it.

"Hurry up!" Moon ordered, standing on the levee and waving aboard the cargo of "Sweet Molasses." He debated what to have painted on the barrels, finally deciding the sloshing liquid of cheap red-eye whisky would never be mistaken for "flour," or "salt pork."

Molasses was the only liquid or semi-liquid substance he could think of which would not raise an eyebrow.

The fact he had just sold an entire cargo of molasses in Saint Louis before coming upriver was not questioned.

At least not aloud.

And certainly not to Captain Moon's face.

With the cargo stowed aboard, the passengers assigned cabins and the departure taxes paid, Blue shoved off with a feeling of relief.

He did not want to go north, yet he did not wish to stand by in Galena.

There were too many Indians, too many staring faces, accusatory glances.

He should not have gone ashore. He should have let Kress do his own hard bargaining.

Taking the risk of being recognized was not worth fifty dollars.

He should have told his partner the whisky came to four hundred dollars. That way, his profit would have come closer to matching the chance he took.

A man only profited from learning by his mistakes if he lived long enough to implement his new knowledge.

"Mister Hansen!"

"Sir?"

The lieutenant approached with some trepidation. The captain's mood was black. He did not wish to run afoul of it.

"From this point forward, until the end of this trip – until we return to Saint Louie," he added for emphasis, "I do not wished to be addressed as anything but 'Captain.' Not 'Captain Moon,' not 'Blue Moon.' Is that clear?"

It was as clear as it went.

"May I ask why, sir?"

"You may not." When the mate lingered, Blue dismissed him.

"Captain –"

Blue sighed and granted him one minutes more additional audience. The twitching in his jaws reflected his displeasure and his discomfiture.

"Does this alteration on your part have anything to do with that 'China'?"

Captain No-Name visibly relaxed.

"No. Why do you ask?" No reply. "Has she been causing trouble? Burning her incense where it bothers the crew?" No answer. "Well?" he demanded, hands on hips, balancing on the balls of his heels in an aggressive posture.

"The men don't like her."

"Tell the men to leave her alone!" Realizing he was shouting without need, Blue made a forced effort to lower his voice. "If everyone *I* didn't like were booted off this boat, I'd be sailing her alone, Mister Hansen. You can relay that message to the crew."

"Yes, sir."

Hansen saluted and departed.

For as long as he lived, the mate would never believe Captain Blue Moon had sung "Rock of Ages," from piety.

When the *Blue Moon* slipped from the Fever River back into the Mississippi and headed north, against the current, Blue made another trip to the boiler room. He critically observed the workings of the machinery, listened with an ear half-cocked to the sounds she made, then grunted his approval.

The engineer joined him.

"How much fuel do we have?" the captain asked. He could see for himself, there was no point in his questioning the engineer.

He did it to irritate the man.

"Enough," came the vague response.

Which was as much of an answer as he expected.

"I bought several crates of pine faggots in Galena. Did you get them?"

Scotty nodded, indicating with a shrug of his shoulder where the crates had been stored.

"If I give the order, I want you to use them. We may need the extra speed."

"Why?"

"I hear the Sauk are restless."

"It's gettin' to be a new moon."

"What does that mean?"

"New moons make Injuns restless."

Which was not what he meant at all.

"Keep yourself available. If we have to put on speed, I don't want the damn engines to blow. If they do..."

He cut himself just in time. There was no point stating the obvious.

"I take yer meanin'" Scott replied through clenched teeth. Whether he did or not was problematic. "Blue Moon."

Blue's brown eyes hardened into points of anger.

"I gave orders that name was not to be used during this trip."

"Jest so you know, Blue Moon."

"Jest so I know what?"

"Comes to it, I'll throw you overboard m'self to save this boat an' my own hide."

"Thanks for the warning."

Scotty smiled.

"I'm jest repeatin' what I heard from others."

"Go to hell!"

Because the engineer was blocking his retreat toward the main companionway, Blue continued along his open path, through the cargo hold. It meant nothing to him if he had to get topside through the bowels of the boat.

He did not give a damn.

If he had, it would have to remain a silent condemnation.

For now.

The captain was almost past the woman when she made a slight movement, catching his eye. Stopping in his tracks, hand on the hilt of his knife, ready for anything, he froze before identifying Ching Lee.

"Good morning, Captain." She addressed him with a shy smile.

He did not return it.

"Good morning." He looked around, the hair on the back of his neck still raised in anticipation of a fight. "Are you alone?"

"Yes." He took her answer at face value. "Why do you ask?"

Instead on answering, he stared at the paper she held in her hands.

"What are you doing?"

"Taking inventory."

"What do you mean?" There was more shock than harshness in his voice. "Inventory of what?"

"Of your cargo."

"The hell, you say."

"There are fifty barrels of whisky, marked 'molasses,' and as many empty barrels. So you can dilute the whisky and sell it as pure. Very clever although it is a common practice and will fool no one." She paused, expecting a protest and received none. "There are two dozen crates of muskets and four cases of ammunition."

"What of it?"

"There are two crates of 'trinkets,' several hogshead of tobacco and clay pipes."

"What I'm carrying as cargo on this vessel is none of your business." When she did not reply, a sudden realization swept over him, causing the color in his cheeks to rise in anger. "What is that man who owns you? An Indian agent? Is that why he's aboard? To spy on me?"

She shook her head.

"No. He is not an Indian agent."

"Why should I believe you?"

"You trusted me, when I said I was alone."

His flush deepened.

"Who is he, then?"

"A merchant."

"He didn't bring any cargo aboard."

"You mistake."

"I didn't see nuthin'."

"You have only your eyes to see with, Captain."

"What the hell does that mean?"

A small, quixotic smile played on her lips.

"It is said Orientals are inscrutable."

Blue shook his head in hopeless confusion. When she did not explain the word, he reached out and grabbed the inventory sheet from her hand.

"I don't want you messin' down here. That's good ol', plain English. If I find you messin' with my cargo, I'll put you ashore. Along with that damn merchant of yours."

"He is not mine; I am his."

"You know what I mean. Who *is* he?"

This time, she frowned slightly before answering.

"A man."

"What's his name?"

"I have never heard him called by a name."

"What do you call him?"

"I call him nothing."

It was an answer he could identify with. But it did not sate the gnawing which had been eating a hole in his belly since first laying eyes on him.

"Where do I know him from?"

"I cannot answer that. Not unless..." she began, then trailed off. "Not unless you let me look into your eyes."

"What good will that do?"

"I may be able to see... what you have forgotten."

"That don't make any sense. How could you see what I don't remember?"

"I have a gift."

"If I were you, I'd give it back. Be an Injun giver." He laughed at his own joke, then decided not to pursue the subject. "Did he tell you to make an accounting?"

"No."

"So why are you? And how'd you know there was whisky in them barrels?"

"I smelled the wood. I made careful observation. There was no spilled molasses around the tops."

"Ain't you one fer observin'. Leave 'em alone. I mean it. Knowing more than you should will get you in trouble. I'll put you overboard," he added, as a reminder.

"Weren't you planning on doing that anyway?"

He jumped back as though she had stung him.

"Who are you? How did you get the power to read minds?"

Again, the smile. He no longer needed a definition of the word "inscrutable."

"Yes. I'm gonna put you ashore, along with the rest of the passengers. Not here. Upriver a'ways. We're going to run aground. Into a sandbar. An' then I'm gonna forget to pick you back up before I steam off. Once my business is done, I'll come back for you."

He did not know why he was telling her his plans.

"It is a bad business."

He shrugged. He did not have to explain to her.

"Money is money."

"Do you believe that?"

"Yes."

To his utter amazement, she laughed. It was a light, tinkling sound, somewhere between joy and good humor.

Seeing no point in prolonging the conversation, he brushed past her and left, feeling confused, betrayed and ill.

It was the same illness he had felt when Mrs. Lang first put a spell on him.

That damned woman had cursed him for life.

He should have left her and her husband to rot. Teach him to do a good deed.

He would find some way to make her pay.

Which reminded him of the gypsy. When he returned to New Orleans, he would have words with her, too.

Returning topside, Blue frowned as he saw Kress and his lieutenant, Hansen, in whispered conversation. They were looking in the direction of the hold. Both turned and separated at his approach. There was an air of guilty conspiracy about their actions he did not like.

"Mister Hansen!"

"Sir?"

"I want a guard posted, watching the shore for signs of Injuns."

"Which Indians?" came the slow, indolent reply.

"Any Injuns. An Injun is an Injun. One can shoot as good as another."

His analogy struck immediate life into Hansen, causing Blue to form the impression the man was afraid of being shot.

"Good," the captain mumbled to himself. Then, louder, "You take the first watch. Four hours at a time. Port and starboard. Ask Mister Miller to stand opposite you."

"Yes, sir."

There was a sullenness in the mate's voice which had not been there before.

No Indian sightings were reported on the first shift. Blue took second watch, starboard side. His eyes scanned the passing landscape with an intenseness he dared not explain to himself.

He experienced the feeling a long-lost wanderer had when returning to his birthplace after many years absence. Excitement, fear, suspicion, anticipation. Much had changed. The river had broadened beyond his child's memory. There were more trees. The surrounding forests seemed thicker, denser. Even the flowing noises the Mississippi made as it gurgled past the bow were ominous.

Once, he had looked out upon the Great River and dreamed of escape. How, he was heeding another call. One as strong and infinitely older:

The summons Home.

It did not matter whether that home was warm with welcome, or cold from bitter memories. No man knew his end, but most had some awareness of their beginning.

Blue Moon was a child of the river, a product, or so he was told, and so he believed, of the god of earth and the god of night sky.

Earthquake and comet.

Not a father and mother he could hold to his bosom or be cherished by, but an orphan, devoid of human companionship.

He was born under the blue moon, stolen from a boat of steam and fire, suckled by the Chickasaw, nurtured by the Sauk, raised by the Fox.

All cycles go in threes. So the Indians said and so the white men preached.

Earthquake, comet, blue moon.

The Holy Trinity.

He was not an Indian.

He was an Indian legend.

For two days and two nights the river was as quiet as the grave. No sign of Indians; no passing steamboats, no floating barges. He saw and had reported to him no suspicious noises, no wisps of campfire smoke, no telltale tracks by the banks.

For all the world, the red men had abandoned their lands and gone further west.

The *Blue Moon* put in at a small trading post, took on wood and water, left several of their passengers. Blue hoped the tall man with black eyes and his charge would disembark, but they did not. When he asked them again how far they were going, the master would only smile.

"To the end of the line."

"I'm not going that much higher up," he was informed.

"I'll know the place when I get there."

The tall man, too, spent time scanning the shore. As attentive, if not as intense as Blue, he watched with the eyes of someone who courted trouble and anticipated great profit.

For whatever he was selling.

"I think I'll put the passengers off around the next bend," Blue confided to Kress. "It's too quiet. I don't like it. There's Injuns around. I kin smell them."

"Not just yet," his partner suggested. There was a casualness to his voice which immediately aroused the riverman's suspicions. Kress might be a Famous Author, but he was a Poor Liar.

One would not have thought they were mutually exclusive.

"Why not? You were the one who didn't want any witnesses around. I think you should be glad we're well shed of them."

"Oh, I will be," Kress agreed.

"Then why not put 'em off here?"

Kress waved a noncommittal hand.

"The tall passenger – he plays a good game of chess. I will miss his company when he goes. It passes the time," he added.

Which did not make the falsehood of his statement wash any cleaner.

Blue almost let it pass. But not quite. He had not survived twenty-three years without developing the skills of self-preservation.

"We'll put the others ashore, then. And the woman. The China."

Kress yawned, which nearly got him a mouthful of river water.

"He won't let her off. He keeps a close eye on her."

"Why?"

"She... has some sentimental value to him."

For which Blue took to understand he was using her for dirty purposes. His fists clenched.

"He better not be doin' that aboard this boat."

"Doing what?"

"You know what I mean."

Blue spat into the river to underscore his objection.

"The man is a gentleman. You mistook my meaning."

Which reassured Blue about as much as a boiler bursting.

He should have kept better watch over that stranger. He would do so in future.

He would keep an eye on the Great Explorer, as well. The jury was still out on the "great" part, but he sure as blue blazes was no gentleman. If Kress was playing games with the tall man, they had set up some deal of their own.

One which did not include the steamboat captain.

Blue was asleep in his cabin when the call came. He had not been resting well, getting no more than a catnap at any one time since they left Galena. He had just begun to dream when aroused by a shrill yelp of alarm. Leaping fully clothed from his bunk, the captain reached the upper deck before the last echoes had died away.

"What is it?" But he did not have to ask.

A small party of Indians stood on shore. It was an hour past dawn. The early morning shadows obscured their numbers but not their intent.

"I make out six," Miller whispered. "Them's Sioux."

"Them's Fox," Blue corrected. "And as fierce a tribe as ever lived. Get Kress up here."

The order was carried out and the Trader met his partner on deck. There was a look of wild excitement in his eyes.

"Here?" he whispered, though there was little chance of his voice carrying as far as shore. "Now?"

"No. Upstream."

"Why?"

"Never meet an Injun on his own huntin' ground. Make 'em come to yours."

"Will they follow us?"

"It's Irish," Blue snapped, meaning the Indians would follow them with the certainty of death following life. "We'll let the rest of the passengers off here."

"No."

"Don't tell me —"

Kress held up his hands in an act of surrender. In another it might have been contrition, but there was no possibility of mistake in this case.

"Captain, please. I meant no disrespect. Merely that a drastic act now would naturally raise suspicions, not only with the passengers but amongst the crew."

Blue was not pacified. He paced away from the man, shaking his head.

"Bad business. Bad business," he muttered. When he turned back to the Famous Writer, his mind was made up. "We're going back," he announced.

"Back? Back, where? To Galena?"

"Back to Natchez."

"We have a deal."

"To hell with our deal. It stinks. It's rotten. I don't want to sell guns and whisky to the damn Injuns."

"Lower your voice!"

"Those damn Fox out there. See 'em? Know what whisky'll do to them? Even watered down whisky? It makes 'em crazy. Fire water. That's what they call it. They get drunk on fire water and they'll take those muskets and start another war. It'll end the same way their last war ended. In bloodshed." The muscles in his jaw shook. "Ask Black Hawk. He'll tell you. The Great White Father in Washington can't be beaten. But he sure as hell can punish. Maybe I don't want to see no more Injuns getting punished. Mebbe there's been enough punishment."

Blue was not through speaking, or at least he did not think he was. The hard, unmistakable feel of a gun barrel between his shoulder blades convinced him otherwise.

"Don't move, boy."

It was then he recognized the voice. He had been trying to identify the sound through a man's ears, when he should have been listening through those of a child's. If it were physically possible, his heart would have sunk through the floor boards.

"I remember you," he hissed in hushed tones. "It took me all this time, but I remember. What happened to your partner?" There was a leer to the question.

"He died. Was he the first man in your illustrious career you ever killed, Blue Moon?"

"No."

"I didn't think so. You were too good with a knife."

"I had good teachers."

"So I was led to believe. Jonas should have been more careful. It cost me a lot of money."

"It cost him his life."

"They want you back, you know. Badly. Very badly. Things have not been going well for the Fox. They need some powerful magic to regain their lands from the white invaders. There is a prophesy. A legend. About a boy born of earthquake and falling star. A boy born on a terrible monster boat belching steam and fire." He paused before adding, "A boy with red hair."

A shout came from shore. As the man with black eyes turned his orbs to give a signal, Blue took his one chance. Without bothering to turn, he kicked back with his leg, striking Canfield a blow to the knee. He toppled but did not fall.

Spinning, then, with the agility of one taught from infancy, Blue grabbed the musket from his hand. Before he could straighten, however, he was struck from behind by another enemy. As his world turned as dark as the evil man's eyes, Blue looked upward into the grinning face of Andre Kress.

No longer a Famous Explorer but a Treacherous Traitor.

CHAPTER 20

"You slimy bastard. You river rat," Blue hissed through clenched teeth.

His hands were tied behind his back and he was propped up against the smokestack on deck. His eyes were bound with a black cloth. With careful maneuvering, he was able to push it back a quarter inch, allowing him to see through the lower portion of the blindfold.

He could not see Kress from his position, but sensed the man was near. There was an unmistakable stink in the air.

Kress confirmed his belief by walking into Blue's limited frame of vision.

"So, you finally wake, my friend."

"I ain't your friend, you dog."

"As you say."

"What are you going to do with me?"

"Exactly what I came to do – trade with the Indians."

"Trade – me?"

"You, as it turns out, are more profitable than any of the 'trinkets,' guns and whisky I brought."

"Who told you so?"

"Your old friend, Mr. Canfield."

"He's slime, too. I should have finished him when I had the chance."

"So you should have," Kress agreed.

"How'd you find out anything?"

"I told you. We played chess together. We came to... appreciate one another's strategies. His, it so happened, was better than mine."

"I don't know what you mean."

"I think you do. Mr. Canfield had one half the puzzle. I had the other. Not in hand, mind you, but as a partner. Quite a bit of luck, he and I meeting like this. He with one valuable commodity to trade to the Indians, I with another. Getting both together makes quite an attractive package. Their 'gods' will be pleased."

"You're crazy; out of your mind."

"Am I? I knew there was something about you. Some mystery. I just didn't believe the legend. When Mr. Canfield confirmed it for me, I knew. And so did he. He recognized you long before you placed him. Unfortunately for you." He smiled. "What will the Sauk and the Fox do with you?"

"You got the wrong man."

"Come, Blue Moon, The time for denial is past. You are the boy they seek. The boy born of earthquake and – what was it? Comet? Falling star? Fascinating, really. I wonder who your real parents were. Do you know?"

"Shut up!" Blue screamed, struggling wildly in his bonds.

"I suppose it doesn't matter," Kress continued, oblivious to the suffering of the man bound and blindfolded before him. "Although a bit of research ought to bring their names to light. Passengers on the *New Orleans,* weren't they?"

"You don't know anything!"

"When I get back, I may look it up. It must be a matter of record. And then, it was only twenty-three years ago. I imagine there must be people still alive who remember the incident. Perhaps even your parents. They might pay to discover what became of their stolen infant."

"Go to hell!"

"You might at least like to know what your last name is. I mean, a grown man ought not to go around calling himself 'Blue Moon.'"

"That's my name. There ain't nothing wrong with it!"

"Perhaps not. I suppose it suits you. Blue Moon: pale-faced redskin. Boy of 'Injun' legend." He laughed cruelly. Blue groaned and was glad, for the moment, his eyes were bandaged.

He would not tolerate Andre Kress seeing him cry for all his life.

"Kress!" It was Canfield calling. Blue heard the man walk away. "They want to see him. To be sure."

"All right. But not too close. Not until we finalize a deal."

The two traders came back and lifted Blue up. He struggled, kicked, nearly succeeded in breaking free before a heavy blow hit him from behind at the level of his right kidney. He stifled a cry and pitched forward. Without the ability to block his fall, he landed heavily on his face, exploding blood vessels in his nose.

He was dragged to his feet and the blindfold removed. Canfield laughed as he saw the blood.

"Drippy nose, little boy," he chided him, rubbing the black cloth under Blue's nostrils to wipe away the wetness.

"Go ahead and trade me," Blue spat, striking the man with a mouthful of red-tinged spittle. "The moment your back is turned, they'll knife you. Both of you."

"As if we hadn't thought of that," Canfield continued. "But I think not." He did not give Blue the opportunity for a rejoinder. "Not after they have been celebrating all night."

A cold chill began in the pit of Blue's stomach, traveling up his arms and down his legs.

"Don't sell 'em whisky," he begged.

"An odd request from a man who can upriver for that very reason." It was Kress' turn to smirk. "But put your mind at ease. We are not going to sell them whisky. We are going to give it to them. Undiluted, inasmuch as you failed to add river water to what we brought. No matter. They will be so drunk, none of them will think about coming after us – if, indeed, any have that idea – until we are long gone."

"If you trade me away, who'll pilot you down river? Going with the current, you'll pick up speed too fast. A man who don't know where the sandbars and the snags are will git you hung up."

"Mister Hansen has volunteered for the job."

"I don't believe you! I'm his captain. That's mutiny."

"He said he was doing it for Mrs. Lang, if I remember the name correctly."

"Sweet Jesus."

Reverend Holly would have been touched at the long-ago influence he had on the red-haired heathen.

It was a night for remembering and forging new partnerships.

The Indians on shore saw Blue being brought to the side of the boat and stiffened with anxiety. Their keen, piercing eyes examined the struggling man, judged, questioned among themselves, then finally one stepped forward.

"Blue Moon!" He called. "Blue Moon."

"The gentleman wants you to speak to him."

Canfield took the stock of his musket and jabbed the bound man in the ribs. Blue groaned with pain, struggled and cursed. For his trouble, he received a second blow, this one by Canfield's fist. He was struck under the left eye. Stars of tremendous yellow and white magnitude imploded in his brain.

"Halt!" the Indian ordered. His voice was controlled, yet reflected the tension of the moment. "No violence."

"You want him, you'll have to pay for him!" Canfield called. "You know our terms."

The Indian stepped back and whispered to his compatriots. There was much gesticulating, low-toned words of anger and warning. Finally, the leader stepped back toward the river to address the men on the *Blue Moon.*

"We will give you the furs and hides you ask."

"What about the other?" Kress shouted back.

Although his left eye was shut from swollen tissue, Blue did not fail to make out the Author's flushed face. He likened it to that of a dog whose master is withholding a bone.

He would not have put it past Kress to slobber.

"Headdresses, necklaces, knives, ceremorial items. I also wish the war bonnet and clothing Black Hawk wore into battle during his late war. His bow and arrows, his quiver, his feathered bonnet."

"No."

"You know what we want. We are not here to bargain. We have the red-haired boy who escaped from your tribes thirteen years ago. If you and your gods want him back, you will have to pay our asking price, or we kill him."

"Kill him and you are dead, white devil."

The tall man with the black eyes moved suddenly to his left, disappearing down the first three steps of the companionway leading to the hold. There, his slave and trading material had tacitly summoned him.

With a cupped hand around her mouth to hide her words from any but the ear intended, she spoke into Canfield's bowed head.

"I know those Indians. You must be very careful. They will kill all of you, if they can. That man Kress irritates them. Do not let him lead you down the path of destruction."

Her words were so soft, so affectionately spoken, the heart of her master was won over. He trusted Ching Lee. She had been his loyal slave for as long as he owned her. Knowledgeable on many subjects, he had utilized her as a man might use a black male slave. She bore the burden of his heavy work, performed the duties of a valet, ran and fetched, delivered goods and brought back gold and messages.

Given her master's confidence, Ching Lee had been granted limited freedom of movement. For this gift, she repaid her master by absorbing all knowledge which presented itself to her. Gifted in languages, she became his linguist. Skilled in the art of penmanship and ledger work, she slowly assumed the accountant duties associated with his various enterprises.

The other services she provided were not those a male slave would generally be compelled to give or receive.

"What do you suggest?"

Canfield knew Ching Lee well enough to know she had a solution to his problem, or she would not have spoken.

"I heard you speaking. I set out ten barrels of whisky. Let the Indians drink and grow careless. When their heads are in the clouds, you may get what you ask for and more, besides."

He gave a curt jerk of his head.

"I'll have the whisky brought up. Hide below."

She remained motionless.

Canfield returned to his partner with the beginnings of a smirk on his tight-skinned face. His thin lips were parted, revealing uneven teeth.

"We have what they want and they have what we want. I suggest a parlay."

"What do you mean?"

"A conversation."

Kress caught the drift.

"Over whisky and a smoke?"

"Exactly. I suggest we send ten barrels of 'fire water,' along with those pipes of yours and plenty of tobacco. Let them mellow a bit, then we go ashore and make a deal."

The Famous Author-turned-Riverboat Captain turned to his first lieutenant and gave the order.

"Bring up ten barrels of that molasses and a keg of tobacco. And some of that flour we brought. Let them make a meal off our generosity, have an evening to sit and smoke over full stomachs, then we trade. And then," he added, "we exonerate the good name of Mrs. Lang by handing over the man who took advantage of her."

If Hansen had doubts, Kress dispelled them.

"Yes, sir," he replied. He saw to it the orders were carried out. It was not a pleasant duty for him, but one he felt obliged to fulfill.

Let the legend of Blue Moon end as it began.

When the Indians were made aware that a good-will gesture was being sent ashore, they met the news with guarded optimism. They stayed well back as a small row boat drew away from the *Blue Moon* and was pulled toward the river bank. Sensing any overt action on their part would be cause for alarm, the red men watched but did not help the rivermen as they unloaded the gifts.

Only after the boat was back aboard the steamboat did they step out and inspect their treasures.

Camp fires were built, the tops of the kegs were broken into and cups were dipped into the precious liquid.

It would be a night to remember.

Kress and Canfield watched from the bow, keeping their bound prisoner close at hand.

"Why do they really want you back, Moon?" Canfield inquired, prodding the captain with the barrel of his musket. "Will they sacrifice you to their gods as an act of devotion?"

Blue remained silent.

"Why don't you tell the man?" Kress suggested. "If you tell an interesting story, perhaps I will immortalize you, as I did Hernando DeSoto. Where did you hide him, by the way? Not that it matters. I suppose any set of bones will do. After all, the ones we used weren't anything more than the remains of an old gimp Injun."

He laughed at his own joke.

"I'll come after you," Blue hissed through the blackness. In the gloom, his body was only vaguely outlined, giving his two listeners the eerie impression they were being spoken to by a disembodied spirit.

"This must be getting to me," Canfield confessed. "You are still flesh and blood, aren't you?"

When Blue did not answer, the man tried harder. "Remember how you gutted poor old Jonas with that Indian knife of yours? I'll never forget it. You were the coldest, most evil looking boy I ever did see. How was it you didn't finish me?"

"I was savin' you for another time."

Again, the voice, floating through air. Canfield stood, crossed to where he supposed the form of the steamboat skipper to be, and reached out a hand. Striking nothing but empty air, the trader nearly lost his balance and fell.

"What the hell?" he muttered.

He was rewarded by hearing the captive make low, victorious noises deep within his throat.

"Bastard."

Canfield struck again, this time hitting the body which had moved two feet to his left. By so doing, he nearly lost himself in the deepening shadows.

"I swore I'd get you, boy, and by God, I have. A bit of luck, it was, too, me having your 'bride' and then finding you by accident aboard the very ship which was taking me north. A nice package to trade the Indians."

The enormity of the statement not only cleared Blue's head but sent waves of goosebumps down his back.

His *bride*.

That, too, had been part of the prophesy. A red-haired boy and a dark-skinned girl who was neither of the Red nor White tribes. She, who was to be part of the package deal ordained by the gods. Not to grow, mate and produce offspring, but to balance the scales.

Male and female.

The symbolic tribute to life and regeneration.

Barely able to wrap his swirling thoughts around the enormity of the situation, Blue forced his mind to calm. The word "inscrutable" came to him. He pictured the letter "I" from the pages of his reading book. "I." It seemed an omen of another sort. His life, whatever he had left of it, was coming together.

"When the Injuns find you got the wrong man – and the wrong woman – they'll be after you so fast you'll be skinned before you stop quivering."

Canfield struck him a vicious blow to the back, then spun him around and kicked him in the groin. Blue exhaled through his nose, keeping his jaws tightly clamped. The pain was agonizing, but he had known pain in his young life. Knew how to endure in silence.

Knew how to suffer without showing emotion.

For the first ten years of his existence, Blue Moon had been raised an Indian. His kind of pride was that which no white man would ever comprehend.

"I've been up and down in my life, Blue Moon, but going after you was the worst I ever had it. You – a mere boy. I took you for granted, no doubt. I didn't consider you were part devil."

"Untie my hands and I'll remind you."

Canfield expected the audacity and was ready. Moving as close as he dared to the bound man he had learned never to trust, he struck him again, this time in the stomach. When he did not get the reaction he craved, he hit again, his fist sinking deep into Blue's abdomen.

"You know how long I waited to have my arm treated? The one you sliced through like it was a slab of meat? It was a week... mebbe more. I lost track of time. Was delirious with fever. You did that to me."

He yanked off the blindfold, rolled up the sleeve of his arm, then shoved it under Blue's closed eyes.

"Look at what you did to me, you river rat."

"Breaks my heart," the captive replied without looking. He did not have to see the scar to know what it looked like. He had imagined it often enough while huddled around a pile of unlit driftwood. He knew what it was like to suffer; to be so poor he did not have match or a live coal with which to light his pitiful fire.

In his life, Blue Moon knew physical cold and physical hunger.

In his young life, he was even more acutely aware of the mental cold of abandonment, the haunting torment of hunger for companionship, for the sound of a kind word, the dream, even the delusion, that someone cared.

Mister Canfield could beat him senseless and not hurt him more than the cruel world had already done.

The Trader spoke of scars.

The Orphan lived a scarred life.

Flinging the cap from Blue's head, Canfield grabbed him by the tufts of his newly shorn head, drawing it back, forcing the intense brown eyes to open.

"How about if I blind you, boy? Does that scare you? Does it make your guts quiver, like mine did?"

"No."

It was the boldest lie he ever told.

Also, the worst.

His life did not have to flash past his eyes to know what losing his sight would mean. Without the ability to watch the river, judge the sky for changes in the weather, read the gauges on the engines, stare into the faces of his crew, Blue Moon would never captain again.

He would never hard-bargain for cargo, solicit passengers with promises of soft beds and French meals, lie to merchants about arrival and departure times.

He would never see his name painted on the side of the great steamboat he owned.

He would never need a book or a pair of spectacles, for without eyes, he could not read.

The only thing he could do was sing for his supper.

Amongst rivermen, that was called begging.

He supposed the same held true for the river cities of Saint Louis, Natchez and New Orleans.

Crippled old soldiers begged for their food. So did river widows, orphans, drunks and dogs.

Of that entire group, only the dog was likely to get a crust of bread.

And even that was not enough to sustain life.

Without eyes, Blue Moon was a dead man. Worse, he was a living man waiting for death.

Of all the ends he imagined for himself, that was the most unpleasant.

No one ever said life was fair, Blue Moon.

Words of wisdom from a consumptive wooder he once knew.

Put your trust in the Lord, Blue Moon.

All others pay cash, he had finished.

And almost laughed.

But it was no longer funny.

And never had been to a runaway boy.

The man with black eyes dug his fingernails into the soft, unresisting flesh at the point where skull recedes into eye sockets. Blue jumped, then readied himself, ashamed of his momentary cowardice. He would face what was to come, even if that direction led to death.

There were worse things than death.

Being blind was one of them.

He jumped again as Canfield's hot breath scorched his face.

"I'll poke your eyes out, then set you loose aboard ship. Think you could find your way around? Inch along, one foot in front of the other, until you trip over a coil of rope, or fall down the stairs. How about that, Moon? How about if I strap you to the bow and use you as a figurehead. 'Blind justice.' Ever hear of that? A pair of eyes for my scarred arm."

Blue struggled, cursed, spat, then swallowed his hatred and stiffened his back.

"You'll know hell, Canfield."

"Never heard of a blind man guiding the way."

Canfield slit the soft tissue under Blue's right eye, drawing blood. It dripped, making a red tear track down his cheek.

"Blind! Blind! Blind!"

"No!" Blue cried, unable to stay his tongue. He was only twenty-three years old. He had lived a dog's life. He did not deserve to beg like a dog, to die like a dog.

Justice could not be blind.

God could not be deaf.

It was not fair.

The deck had been stacked against him since the earthquake and the comet had mated.

"Leave me alone!"

Unlike Andre Kress, Canfield understood when a man was begging.

"First one eye and then the other."

Like Andre Kress, Canfield possessed no mercy. Mercy went hand in hand with soul.

All men were not created equal.

There was a soft, shuffling noise behind the pair. Unable to place it, Canfield jerked his head around, eyes wild with lust. He saw Ching Lee appear out of the stairwell, carrying a bottle and two glasses. Without the slightest acknowledgement she was interrupting anything, she made a low, subservient bow.

"I see no reason why you should not celebrate, too, master. Will you take a glass of whisky?"

Her long, silken black hair was worn loose, about the shoulders. Several long tresses covered her forehead, then draped over one eye, giving her an alien expression in the moonless night.

In his tortured agony, Blue understood her symbolism and hung his head, heart pounding.

He was alone and not alone.

It was an awareness never before experienced.

As if reading Canfield's thoughts, Ching Lee spoke again, never taking her one good eye from his twisted face.

"It will be a night of great adventure, master."

He laughed crudely.

"I'll miss you, you know that, little vixen?" He was breathing deeply. His foul exhalations filled the confined space called earth. Licking his lips, he sheathed the knife and drew her to him, placing his arms across her breasts.

"How will it be for you, going from the bed of a great white man to that of a red breed Indian?"

Ching Lee pulled away, turning her back on him, as though in modesty. Drooping her head, she appeared to contemplate the question. When she had seen all she needed to, the slender, sinewy woman turned back.

Her eyes were shining.

Canfield assumed the phenomenon was from reflected glory.

"You mistake, I think, sir."

Kress, who had been leering at the scene, jabbed his partner with an elbow.

"You mistake, I think, sir," he imitated. Canfield glowered at him, then redirected his attention to the young woman.

The night had grown quiet. The crickets and mosquitoes fell silent. The lapping of the river current against the bow diminished. The only things left in the universe to create the impression of sound were the stars. Their song was played with lights.

It was a new moon.

An invisible moon. Invisible to the naked eye.

"What do you mean, 'you think I mistake'? I know who you are. I know *what* you are. Don't try to lie to me, now. It's too late. Those Indians took you to be *his* bride."

He kicked Blue Moon. For all the response he got, he might as well have kicked the side of the boat.

Both Blue Moons felt the blow.

They were twins, after all. Both born of the Mighty Mississippi. Both with hearts. One of wood, the other in splinters.

Both considered less than human.

Neither responded.

They had both said all there was to say.

"It is the word 'bride' which confuses you," Ching Lee pursued. Her words were deliberate, carefully articulated. For all appearances, she was unfamiliar with the language, compelled to choose her words with forethought.

Malice aforethought.

But that was a legal term with which neither Indian Trader was familiar.

No matter.

It was her smile they stared at, not her sentence. Nor her thoughts.

"I think we know what 'bride' means." It was Kress who spoke. The woman turned her eyes on him. The orbs were dark pools of dilated color.

They were not black eyes, for black was the absence of color. It could not be said she lacked color.

But that, too, was obscure.

"The word is not meant to convey the idea of a husband and wife."

"No one said anything about a preacher."

More crude laughter. Ching Lee appeared not to comprehend the levity. She swayed her hips seductively, taking the captors attention from their victim.

"It is the ancient concept of yin and yang. Opposites. The strength of the male pitted against the power of the female. To the death."

"Then I wouldn't want to be in your moccasins," the Great Explorer commented.

She turned her darkness-shrouded face toward the speaker.

"For as long as legend exists, the female has never lost."

"What does it mean?"

"The contest symbolizes the struggle between Mother Earth and Father Sky. I, of ancient races, he of comets. The winner of our contest determines how the earth shall be ruled for another hundred years."

"That isn't the story I heard."

"There are many stories. Perhaps none of them are true."

Ching Lee made a gentle bow with her head, reaching out, while positioning herself between Canfield and Blue, to pour her master another drink. She had almost succeeded when the lee side of the boat listed heavily.

"Indians!" screamed Deke Miller.

Shoving Ching Lee aside with a vicious blow to her shoulder, the tall man with black eyes grasped Blue by the back of his shirt collar. He hoisted the captain to his feet. They turned as one, the flesh and blood counterpart of the *Blue Moon* acting as a shield for the Trader, who stood half a head taller than he.

The knife blade struck wood a quarter inch from Canfield's ear.

"Indians!" he screamed.

Too late.

Before Kress or any of the crew could defend themselves, the *Blue Moon* was swarming with Sauk and Fox braves. One cry, another. The nearly noiseless perception of throats being slit, iron being driven through unresisting flesh.

"Stop!" Canfield ordered in panic. "What is this treachery?"

"You have bargained in bad faith."

His head spun in all directions at once, unable to locate the owner of the voice. Blue broke away from his grasp, leaving Canfield defenseless.

"No! I swear!"

"There was no whisky in those barrels," the warrior pursued. "They were filled with river water. You lied. You did not mean to give us that which is ours."

"No. Some mistake. Kress!" Canfield roared. "What is the meaning of this? You told me those barrels were filled with whisky."

Kress could not answer. The Famous Author was writing his own funeral oration.

By the light of hell fire.

No longer floating on the waters of the Great River but on those of another.

His death had come as a shock.

A Great Surprise. Proving, at least, he had done something wondrous in his life, even if it were on his passage out of existence.

"Mister Scott!" It was Canfield's high-pitched voice. "Come up here and tell them. These *was* whisky in those barrels."

He had no pity for Kress, no time to contemplate his partner's death. He had his own life to protect.

"He cannot come." It was a strange, alien, yet familiar voice which answered his command. Canfield shuddered. "He is visiting his ancestors on a trip from whence there is no return."

"You!" the gaunt man hissed, turning to face Ching Lee. "You! You did all this. I trusted you."

"That was your mistake. One should never trust a slave. That is, by definition, an oxymoron," Ching Lee coldly replied.

"Damn you!"

In an act of demented self-preservation, Canfield lunged at Ching Lee, knocking her down, falling heavily atop her. His fingers struggled for control of her body, ripped at her tunic, shredding the cloth from neck to waist. She rolled from beneath him, unconcerned about her nakedness. There was no modesty when Death came knocking.

"Do not touch her!" Blue called in tortured command. He diverted his eyes to her for no more than a second. It was enough.

Too much.

Canfield, seeing opportunity, hurled himself over the body of his partner to tackle Blue. The captain went down from the force of the blow, striking his face against the hard wood of the deck. The Trader straddled him, grasping his short red hair with one hand, wrapping the other around Blue's throat.

It was a night of strangulation and suffocation.

For the lucky.

"Halt!" he ordered the Indians, who moved in with the stealth of their kind. "I have Blue Moon. Listen to me or I kill him! I mean it. I have nothing to lose."

"Stop!" It was Ching Lee who commanded the warriors. Sensing her wisdom, they froze, eyes shifting from the woman to the two men on deck.

"Give him to us." It was Hatchet Nose, the leader, who spoke. Canfield glowered at him with hatred. It had all gone bad, somehow. Blue Moon would pay. Ching Lee would pay. All the redskins in the world would pay.

He was worth them all and then some.

"Blue Moon belongs to me. Make a move against me and I kill him. Then see how your prophesy flies." Activity on the boat ceased. "Hansen. Light a lamp. Let us see what we have here."

No one moved. No one went to obey the order.

"Hansen!"

"You call in vain," the Fox chief replied. His English was well executed. "There shall be no light. Give the boy and the girl to us."

There was the sound of death in the red man's voice.

"I'll kill him! I swear, I will kill him. Stand back."

There was the sound of desperation in the white man's voice.

"Return Blue Moon to those who understand his ways. He belongs to us. So it has been said. So it shall be."

Canfield drew his arm tighter around Blue's throat. The orphan struggled, as much to be free from his grasp, as saved from the fate of being returned to the Indians. Canfield delivered a punishing blow to the captain's left ear. A gasp of tortured air escaped the prisoner from the unexpectedness of the attack.

Blood spurted from Blue's ear. The left side of his face went numb. The noises of the world dimmed by exactly one half.

Canfield felt, rather than saw, the attackers disappear.

"Over the side," he commanded. "Back where you came from. I will deal with you in the morning. Not until then. Or I kill him."

"Kill him and you die."
Canfield snorted, too frightened to reply.
Death was in the air. He needed light to see.
It would not improve his vision.

CHAPTER 21

It was a cold night. The fingers of the wind were cruel to Blue Moon. With his arms tied tightly behind him, he could not use the body heat from the palm of his hand to protect his ear. While his face was numb from the vicious blow, it was not a comforting lack of sensation. It made him feel as though he were listing to port.

Shifting slightly from side-to-side to ease his cramped muscles, he lost his balance, nearly falling over.

"Stay where you are," Canfield growled. He was in a black mood. It would take very little provocation to kill the man who had come, through no fault of his own, to represent Canfield's salvation.

The words sounded distant, far away, although Blue knew the speaker could be no more than three feet from him. The realization was frightening.

He saw, rather than heard, Deke Miller, his mate, come on deck. The man's face was waxen and drawn.

"He's dead."

Blue almost responded, before realizing the man was not talking to him. He had joined the other side.

Or perhaps, it was more correct to say, Blue was no longer part of his boat.

That pain was worse than the agony in his ear.

"Who's dead?"

It was Canfield who spoke.

"Mister Scott. The engineer. His head's been bashed in. From behind."

Miller gave his former skipper a look of utter hatred. Canfield noted it. Had he been less scared and more in control of his emotions, he would have known to let the matter drop. It was far safer for him to have the mate believe the worst of his former commander.

"She did it."

"She?"

A foolish question, for there was only one "she" aboard.

Discounting the boat, which could not rightfully be said to be "aboard."

"The China."

He could not bring himself to speak her name, inasmuch as he could not now rightfully be said to be her master.

"How could she have done it? She's nothin but a girl."

Canfield snorted. He had believed that once, himself.

"She did it." He directed his dark gaze toward her. "You emptied the whisky from the barrels, didn't you?" She did not reply. "It was your idea. You picked out the whisky barrels. As a sign of good faith. I listened to you."

Ching Lee did not move.

"I saved you from a life of savagery. I took you away. I taught you all you know."

"You taught me many things," she agreed.

"And this is how you repay me. Why?"

The answer was too obvious to bother with. Therefore, she said nothing.

"You did this for him? For that river rat? What is he to you?"

"He is a man. He has a heart."

"He is nothing."

Canfield felt a twinge in his arm. The sensation was familiar. He jerked it, more to see if he possessed the power, than to rid himself of pain. It was that old wound acting up again. The knife cut which had never healed quite right. It had not been treated by a surgeon. The torn muscle had atrophied over the years.

The trader's eyes snaked toward Blue, suspecting him of sending evil thoughts. He met his eyes but could not hold them. He turned to the woman. She stared him down. His head hung in bitter shame.

It was a bad business.

A business which was not finished. The night air was cold but it did not chill his inner desires. He had seen death, played with death, faced death. In death came the desire for life.

The craving to engender life.

His mouth watered as his eyes narrowed.

"So. You would risk your life for him and he for you. I am touched." A low growl of animal lust rumbled deep within his throat. "Submit to me, Ching Lee, or I kill him. Does your new loyalty run that far?"

"No!" Blue strained against the ropes, burning his flesh as his heart seared his soul. "Do not touch her!"

"You do not give the orders, Captain Moon. You are impotent."

Blue did not know the word but understood its meaning. His face flushed red with anger.

"Touch her and you die. A horrible death. I swear."

"Swear what you will. The days of prophesy are past."

Canfield stood, towering over the man on the deck and the woman by his side. He rubbed his groin, arousing himself. Without ever having seen the deed perpetrated, Blue Moon understood. It was the worst revelation he had ever experienced. Here was evil in a living, breathing form.

"Remove your shift, Ching Lee," or I shall forever render him powerless."

"Do not do it!" Blue pleaded, struggling madly against the ropes. "Not for me! Not to save me. Run. Jump overboard."

It was an order she could not obey.

There were tears in Blue's young voice. "I don't care what he does to me!"

She understood what he did not.

She reached up and pulled the tunic over her head, removing it. Blue sobbed. She wore nothing beneath but a thin white undergarment. As Canfield watched with greed, she slipped that off, as well. Standing naked before him, Ching Lee was ten feet taller than man who would violate her.

Blue Moon had never seen a naked woman before. He stared with numb disbelief, not at her unfamiliar form but at the knowledge his own body transmitted to his frozen brain.

He understood now exactly what Mrs. Lang had offered him. The realization made him gag with horror and shame.

"In the name of God," Blue whispered hoarsely. "Do not touch her."

There were other, deeper sensations of awareness. His own flesh crawled with ten thousand million needle pricks.

"Take me."

He was a boy, again, in the hands of missionaries and he knew what he was saying.

He knew he was offering that which was worse than blindness to save her.

Blue Moon dared not breathe for fear of missing Canfield's answer. He turned his one good ear toward the devil fashioned in God's sacred image.

He need not have held his breath.

The god, with two good ears, was not listening.

Canfield removed his trousers, stripping down to bare skin. His male anatomy was hard, erect. He looked like a missionary man.

"Down." He pointed to the deck.

Ching Lee lay upon the wood of the *Blue Moon,* her own form stiff, unyielding. She knew what she was doing.

She had heard the story of Mrs. Lang.

Canfield dropped on top of her. He kissed her lips, tore at the tender flesh of her neck, bit her breasts. He gasped, panted, rose up and fell down. His male animal noises were lost to the moaning of he who was not touching her.

She did not close her eyes. They snaked beyond the rapist to the men who had gathered to watch. Cold, hard, stiff men. She caught their stares and held them as surely as she held Canfield between her thighs.

Remember, Ching Lee drilled in silent communication between their reddened eyes. *Remember Mrs. Lang. Remember what has happened here.*

Remember what you did not hear behind the doors of Blue Moon's stateroom.

She moaned and cried to underscore the pain. She thrashed, struggled, acted out the panic of a proud woman.

Her hatred was as tangible as a living beast.

Deke Miller turned away from the spectacle and vomited over the side of the railing.

As he wretched, Ching Lee gasped, choked, endured as another had not. She had to be certain.

And prayed the bound man who had once exhibited mercy on another woman would understand.

Sacrifice.

They would wash together in the river.

In the waters of the Mighty Mississippi.

The stars winked out. The new moon wept.

It was almost dawn. With first light came the time for decisions.

"Mister Hansen."

Canfield was dressed and tired. The air coming in off the river did not revive him.

It was against his nature to address anyone by title, but circumstances had changed much. He needed Hansen and Miller to operate the steamboat if he were to have any chance at escape.

They were men. He expected them to understand.

The mate, who had not perished in the Indian attack, although was wounded, approached.

"Yes?"

"Come with me. We must make plans. Leave a guard here. If Moon or the Chinese make a move, shoot them in the leg."

"I will give the orders."

"Very well." Canfield was relieved. 'We must speak. It will soon be light. The Indians will not wait past dawn for a reckoning."

The two crewmen and the trader went below. A guard was placed to watch the prisoners. Neither the Captain nor the China made any attempt to communicate with him.

He could not be trusted. A mutineer was beneath contempt.

One did not negotiate with a traitor. Not even to save one's own life.

It was one thing to die.

Another to perish without honor.

For those who were born without, for those who had sacrificed, to die with the perception of one's dignity was an achievement worth the risk.

When the three men returned, the first pale streaks of sunlight were shafting their way through the cover of night. The disquietude of darkness was being overtaken by the uneasiness of morning.

"White skins on the boat!"

The voice came from shore. Each person on the riverboat reacted differently.

Those who did not react were beyond the reach of the red-skinned Grim Reapers. They had left the waters of the Great River to sail those of another.

The River Styx.

"We hear you," Canfield shouted back. There was no need to raise his voice. He did so from force of habit.

"Send us Blue Moon and the woman."

"I will dump their headless bodies overboard if you do not do as I say."

Blue watched as Miller disappeared below. He did not have to wonder where he was going. To escape aboard the *Blue Moon,* they would have to stoke the boilers, get up a head of steam. Such an action could not be undertaken in stealth. Even a savage could tell when a steam engine was being primed.

The boat had drifted during the night. A long, only partially submerged sandbar had arisen between the *Blue Moon* and shore. As a half way point, its appearance seemed providential.

"Did you prepare the furs? The hides? You will not get my hostages without payment."

An eye for an eye, a tooth for a tooth.

"We have them."

"Bring them aboard."

"Give us Blue Moon and the woman."

It was Hansen's idea. He pointed to the sandbar.

"Let them put the hides and fur there. We will then bring Captain Moon and the China to the sandbar. An equal exchange."

His use of the word "captain" was not lost on he who had so recently been stripped of the title.

Canfield, who was not a captain, paid no heed. He nodded. His full attention was in conveying the terms to the Indians. When presented with the terms, they agreed.

Without reservation.

It took an hour for twenty-seven bundles of fur and hides to be brought from shore. A veritable gold mine. A man owning that amount of tradable goods was a King. Canfield's mouth watered. Without a partner, he ruled the Kingdom alone.

"We have paid your price," Hatchet Nose, warrior chief, warned. "Bring out Blue Moon and the woman."

It was time.

Always a reckoning.

"Let's go."

Canfield grabbed Blue, dragging him to his feet. The captain swayed but did not fall. Born the son of earthquake, he would keep his balance.

Standing upright, his ear began to bleed once more.

His blood was red.

As red as his hair.

As red as his heritage.

He was going home.

What neither warring faction understood, was that an orphan had no real home.

Only the one which he made for himself.

Blue and Ching Lee were forced into the small rowboat belonging to the *Blue Moon.* Canfield joined them, keeping his musket leveled at the back of Blue's head. Blue's hands were tired but hers were not. The "China" was kept close by an occasional lateral movement of the barrel from right to left.

She was very quiet, very still. When the boat swayed from the unevenness of the rowing, she went with it, without adjusting her position for the motion. Blue understood that it was a ritual, a preparation for a great trial, rather than an unfamiliarity with water craft.

He did not know why he understood. He did not question his knowledge. Their eyes did not meet.

Deke Miller rowed. It was a short trip, no more than fifty feet. Had the water been shallow, they could have walked the distance in half the time. An Indian was waiting for them on the sandbar.

"Go back!" Canfield ordered with disdain. "I will inspect the furs and hides before we make the trade."

"I will inspect the Blue Moon and the woman, before we make the trade," came the reply. "First."

Alone in a row boat with one crewman and two prisoners, one of whom had his hands tied behind his back and the other a woman, Canfield realized his precarious position. It would not take much to have a dozen Indians down his throat.

Literally.

"All right."

It was always easy to be magnanimous when there was no choice.

When the bow of the boat touched the temporary, shifting *terra unfirma,* Ching Lee stepped off, then turned and gave Blue a hand. Without use of his arms, it would have been both awkward and undignified for him to struggle out. That was a thought which had not occurred to the Trader or the Oarsman.

Possibly because they did not care.

The only dignity which mattered was their own. It was beyond the sensibilities of the two men to consider that the value of their merchandise depended, to a large extent, on how the red-haired boy and the slant-eyed girl maintained their pride and mystique.

No words were passed between the prisoners.

When Blue planted his feet in the sand, Canfield and Miller stepped out.

"Back up," the tall man ordered.

No one moved. The time for orders was growing short.

Canfield realized his mistake. Like a sensible man, he ignored it. Failing to acknowledge an error was the same as not having made it. At least, from the world where he originated.

The twenty-seven bundles were tightly bound together with leather straps. He did not have a knife to cut the binding and inspect the hides and furs. The ones he could see on the outside were well tanned and preserved.

"I accept," he said.

He was without awareness that was the only answer possible.

Hatchet Face turned to the two prisoners. His eyes did not linger on Ching Lee. He had seen her more recently than the boy. When the man with the black eyes had brought her to the attention of the tribes and spoke of the Prophesy. He knew her as a woman. Blue he knew only as a child.

He asked a question in Sauk. Blue did not answer. He understood the words but knew the question could not be directed at him. He was never to be spoken to. Memories came alive.

The red man reached out a hand, Blue barred his teeth.

Once a river rat, always a river rat.

From the inner recesses of his dress, the Indian removed a square of leather. On it were a series of small points, seared into the material by a red-hot wire or the burning point of a stick. To the uninitiated, it might have represented the astrological depiction of a night sky.

Taurus. Pegasus. Perseus. Gemini.

Except there was no larger object to indicate the moon.

The brave held the map to Blue's face. He did not speak again. He studied the similarities between the marks on the leather and those on the man's face.

The landscape had changed with time.

Some of the points had moved.

Some had faded, others taken their place.

Freckles.

Close enough.

The Indian nodded. He was satisfied.

"I will take them now."

"Not yet," Canfield warned. "Miller: load the boat."

Miller did as he was told. When the rowboat was filled with hides and furs, Miller rowed it back to the *Blue Moon.*, Canfield remaining behind to guard his two living investments. Not until the cargo was stowed aboard did anyone on the island move. Miller gave what appeared to be the all-clear, signaling Canfield to return.

Contrary to what the man with black eyes expected, a terrific blast of steam shrieked forth from the riverboat. The Mighty Paddlewheel began to turn. The waters of the Great River churned.

"No!" Canfield screamed, pale face stricken with horror. "Come back for me! Don't leave me here!"

The deceiver had been deceived. He had failed to understand the message Mrs. Lang had left in her wake.

He plunged into the water, wet himself to the waist, then floundered.

"Come back!"

"Swim for it."

It was Blue Moon who spoke. They were the first words issued from his mouth since the stars had paled. His voice was deep, hoarse.

"I cannot swim!" the Trader protested.

"I know."

Blue's face twisted into part grin, part sneer.

It was as close to a smile as the red-haired, freckle-faced man could come.

His words triggered Canfield into panic. They held within them all the hatred of a tortured soul.

They held within them all the torture of a hating soul.

More steam from the boilers of the steamboat. The whistle blew. Mechanically manufactured waves washed over the island, wearing away the loose sand. In a minute, the sandbar was half what it had been.

"Help!"

Canfield turned wide-eyed orbs to the woman. He appealed to her gender. She stared at him with her own cark orbs. The great difference between them being the whites of the male's eyes were now full and dominant.

Resembling full moons.

Two full moons.

The equivalent of a blue moon.

There would be no help from her.

"Swim for it," she said.

Canfield plunged into the wildly churning water, splashed helplessly, disappeared beneath, bobbed up, swam a foot, then was lost from sight as a wave crashed over him. No one made a move.

He re-emerged, screamed, choked, gesticulated to the men on the riverboat. No one was watching. They were too busy preparing for departure. They were looking ahead, not back.

The *Blue Moon* inched away, creating larger, more powerful waves. The sandbar all but disappeared, soaking the remaining occupants to the knees.

Canfield cried, made ineffectual swimming motions, caught himself in the downward flow of current. He was swept toward safety.

The security of death.

In the form of an aging, 200 ton riverboat named *Blue Moon*.

In a moment, his helplessly flailing body was pushed into the rotating paddlewheel. Caught in the wooden planks, he was lifted up, torn asunder, then ignobly dropped. His body plunged into the water, staining it red. He floated a moment, then was caught a second time.

There came the sound of splintering wood. It masked the more subtle noises of breaking bones.

For the onlookers, it was over in a moment.

No one thought to wonder how long that moment had been for Canfield.

In death, he passed out of their existence.

Hatchet Face made a curt move with his hand.

"Come," he said to the woman. He was referring to both red-haired man and woman, but addressed only the China.

They would have to swim to shore. He did not have to ask if the boy and his bride could swim. He already possessed that knowledge.

He knew them well.

The pieces of the puzzle were falling into place.

"I will cut his bonds."

It was Ching Lee who spoke. Her voice was deep, resonant.

The Indian nodded.

She reached into a pocket of her tunic and withdrew a knife. Opening it with deliberate care, she cut the leather tongs, freeing Blue's hands. As circulation returned, he took one deep sigh.

"Come," Hatchet Face repeated. The water was deepening. It was time to leave. He was growing impatient.

"No."

Again, it was Ching Lee who spoke. This time, her voice was commanding, haughty. Superior. They were the children of the gods, brought together for a great and wondrous purpose. They would not be commanded by mere mortals.

It was time to remind their subjects.

The Indian turned, head thrown back, mouth tight.

"You are to come." He spoke slowly.

"We are *not* to come."

The warriors on shore drew closer, inching their way into the water. If their pair would not come willingly, they would be brought to shore.

Taken home.

There were ceremonies to perform. The tribes had waited long enough. They had lost their lands, their hunting grounds, their dignity.

It was time to wage a new war. Not Black Hawk's War. A war blessed by the gods.

A war they could not lose.

"Stand back!" Ching Lee warned.

The Indian stood back. The sand beneath his feet washed away. He would wait for the others.

There could be no mistake now.

Ching Lee watched the Indians come. She bided her time.

There must be no mistake now.

When they were close, when she could feel the hot breath of their exhalations on her skin, she made a move. Holding up her empty hands, palms outward, she warned them off.

"It is told," she declared with omnipotent authority, "That a boy born of earthquake and comet will come to you. This is that boy, grown to manhood. You have waited too long to find him. He is no longer yours to command. He belongs to himself. Go back, I warn you. If you attempt to take him, he will punish you."

"We will have him."

It was the Chief who spoke. He was known to both the boy of the blue moon and the girl who was not a squaw.

The legends faced those who had not come to worship but to rule.

"Leave us," she said.

There was five hundred years of prophesy in her voice. She pitted it against the present moment.

The quick and the dead.

The quick against the dead.

The spirits of what Were and What Will Be.

The warriors hesitated. The Sands of Time were against Blue Moon and Ching Lee.

"One step further and we will display our power. Go back or we shall destroy."

She crossed to him, suddenly beginning a loud chant. Blue responded, raising his voice to the gods in the evangelistic style which Man had also incorporated into his heritage. There were no words. None were needed. They were communicating in a language older than the earth.

More ancient than the stars.

A wave washed high over the man and the woman, soaking them to the waist.

"The river has spoken." The Chief broke the silence. He did not have language older than the stars. "Come now or the gods will drown you."

The Mississippi gave the gods courage. They understood the river. They would take what was theirs.

Take back what had been promised so long ago.

"Remember the legend," Ching Lee warned. "The stories of your ancestors. The boy with red hair. Touch a straw to his head and it will burn. His hair is fire."

She took from her pocket a handful of straw and held it to his head. The dried grass immediately burst into flame.

Blue Moon screamed.

The Indians fled in panic, turning their backs on the horrible apparition of the prophesy they had waited so long to behold.

Throwing the burning straw toward shore, Ching Lee and Blue Moon dove into the swirling waters of the river which had given him birth. They swam for the riverboat, which he had made his home.

It was a race.

The *Blue Moon* was a quarter mile away and picking up steam. The two swam with power, away from the world not of their choosing.

Seeing that the burning straw fell into the water and extinguished, the Indians woke from their fear and followed, howling with rage.

They drew close but could not catch the Progeny of the Past. With powerful strokes, Blue and Ching Lee swam through the white-frothed water, then around to the side of the riverboat. Grasping hold of the slippery side, Blue clung to it by his nails. He offered her a cupped hand to use as a step up. She accepted, scrambling over his wet body, pressing flesh to flesh in a momentary marriage of bodies.

He did not move until he saw her aboard.

It was the captain's right. Last off a sinking boat, last aboard.

He had come back home and taken her with him.

"We will need full steam," he said through clenched teeth. "We must outrun them."

Those men of his former crew stood shock still, eying the captain as water dripped off his clothes. There had been many bad decisions made. There was only one left. To correct those made in error.

Bic Hansen squared his shoulders, cleared his throat and stepped forward. Blue's hand went for his Indian knife, forgetting, for the moment, the sheath was not attached to his belt.

"Captain."

The salutation was not what the captain expected. He raised an eyebrow.

"Yes?"

"One question, sir."

He did not enunciate the statement as an interrogative, yet there was an obvious tone of inquiry in his voice.

"What is it?"

"About Mrs. Lang, sir."

Blue had expected something, but not this. He nodded his approval for Hansen to continue.

"What did she pay you to take her and her husband to New Orleans?"

Blue stared at the lieutenant as though he had gone stark raving mad.

"Pay me? What did she pay me?" He started to shake his head when lightning struck. "You think she gave me money? Money you are entitled to a cut of?" His voice rose an octave.

"No, sir."

Blue tried again. His hands clenched into fists, then slowly untangled themselves.

"You wonder why I left the cargo of the *Bell Bottom?* Is that it? You think *I've* gone mad?"

Hansen was clearly unable to articulate his question. He shifted his eyes to Ching Lee. She did not have to read his thoughts to understand his dilemma.

"Blue Moon."

Blue jumped as though she had stung him with the lash of a whip. Ching Lee gave him a moment to collect his dignity before continuing.

"Mrs. Lang is a woman. She was seen coming out of your cabin. The men thought... they *supposed* she offered you what I offered Canfield – and, like that devil out of hell – you accepted. As he accepted."

Blue's eyes welled with river spray. He shook his head slowly, as comprehension finally struck pay dirt.

"They think I... I... am a beast?"

"Yes."

"That I touched her?"

"Yes."

"That I took her body as payment for the trip to New Orleans?"

The river spray leaked down his face.

"Yes."

He sniffed, then began to quiver.

"No...." he whispered. Then, holding his arms out, motioned for Ching Lee. She came to him and he hugged her, holding her body close to his. "How can they think that?" he cried. "I was raised like a dog, but I am not a dog."

"No, Blue Moon," she whispered back. "You are not a dog. Not a devil. And you are not alone. Never again."

His eyes met hers. He raised a hand and touched her cheek. Had her skin been as delicate as a bubble, he would not have burst it.

"I have heard it said," he continued out of earshot of his crew. "That no good deed goes unpunished. I did a good deed for Mrs. Lang. She put a curse on me. I thought that was my punishment. I see now it was not. My punishment was to see you suffer."

"And my punishment was to see you suffer. Shall we now begin again?"

"We shall do fewer good deeds in future," he promised, wiping his nose with the back of his hand. Then, raising his head. "Mister Hansen."

"Yes, sir!"

"I think we had better get out of here. My order was, 'full steam ahead.' Are you with us or against us?"

"I am with you, sir."

"And the rest?"

"We are with you, sir," Mister Miller responded.

"Very well. Then carry out my order, before we are boarded and attacked."

"Very well, sir!"

The order was carried out with alacrity as the newly re-enlisted crew ran to carry out their requisite tasks. The *Blue Moon* shuddered, quivered as a thing alive.

Behind them, the Indians came in canoes, reprising a drama which had taken place exactly twenty-three years earlier. Neither Blue Moon nor Ching Lee remembered the play.

But they were unknowingly rewriting the ending.

Shouts and screams of holy indignation followed them as the Fox and the Sauk and the Winnebago refused to lose that which they had waited for so long. The canoes swift, the paddlers strong, they raced against the monster belching steam from its belly, their faces mad with passion.

Closer, closer, came their encroaching enemy, fueled by thwarted prophesy.

"The pine knots. Throw the pine knots in the fire," Blue shouted into the communications pipe leading to the bowels of the boat.

There was no one in the engine room. The engineer was dead.

"Go!" Ching Lee ordered.

He did not question. Running like a man possessed, Blue leapt through the companionway and jumped, three stairs at a time, down the narrow passage. Stumbling, nearly tripping but not falling, he grasped handfuls of the small, highly combustible fuel and threw them into the fire. A roar of hungry flame accepted his gift.

His burnt offering.

The *Blue Moon* sped with the current, her direction straight, her path controlled. Blue sensed the boat was guided by unseen hands. There was no time to question. He threw in more knots, then tossed in wood, singing his eyebrows, turning his skin a florid red from heat.

Faster she flew, faster, the fire consuming all it was given, producing steam which powered the engines, spinning the damaged paddlewheel, driving the boat.

An hour he stoked the flames until the metal was red hot and he dared not push it further. With a low moan of total exhaustion, Blue Moon, captain of the *Blue Moon,* gave a nod of acceptance and staggered away.

He had given her his life.

Only topside would he know if she had given him his.

The air was brisk and clear as he emerged, billowing clouds of man-made steam trailing in their wake, like the spidery lines of a map. The crew was at their accustomed positions. They acknowledged him with salutes as he went past. He took that for a sign of triumph.

Walking with rubbery legs, Captain Blue climbed to the wheelhouse. Ching Lee was there.

Had he suddenly discovered himself on the dark side of the moon, he knew he would have found her there, as well.

"We have outrun them," she announced.

She was holding the wheel with two hands, her own face streaked with lines of sweat, arms taut, spirit undaunted.

"You?" he questioned. *"You* held the wheel?"

She nodded.

"You navigated this boat?"

She nodded.

"How?"

"Did I not tell you I had many talents?"

He blushed, the red creeping over his already flushed face.

"Have we outrun them?"

"We have."

He leaned against the boat, suddenly weak and shaking. His solitary world had come to admit another.

"You saved my life." It was not an easy admission.

She nodded once more.

There was the prophesy to fulfill. Not the entire legend. Just one part of it.

"There is a tradition with my people, Blue Moon," Ching Lee began. The speech was not prepared, yet she did not hesitate. "When a person saves the life of another, that life belongs to the savior. Do you acknowledge as much?"

"I do."

Two words of a marriage ceremony.

"Then your life belongs to me."

"It does."

It was not a vow he made without thought. Nor one he fully understood.

"Then I accept it. And give it back. With one condition."

Ching Lee stared at Blue Moon. He met her gaze. His body tingled with new life, but it was his heart which prompted his words.

"Name it."

Unconditionally.

"A half moon."

"You are asking for one half my boat?"

"I am asking for a half moon. Call it what you will."

"You wish to be my partner? My equal partner?"

"Either that, or I will take it all. That is my right."

"Irish," he growled.

Which was as close to an agreement as he was capable of making.

Walking unsteadily to the railing, Blue leaned over the side and stared out, into the new day and the white-churned water.

"How did you do it?"

She did not need further elucidation.

"Is it not said, touch straw to red hair and it will burn?"

"How did you do it?" he repeated.

"With this."

He turned slowly. She held out a small splinter of wood.

"A lucifer match. I struck it with my thumbnail."

Reverend Holly could not have put it better.

She would prove worthy.

His body quivered as a sudden chill swept over him. His palms began to sweat.

The explanation was as clear as the freckles on his face.

With the beginnings of love came an older, more familiar realization.

"The furs and hides! We're rich."

He jumped like a live wire touched to a Galvanic battery and he raced down the ladder to the deck, she following. The Great Wheel held steady in their absence.

"Look at all this treasure! Canfield and Kress knew what they were after. They just didn't realize it would be us who would profit." He shouted his revelation to the Four Winds.

His mind was awhirl, not totally connected to his actions.

Blue reached for his Indian knife, forgetting again it had been taken from him. Since he was a boy, the knife had been a part of his body. Ching Lee removed the pocketknife she carried and handed it to him.

An eye for an eye.

Accepting her gift without a word, he sliced the blade through the leather tie, freeing the bundle. With a joyous exclamation of the suddenly wealthy, Blue dove into the pile, tossing furs left and right.

"A fortune!"

He chuckled with pleasure. Life and possibilities were swirling around and within him.

Only partially understood.

He put his concentration on the moment. Wealth he could understand.

Blue Moon. Former river rat, rich man.

That explained the queasiness in his stomach.

He would get his suite of rooms at the Impressed. He would parade the levees of Saint Louis with gold in his pockets. He would run his own *line* of riverboats.

Let anyone dare call him "Baby Blue" now.

He stopped as suddenly as he began, eyes wide with disbelief. Discarding the pile he had opened, he set at a second, then a third and a fourth before finally lifting up his head and howling like an abandoned wolf cub at the full moon.

"Cheated! Those damn Injuns cheated me."

Ching Lee critically observed the scattered mess he had made. The top fur of each pile was perfect. All the others were rotten, useless.

Captain Moon inspected the hides. The same trick had been perpetrated with the hides. The top leather was perfect, those below inferior.

"Ruined!"

"You have lost nothing," she observed with careful calm. He turned to her with righteous indignation. "There are other considerations."

"What considerations?"

"Think of the money you have saved."

"Saved how?" he demanded. It was not an easy thing to lose a fortune so easily obtained.

Sweat trickled from his armpits. It was an uncomfortable feeling.

"You need not pay a mutinous crew. You have them for the season without pay."

He held his breath to quell his madly beating heart.

When time began again, he burst out laughing.

"You are right," he said. "I had not thought of that." And then he remembered. "Who's minding the helm?"

They returned together to the Great Wheel.

"If you're so good at navigation, you take it," he suggested in the form of an order.

He did not have to say he had no strength left to do it himself. She already knew.

Ching Lee obliged, not because he had ordered her, but because she was better at it than he.

The subtly was lost on the captain and half owner of the *Blue Moon.*

Blue Moon and Ching Lee and their inspired crew steamed down the Mighty Mississippi until dusk, then set the lines and made secure for the night. A guard was posted. Supper was served. With it a bottle of whisky. The same bottle which had seen service before.

When it was half drank, Blue's eyes began to sparkle. One aspect of his life had been put behind him; another remained.

A man is half memory, half hope.

He summoned the crew with a beckoning of his hands. They came without question, watching, settling in as the captain dragged a crate into the center of their circle.

Standing on the overturned wooden box, he waved his hands in the grandiose style of an evangelistic temperance preacher.

"Brethren," he announced, staring out at the faces of those who had betrayed and come back to the fold. "Whisky is for the damned. I pour this poison into the water."

So saying, he dumped the contents of the bottle into the Mississippi.

"Amen," Hansen shouted.

"Brethren," Blue continued, "I ask you to dump all the whisky in the world into the river."

"Amen," Miller replied.

"Brethren, when we get to Saint Louie, we shall empty the taverns of all evil spirits, filling the river with wine."

"Amen," Ching Lee agreed, eyes shining.

She had heard this sermon before.

"Brethren, when we get to Natchez, we will break open the barrels of bourbon and scotch, raising the water levels of the Great River."

"Hallelujah!"

With eyes glinting in religious fervor, Blue waved his fisted hand into the air.

Inspiration was upon him.

"John 7: 37." He quoted. "On the last day of the feast, the great day, Jesus stood up and proclaimed: If any one thirst, let him come to me and drink. He who believes in me, as the scripture has said, 'Out of his heart shall flow rivers of living water.'

"The 'Rivers of Living Water' we have created by filling them with beer and whisky and wine!"

"Praise the Lord!" his newly converted crew responded.

"Let our hearts flow with gratitude!"

"Amen, Brother Blue Moon!"

A new family had been forged from Temperance.

Or a reasonable imitation thereof.

"Brethren, we shall sing our praises to the Lord, while drinking from the Waters of Life!"

He did not need to add, those waters newly filled with beer and whisky and wine.

A song welled up in his heart. He began to sing.

> "Rock of Ages, cleft for me,
> Let me hide myself in thee;
> Let the water and the blood
> From thy wounded side which flowed,
> Be of sin the double cure,
> Save from wrath and make me pure."

Ching Lee blended her voice with his.

Ironically, she knew the lyrics.

Just as she appreciated the joke.

> "While I draw this fleeting breath,
> When my eyes shall close in death,
> When I rise to worlds unknown,
> And behold thee on thy throne,
> Rock of Ages cleft for me,
> Let me hide myself in thee."

Never had a Revival Meeting been so successful.

A barrel of undiluted fire water was procured from below and its contents passed around.

As the *Blue Moon* swayed in her moorings under the flowing current of the Mighty River, the lapping of the waves provided the accompaniment.

The Spirits of Adventure were in the air.

Intoxicating the Believers.

The End

GSFE

ALSO BY: S.L.KOTAR AND J.E.GESSLER

"The Hugh Kerr Mystery Series"..
- I   The Conundrum of the Decapitated Detective
- II   The Conundrum of the Absconded Attorney
- III   The Conundrum of the Sins of the Fathers
- IV   The Conundrum of The Two-Sided Lawyer
- V   The Conundrum of the Clueless Counselor
- VI   The Conundrum of the Loveless Marriage
- VII   The Conundrum of the Executed Defendant
- VIII   The Conundrum of the Jettisoned Jury
- IX   The Conundrum of the Perjured Pigeon
- X   The Conundrum of the Haunting Halloween
    - Party
- XI   The Conundrum of the Tuneless Tunesmith
- XII   The Conundrum of the Meddling Motorcar
- XIII   The Conundrum of the Blundering Bear
- XIV   The Conundrum of Shooting Fish in a Barrel
- XV   The Conundrum of The Girl with the Emerald
             Eyes
- XVI   The Conundrum of The Vanishing Cream
- XVII   The Conundrum of the Convoluted Confession
    -
    - o   To Be Continued!

"New Beginnings Series"

- I   The Believer
- II   The Heretic
- III   Arrow Song
- IV   Peas In A Pod
- V   The Agnostics
-
    - o   To Be Continued!

"the ReproBate saga"

- I   **Beneath the Rose**
- II   **skull and cRossBones**
- III   **Redefining Bastions**
- IV   **thicker than Blood**
- V   **prioR Battles**
- VI   **Requited Blasphemy**
- VII   **The waR Between**
- VIII   **To Richmond or Bust**
- IX   **carrying Battlescars**
- X   **RamBlings**
- XI   **Retrieving Ballast**
- XII   **captain's RB**
- XIII   **wondeRous Backdrops**
- XIV   **ReproBate**
- XV   **time and tRouBle**
- XVI   **the Road Back**
- XVII   **oveR the Brink**

  - **To be Continued!**

"the Hellhole saga"

- I   **First Draw**
- II   **Audition for a Legend**
- III   **Strange Bedfellows**
-

"The Kansas Pirate Series"

- I   **Pirate Treasure**
- II   **Strawberry Fields**
- III   **The Drinking Gourd**

- **Catman**
-
- **ONE**
-
- **Shepherd of the Kingdom**
-
- **Wolf Eyes**
-
- **I Am the Ship**

Non-Fiction
"The Kepi Magazine," :

- **Volume I and II**
- **Volumes III and IV**

www.ingramcontent.com/pod-product-compliance
Lightning Source LLC
Chambersburg PA
CBHW020610180626
46810CB00007B/2716